Change of Venue

Also by James J. Griffin and available from
Center Point Large Print:

Desperate Ride
Trouble Times Two
Ride for Justice, Ride for Revenge
Bullet for a Ranger
The Zombies of Zapata
The Ranger
To Avenge a Ranger
Murder Most Fowl—Texas Style
The Ghost Riders
Tough Month for a Ranger
Fight for Freedom
Renegade Ranger
Blood Ties
Texas Jeopardy
Ranger's Revenge

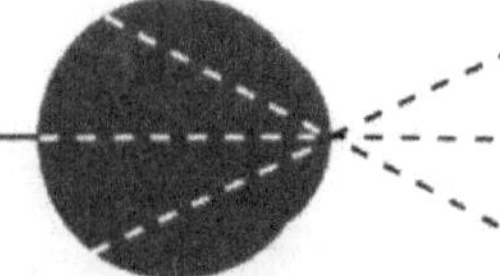

Change of Venue

A Texas Ranger James C. Blawcyzk Novel

James J. Griffin

Center Point Large Print
Thorndike, Maine

This Center Point Large Print edition
is published in the year 2023 by arrangement with
the author.

The text of this Large Print edition is unabridged.
In other aspects, this book may vary
from the original edition.
Printed in the United States of America
on permanent paper sourced using
environmentally responsible foresting methods.
Set in 16-point Times New Roman type.

ISBN: 978-1-63808-717-5

The Library of Congress has cataloged this record
under Library of Congress Control Number: 2023930125

In memory of four great horses:
Sam, Mister T, Sizzle, and Yankee.

1

Sixth generation Texas Ranger James C. Blawcyzk had just returned home from work. He walked through the back door of his house. His family's two dogs, a light tan Cairn/Wheaten terrier cross named Frostie, and a black and tan Dachshund named Fritz, bounded along beside him.

"Kim, I'm home," he called. "Where are you?"

"In the living room, with your mother," his wife answered. "And please keep your voice down. I just fed Katerina, and she's asleep in her crib."

"Daddy's home!" Josh, their four-year-old son, screamed. He ran for the kitchen and jumped into his father's outstretched arms. Jim grunted from the impact.

"Oof. Josh boy, you're gettin' awful durn heavy," he said. "And shush. We don't want to wake your baby sister up."

"Aw, she sleeps all the time," Josh complained. "That, and does poo."

"Well, that's what babies do," Jim answered, chuckling. "You did the same when you were Katerina's age. And you still need your naps."

"You need yours too, Daddy. Sometimes you sleep all day long."

"Only when I've been out all night looking for the bad guys."

They had reached the living room. Jim put Josh down. He leaned over and kissed his mother, then Kim.

"Jim, you look tired," Kim observed. "Was it a rough day?"

"Lots of paperwork that had to be finished. That always wears me out. I'd rather be on an investigation any day of the week. How about you?"

"It was mostly routine. Following up on some matters," Kim answered. "I didn't make supper. I thought perhaps I'd treat you to a night out. Betty has already agreed to watch the kids. How does Jimmy Jack's Road House sound?"

Jim laughed before replying.

"I guess great minds do think alike. I was going to ask you if you wanted to go out to dinner. I thought you'd enjoy a nice meal at *L'Escargot Noir*. I know the service can be slow as a snail there, but you do enjoy the food. And, hard as it is to believe, they have tables available. I checked."

"Only if you promise no more bad snail jokes," Kim said. "And what's this? *You* offering to take me to an exclusive French restaurant? You've either done something that's going to land you in hot water, so you're trying to head that off at the pass, or you want something, awfully badly."

Jim put a completely innocent look on his face.

"Kim! I'm so hurt. Not to mention shocked you're so suspicious of my motives. Can't a husband take his wife out for a nice evening just because he loves her?"

"Most husbands, yes. And if it was an expensive steakhouse, perhaps a place like Saltgrass, I might believe you just want to treat me to a nice meal. But French? That's just not you. And if we do go *L'Escargot Noir*, don't you dare make that same awful joke to any of the staff."

"Okay. Only jokes about good snails."

"Jim . . ."

"It sounds to me like you two have a decision to make," Betty said. "A rowdy cowboy honkytonk, or an elegant French bistro. Which will it be?"

"I'll leave the choice up to you, Kim," Jim said.

"That's not fair, putting all the pressure on me," Kim objected.

"Well, it shouldn't be just my decision," Jim answered.

"Oh, sometimes the two of you are infuriating," Betty said. "Just impossible to reason with. Particularly you, Jim. Your father was the same way. So instead, I'll deal with the situation myself. Otherwise we'll be here all night, and y'all's dinner will end up being bologna sandwiches on stale bread. There's a deck of cards in the end table drawer. I'll get those. You can cut the deck. High card wins. Whoever loses gets to go to their restaurant the next time."

She removed the cards from the drawer, shuffled them, and held them out.

"You first, Kimberly."

Kim cut the deck. Her card was a four of hearts.

"Looks like it's the honkytonk," she said.

"Not so fast. Your husband still has to cut."

Jim took his turn. He ended up with the deuce of hearts.

"You win, Kim. *Aux moines les cartes sont les deux coeurs. Cela montre que nous sommes toujours amoureux, ma cherie*."

"Jim, if you must speak a foreign language, stick to Spanish," Kim advised.

"And waste all those high school French classes? Not a chance."

"You can have that discussion over your appetizers," Betty said. "Just go, and have a good time. I'll give Josh his bath, then put him to sleep with a bedtime story. He and Katerina will be just fine."

"I'll have to shower and change," Kim said.

"I won't. I'm already wearing the jacket and tie *L'Escargot Noir* requires for gentlemen," Jim said. "Thanks to the goldang Ranger dress code. All I need do is splash some water on my face, and scrape off my five o'clock shadow. If you'd like, Kim, I could help you shower."

"Jim! You just called yourself a gentleman," Kim pointed out. "And I would like to get to the restaurant before they close. That won't ever happen if you get in the shower with me."

"I wasn't referring to me being a gentleman, merely the dress requirements," Jim shot back.

"Just get ready and go, before I take out my shotgun," Betty threatened.

Jim grimaced.

"All right, Ma. We're goin'. We're goin'."

After finishing their main courses, Jim's being *Cordon Bleu au Poulet*, Kim's *Coq au Vin*, they were sharing an airy, feather-light *Soufflé au Chocolat* for dessert. Although, truth be told, Kim was just picking at the elegant dish, while Jim was downing huge forkfuls. This despite the fact he had already eaten a *Mousse au Chocolat*, which was served surrounded by thick sweetened *creme fraiche* and topped with heavy whipped cream. Both had cups of coffee, Jim's black and strong, Kim's sweetened with a half tablespoon of sugar, and lightened with a dollop of cream.

Kim paused with her fork halfway to her mouth, then set it back down on the dessert plate. She and Jim both started to speak at once.

"Jim, you've been awfully . . ."

"Kim, you seem to have something . . ."

They both stopped and laughed.

"You go first, Kim. I didn't mean to interrupt you."

"Jim, you don't seem to have your usual appetite," she said. "And you've been awfully quiet all evening. The past several days, for that matter. Is there something on your mind?"

Jim put another piece of *soufflé* in his mouth, savoring it before answering.

"That's funny. I was just about to ask you the same thing. Whether you realize it or not, you haven't been yourself recently. You've also been on the quiet side. I think maybe we're both worried about something. Or am I missing my guess?"

"No, you're not wrong. Sometimes I hate that lawman's intuition of yours," Kim answered. "I need your advice about a major life change I'm thinking of making."

"You're transitioning genders, and are running off with RuPaul."

"Jim, will you be serious for once in your life? This is not the time for joking. You've already realized something's troubling me."

"Well, your woman's intuition is working just as well," Jim said. "I do have something important I need to discuss with you. Real important."

"Do you want to go first, or shall I?" Kim asked.

"The old adage is 'ladies first.' Why don't we go by that, unless you'd rather not," Jim replied.

"No, what I'm worried about has been eating at me for quite some time," Kim said. "I'd prefer to get it out in the open. Perhaps it will help you with your problem."

"I'm waiting."

Kim took a deep breath before continuing.

"I've had an offer to buy my company. A very good offer. I'm seriously contemplating accepting it. I'd like to hear your thoughts."

"This is a surprise," Jim said. "Give me a minute to gather said thoughts."

"Of course."

Jim was silent for a few moments. He drank most of his remaining coffee before he spoke again.

"First, Kim, I want to emphasize whatever decision you make I will respect, and back you one hundred percent. You started Tavares Consulting, worked hard to make a go of it, and the company was already a success before we even met. It's your baby, so to speak."

"But you must have something to say."

"I do, but not a whole heckuva lot. First, is selling the business something you were planning? Did the offer come out of the blue? And most important, at least it would be to me in this situation, is how you feel, deep down in your gut, about giving up the firm you started from scratch, and built from the ground up."

"There are pros and cons, of course," Kim said. "The buyer would ask me to stay on as a consultant, with a five-year contract. After two years, I would have the option to be released from that. Of course, except for occasional travel, I'd still be working from home."

"You do that now," Jim pointed out.

"That's true. However, my workload will be much less. That's a plus. Also, the price they're willing to pay for the business is more than generous. It will assure financial security for well into the future, even during our retirements. We won't have to worry about college tuition for our children, either."

"Which I certainly can't say on my Ranger's salary, even with the pension and 401k," Jim said. A slight scowl played briefly across his face, gone so quickly Kim couldn't be positive she'd seen it.

"Jim, this has nothing to do with how much money either of us makes," Kim protested. "It's about my making the correct choice, in a matter that will affect our entire family for the rest of our lives."

"I know, honey. Go on. What else is part of your considerations?"

"The biggest downside is I would no longer own my company. It would be a division of the buyer's corporation. I'd be giving up control. However, I'd have much more free time. That means more time with our children. Even with you. We would no longer have the problem we have now, scheduling a few days off at the same time when we want to get away."

"Which might not be easy for you, handing over the reins of Tavares Consulting to someone else," Jim said. "However, you *would* be able to start another firm if you so desired, at least once your two-year commitment is up."

"Except the agreement includes a fifteen year no compete clause."

"Even with that, you could go into business in another area, couldn't you?"

"That's true. Which is an interesting proposition. However, this to me is the overriding consideration."

Kim hesitated.

"Don't keep me in suspense," Jim urged.

Kim took another sip of her coffee before replying.

"This is the part I'm most concerned about, because it involves you directly."

"Me? How?"

"Jim, I don't want to live in the Austin area any longer. In fact, I don't want to live anywhere along the I35 corridor from Dallas-Fort Worth down to San Antonio. Every time I make a business trip to New York, Boston, or Washington, the more I realize this part of Texas is turning into the Northeast. It's more crowded, more polluted, and more crime ridden every week. More and more land is being destroyed just to put up cookie cutter tract houses, industrial parks, and big box stores. I haven't even mentioned the traffic. The only difference between Austin and New York is there are more pickup trucks on the road down here. That, more cowboy hats and boots, and more gun racks. I don't want our children growing up in this environment. I want them to grow up with fresh air, wide open spaces, in a town where they can make close friends, and where they can play outside without someone having to keep an eye on them every minute. I want Josh and Katerina to have the freedom to walk around town, ride their horses or bicycles, and not have to stick close to our house. I'd prefer to make the change before Josh starts kindergarten next year. I want them to grow up in the Texas our parents remember. That's not possible here, not any longer. This is the real reason I'd like to sell my company. I can't leave Austin until I do."

"It sounds as if you've already decided," Jim said.

"I have. The deal has been completed. It's just awaiting my signature. However, I can't make the final decision without your input. I know how attached you are to your family's homestead land, and the fight you had to keep it after your father was murdered. Would you want to leave your home behind? What about your job? Would you be able to make a transfer?

Would you even want to? If you aren't, then I'll turn down the offer. Our marriage is my top priority."

"Then you'd resent me for a long time, perhaps the rest of your life, for holding you back," Jim said. "Don't say you wouldn't," he continued, when Kim started to object. "However, what you've just said brings us directly to what's been troubling me. I've been asked to transfer to Company E. I'd be stationed in Alpine, in the Big Bend country. Alpine's worlds apart from here. As Texas Tourism says, 'It's like a whole other country.' It's exactly the kind of environment you seem to be looking for."

"So *you've* been preoccupied, all the while, about breaking the news to me you are also looking at making a move," Kim said. "It seems like we're both a couple of cowards."

"I wouldn't go that far," Jim answered. "I'd say more like anxious about uprooting the life we have now, and making some major changes. You'd have to make more of those than I would, of course. And I haven't said 'yes' to the transfer yet. I told both Major Voitek, and Major Alejandro Trujillo, Company E's commander, I needed to discuss it with you first, that accepting the new post would have to be a family decision. That includes my mother. What?"

From the look on Kim's face, Jim realized she had already talked to his widowed mother.

"You already have, haven't you? You've already spoken to Ma."

"Yes, Jim, I did. Please understand, I had no choice. It would have been impossible for me to keep the discussions under wraps. Your mother is one of the major reasons Tavares Consulting is so successful. She's been invaluable during the negotiations."

"But you didn't drop even the slightest hint to me. Don't you think I should have known?"

"You didn't mention your possibly being transferred to me, either, Jim."

"I only learned about it last week. I spent the past several days considering how I felt about moving to west Texas, and how it would upend all our lives. I didn't want to upset you by mentioning it before I was certain leaving home was what *I* might want. I saw no point in getting you or Ma all worked up until I was positive I might accept the new post. It's plain you've been thinking about this for a lot longer than I have."

"All right, I have," Kim admitted. "I didn't want to mention it to you, until I also was certain the change was something I would even consider. You have enough on your mind just from being a Ranger. The last thing I wanted was to burden you with another distraction, that might well affect your ability to do your job. If that makes you angry or upset, I'm sorry. However, I still would not have handled things any differently."

"I'm not all that upset, well, perhaps just a tad, but I don't want to be, although it may sound that way," Jim answered. "More like a bit surprised, and a little perplexed. So, the bottom line: You want to get away from Austin, you've had an offer for your company which will allow you to do just that, and I've been offered a transfer to west Texas, which would be a new challenge and opportunity for me. I'd also be working in an area I love. Is that right?"

"Yes, it is."

"Then do we make the move?"

"It seems so, but there's a lot of details to iron out," Kim said. "For starters, once you accept the transfer, how soon will you need to report to Company E?"

Before Jim could respond, their server approached.

"*Monsieur*, *Madame*, would you care for more *café*, or anything else?" he asked.

"If you don't have any other customers waiting for this table, we would appreciate more coffee, *s'il vous plait*," Jim answered.

"*Oui*, *Monsieur.* There are no more reservations *ce soir.* Linger over your *soufflé et café* as long as you like. I will bring another pot of *café*."

"*Merci beaucoup*.

"Kim, if we're going to be here a while longer, I figure we needed to at least order more coffee," Jim said, once the server departed. "To answer your question, officially, I would take over the Alpine office in thirty days, when Leon DaSilva retires. However, I'll be bouncing back and forth between Buda and Alpine until then. I'll have to spend time reviewing my active cases with whomever takes my place in Buda, and I'll also have to spend time in Alpine so Leon can bring me up to speed on his active cases. He'll have to introduce me around to the local law, just like I'll have to do with whoever is assigned to my current territory. So I'll start working in Alpine in three weeks. I know, that's not much time. I'm certain you can't get everything wrapped up that quickly, and we damn sure can't find a house and move that fast, especially since we need a spread big enough for our animals. I figure I'll get a hotel room and live out of a suitcase until we find a place to buy. I'll be able to come home weekends until then. You should probably take a trip to Alpine to make certain you'll like the town. It's really isolated. Heck, it doesn't even have a Walmart. The nearest one is up at Fort Stockton, over sixty miles away. It takes about an hour to get there. When you need to make a business trip, the closest major airport is El Paso. That's about three and a half hours by car. There is a small airport in Alpine. I would imagine you could charter a plane there to fly you to El Paso, Austin, or Dallas, where you'd make connections to wherever you were headed. But Alpine's not a complete backwater. Sul Ross State University is located there, along with the Museum of the Big Bend. The town's also got quite a number of restaurants, ranging from fast food chains to exclusive eateries. True, there won't be the cultural offerings like in Austin, but there's nothing which says we can't make trips back here."

"We'll plan a family day and do just that," Kim said. "The main thing I'll need will be decent internet access. Once my contract is up with the buyer, I don't plan on needing to make any more trips, except for vacation."

"Speaking of the buyer, you haven't given me their name yet," Jim pointed out.

Kim leaned closer. She lowered her voice to just above a whisper.

"This has to be kept confidential until the merger papers are signed and the announcement made. It's a company called Denali Financial and International Business Consultants, out of Anchorage, Alaska. It's a native Tlingit owned corporation. Their goals and mission statement are complementary to my own. It will be a good fit. Now I've got a question for you."

"Shoot."

"Jim, how many times have I told you I wish you wouldn't use that expression? It always brings to mind the time you were shot, and almost died."

"I'm sorry, Kim. Go ahead and ask your question."

"What will we do about our home? Do you really want to leave it, or sell it?"

"I guess before I answer that, have you asked my mother what she wants to do? Remain in her house on our property in San Leanna, move into ours, stay in the Austin area but find another place, or move to the Alpine area with us?"

"She's eager to make a change. There are too many bad memories for her here, about your father's death. Plus, even as a consultant, I need her to continue as my executive assistant. She's invaluable to me."

Jim's father had been killed during a failed attempt by a group of domestic terrorists to blow up the Alamo, which would have caused horrendous death and destruction. He had intercepted the men on their way to San Antonio. In the ensuing gunfight, Jim's father had killed four of the terrorists, but was gunned down by their two surviving partners. It took several years after his father's death for Jim himself to track down his murderers. He was forced to kill them when they refused to surrender.

"I'd also imagine she doesn't want to see her grandchildren move away," Jim said. "As far as the homestead, I legally can't sell it. That's the agreement made when those crooked county commissioners attempted to swindle Ma out of the property. I don't want to turn it over to the county for a park yet, as the deed requires if my family line dies out. We might want to move back some day. When my time comes, I want to be buried in the family cemetery. Probably the best thing to do would be find a good property management company, and rent out the houses. We can place any restrictions on the rental contract we deem necessary."

"So you don't mind leaving your family homestead behind?"

"In many ways, yes. Mostly leaving the family cemetery. In others, no. Just like you, I'm not fond of living in the Austin area anymore, either. Let's face it, we get squeezed in tighter more and more every year, as Austin keeps growing, and Travis County gets overrun. There's no decent places to ride our horses any longer, except for Seabright Park. Even getting over there from our place has become a hassle. Not many safe places left for kids, either. Look at the timing, both of us being offered the chance to move on at the same time. I think God has given us this opportunity. We should listen to Him, and take it. Look, I'm free the next three days. I don't have to give Major Voitek my answer until Monday. Why don't we take a drive over to Alpine tomorrow, the whole family? We'll spend the weekend, and look around. If you decide you like the town, we'll hunt up a real estate agent and have them start looking for a new place for us. If you don't, then I'll turn down the transfer, and you can decide whether or not you still want to sell your company."

"That sounds like a fine idea," Kim answered. "If we can get things decided over the weekend, it will ease my mind greatly."

"Then that's settled. We'd better ask for the check. The *maître d'* and our waiter have been glaring at us for the past fifteen minutes. I think they want to go home. We'll get a good night's sleep. There'll be plenty of time to talk in the car tomorrow. However, there is one thing we have to do before we make the move."

"What's that?"

"You still owe me a night at Jimmy Jack's."

2

Early the next morning, the entire Blawcyzk family, including their dogs, piled into Kim's hunter green Chevy Suburban. Jim took the wheel, with Kim riding shotgun. Katerina was buckled in her carrier in the middle seat, with her grandmother beside her. Josh's request to ride in the rear seat had been granted, so he was buckled there, in his child seat. Frostie and Fritz were on either side of him. The dogs' harnesses were fastened securely to seatbelts.

"Everyone ready? Then let's go," Jim said. He put the Suburban in gear, and headed out of the driveway.

The route to Alpine took them along several Texas Farm to Market and Ranch Roads to Dripping Springs, where they would pick up U.S. 290, which would take them to Johnson City, then roughly due west by northwest until they picked up Interstate 10, approximately thirty miles west of Fredericksburg.

"If none of you mind, we'll make a short stop in Fredericksburg, to see if Mike and Annie are home," Jim said, as they neared the city, which had been founded by German immigrants. The city still celebrated its Germanic roots, and was a major tourist center. Spur Award–winning Texas singer-songwriter-author Mike Blakely and his wife, Annie, had a ranch just outside of town. They and Jim had become acquainted several years back.

"Not at all," Kim said. "Katerina will be ready to be fed by then, and it will be time to have her diaper changed."

"I'm hungry too, Mommy," Josh called from the back.

"Then it's settled," Jim said. "We'll stop in town to grab a quick bite and stretch our legs. If Mike and Annie aren't busy, we'll visit with 'em for a little while, then be on our way again."

After a snack at one of Fredericksburg's German *konditoreis*, a pastry shop which Jim could never pass by, they made the short drive to the Blakely ranch. Mike and Annie were indeed home. Besides having a reunion conversation, the Blakelys entertained Jim and his family, particularly Josh and Katerina, with a few songs. Katerina had been fussing, but Mike and Annie's soothing harmonies soon had her mesmerized, then sleeping. After making their goodbyes, the Blawcyzks resumed their journey.

The small city of Sonora was at almost the half-way point of their trip. They stopped at the Road Ranger Travel Center and Truck Stop, where Jim filled the Suburban's tank, and they had lunch.

"Boy howdy, I wish I could charge this trip to the state," Jim said, once they were back on the highway. "Did you see how much it cost to fill up?"

"Not as much as in downtown Austin," Kim pointed out. "And at least we're making good time."

Jim yawned.

"If you say so. Havin' to drive so slow is killin' me. We could've been in Fort Stockton by now."

"Jim, you've been driving fifteen or twenty miles per hour over the speed limit most of the way," Betty pointed out. "That's plenty fast enough. Too fast, as far as I'm concerned. You inherited your father's lead foot."

"Particularly with our children in the car," Kim added. "I'd rather reach Alpine a little later, but alive, than not at all. There's no reason to hurry. We've got the entire weekend."

"If both of you would kindly not mention lead in my foot I'd appreciate it," Jim said, laughing. "I've taken enough lead bullets to last me a lifetime."

After passing Fort Stockton, Jim took Exit 246 off the interstate onto U.S. 67 South, which would lead directly to Alpine. The terrain was still mostly a semi-arid, almost table-flat high desert plain, cut by dry washes and shallow arroyos. However, more mountains and flat-topped mesas were now appearing in the distance.

"It's only about an hour to Alpine from here," Jim said. "Soon as we check in, I figure we can rest awhile, then maybe do a little exploring before supper. How does that sound?"

"Want to swim," Josh said.

"You'll be able to, little pard, once we get there," Jim answered. "The hotel has a pool."

"It wouldn't be a bad idea for you to take Josh for a swim, and burn off some of his energy," Kim said. "He's slept for the past two hours, so he'll be a bit wound up. Betty and I will rest in the rooms while you do that. I don't want Katerina to get too much sun."

"She's got your complexion," Jim said. "I would think she wouldn't burn that easily."

Unlike her older brother, who had Jim's blond hair, blue eyes, and fair skin, Katerina had mostly inherited her mother's features. She had black hair, deep brown eyes, and light tan skin.

"Perhaps when she's a few years older, but no infant should be overexposed to sunlight, especially bright sunlight at this altitude," Kim answered. "That could damage her skin, or worse, her eyes. We'll be just fine while you and Josh take your swim. Just make certain to use plenty of sunscreen. You *gringos* burn so easily."

Jim looked at Kim and grinned.

"*Si*, *madre gallina*. Even though it's an indoor pool."

Kim reached over and slapped his arm.

"Why didn't you say so? That means we can all head for the pool."

"You didn't ask."

Kim slapped him again.

Slightly less than sixty minutes later, after driving through Alpine, Jim pulled the Suburban into the parking lot of The Hotel Parker at the Quarter Circle 7, which was southwest of town, just outside the city limits.

"Here we are," he said. "You ready for that swim, Josh?"

"I sure am, Daddy."

"Then let's get checked in."

After having their swim, Jim took his family on a quick tour around the area outside of Alpine.

"Kim, Ma, I think we'll head on down to Marfa, then come back here and have supper at the hotel's restaurant," he said. "That will give you a quick overview of the region, and get us back in time to eat, then turn in early. That'll leave us all of tomorrow to explore Alpine itself. Unless either of you had something else in mind."

"You're the tour guide, Jim," Kim said. "I don't know anything about this part of the state."

"I've only been here a few times, once on a vacation with your father. That was before you were born," Betty said. "You're in charge."

"*I'm* in charge? Boy howdy, *that's* somethin' I don't hear very often around the house," Jim answered, laughing. "Everyone buckled in? Let's move on out."

The first portion of U.S. 90's stretch from Alpine west to Marfa wound around eroded mountains, mesas, and buttes. After traversing Paisano Pass, the road once again crossed a level to slightly rolling semi-arid plain. At this altitude, over four thousand feet, the vegetation was slightly thicker. In places where sufficient underground moisture was available the land was even tree covered.

"It's certainly stark out here. Not at all like east Texas, or even central," Kim said. "But the land is beautiful in its starkness. The air is so fresh and clear. Look how blue the sky is. I'll bet at night the stars look so close you'd think you could almost touch them."

"Not to mention the Marfa Lights," Jim said. "We'll have to spend some nights watching for them, if we decide to make the move."

"I've already decided, if I have a say," Betty said.

"Of course you do, Betty," Kim assured her.

"I think we should move away from Austin. Jim, your father always talked about it when he was younger. But he never would. He couldn't bring himself to leave there. Perhaps if he had, he'd still be alive."

She took out a tissue and dabbed tears from her eyes.

"You have no way of knowin' that, Ma," Jim said. "He could just as easily been killed out here. Or died in bed. God wanted to take him home."

"I know. If I didn't believe that, I don't know how I could have survived the last few years. In one way, if you move out here, you'll be fulfilling your father's wish."

"Jim, right now I'm leaning toward saying 'yes,' also," Kim added. "It seems like this would certainly be a healthier environment for our children. And for you. It appears there would be much more need for working on horseback out here, which is what you love most about being a Texas Ranger. And lots of riding trails for all of us."

"Well, maybe just a little more horseback work," Jim said. "Those days are mostly gone. However, let's not be too hasty. Wait until tomorrow, after you've had the chance to see more of Alpine. We're only a few minutes away from Marfa. It's a smaller city than Alpine, and the seat of Presidio County. Presidio will be one of my counties if I accept the transfer. Marfa's small, but has a fairly lively and active arts community. Some good restaurants, too."

"Jim, if every crime in Texas happened in restaurants, the criminals wouldn't stand a chance," Betty said. "If there's one thing you know, it's the location of every decent restaurant in the state."

"Also a lot of the not so good ones, greasy cafes, rough roadhouses, and every wild bar and honkytonk in Texas, not even mentioning just plain dives," Kim added.

Both women laughed.

"All part of my job," Jim said. "We're coming into Marfa now. Do we need to stop for anything? If not, I'll just drive through town, then turn around and head back to Alpine."

"Unless Katerina wakes up, there's no need to stop," Kim said. "If she does, I can feed her without having to pull over, as long as she doesn't need a diaper change."

"I want to swim some more," Josh called from the back of the Suburban.

"We'll see when we return to our hotel, little pard," Jim answered. "It might be too late. But we'll hit the pool again tomorrow. I promise. Right now, I'll go a few blocks past the center of town, then swing up to show everyone the Presidio County Courthouse. After that we'll return to Alpine, and call it a day."

He drove farther into the city.

"That's the City Hall, just ahead on the right," Jim said. "It's on the only intersection in the entire city that has a traffic light. Even that's only a four-way blinking red one, to make certain no one misses the stop signs."

Jim rolled up to the intersection of U.S. 90, U.S. 67 South, and Texas 17 North. He stopped, waited for an eighteen-wheeler to clear the intersection, then proceeded. He was under the flashing red light when a Marfa Police Ford Explorer pulled out in front of him, making a right-hand turn. Jim was forced to swerve to avoid a collision. He blew his SUV's horn. The police car pulled to the curb, waited for Jim to pass, then its flashing lights came on. It pulled up behind the Blawcyzks' Suburban. The officer driving hit the vehicle's siren.

"I think he wants to give you a ticket, Jim," Kim said.

"I don't know what for," Jim answered. "If anyone deserves a citation, it's whoever's behind the wheel of that car. I made a full stop, and was already halfway through the intersection when they made that dumb move. Well, let's see what they have to say. And let me do the talking."

Jim pulled the Suburban to the curb. The police Explorer parked right behind him. The officer waited for a few minutes before he emerged from his vehicle. Jim lowered his window as the officer approached.

"Good afternoon, sir," the officer said. "Driver's license, registration, and insurance, please."

Jim took his wallet from his pocket and removed his license. Kim took the Suburban's registration and insurance card from the glove compartment and handed them to her husband, who passed them to the policeman. Frostie and Fritz were both barking furiously from the back of the Suburban.

"May I ask why you pulled me over?" Jim said, as he handed over the documents.

"You didn't stop at the intersection. You nearly caused an accident by almost hitting my vehicle," the policeman answered. "And you need to quiet those dogs."

"Sorry about the dogs, but they're barkers at any strangers. As far as not stopping, I beg to differ, Officer . . . Bradford," Jim said, reading the man's name tag. "I not only came to a full stop, but I had to wait for a McLane Kitchen semi to clear the intersection before I could proceed. There was also a Union Pacific Chevrolet Silverado pickup, with conversion units so it had wheels to ride on railroad tracks, making a right hand turn from 67 North onto 90 East. There was another, older Union Pacific Silverado right behind that one."

"You saw all that?"

"I certainly did. I pay attention when I'm driving, unlike some people."

Jim's barb didn't go unnoticed.

"I'd advise you to watch your tongue. Also, don't try and deny you failed to stop, Mr. Bluh . . . Bluh."

"BLUH-zhick," Jim offered. "And I am

denying it. You're the one who's clearly in the wrong, Officer."

"Mr. Blawcyzk, this conversation is over, unless you'd prefer to continue it at the station. Please wait a moment while I run your registration and license."

The officer returned to his vehicle with Jim's documents.

"He's a liar," Kim said. "We all know it."

"Yes, he is, but there's not a heckuva lot we can do about it, at least not today," Jim said. "The whole thing's recorded on the dashcam. When I show the video in court, the ticket will get tossed."

"Why don't you show it to him now?" Kim asked.

"He'd probably refuse to look at it. Also, I want to show him up for the liar he is. Even a little matter like faking a traffic ticket is a smudge on the badge."

"You could identify yourself as a Texas Ranger," Betty suggested.

"That would be unethical, although things like that are done all the time, particularly among local and county jurisdictions, and of course if a politician's involved," Jim answered. "And if I did, this bozo might file a complaint against me with the D.P.S. That would get me in hot water. No, if he gives me an actual ticket, instead of just a warning, I'll wait for my day in court."

"I gotta go potty, Daddy," Josh said.

"Can you hold on just a minute?" Jim asked. "There's a convenience store on the corner. Soon as this policeman finishes, we'll use the rest room there. I'll even buy you a popsicle if you'd like. Orange."

"Okay, Daddy. Not too long, though."

"It won't be. Here he comes now."

"You and your family seem to be a long way from home, Mr. Blawcyzk," Bradford said. He handed Jim back his license, registration, and insurance card. "Where exactly is San Leanna? I've never heard of it."

"It's in Travis County, just south of Austin."

"What brings y'all out here, if you don't mind my asking?"

"We're just taking a few days for a road trip," Jim answered.

"I see. Well, sir, out here, we don't take much to folks driving like they do back in east Texas. We expect them to obey the law. This is a citation for failing to stop at a traffic control device. There's an additional charge of failing to yield to an emergency vehicle."

"You didn't have your lights or siren on," Jim protested.

"I turned my emergency lights on just as I entered the intersection," Bradford answered. "If you'll just sign here, acknowledging receipt of the ticket, you can be on your way. The court's address is on the citation. You have ten days to pay it. If you intend to contest the charges, you will need to return to Marfa on the date indicated. Court is held in the Presidio County Courthouse."

"Oh, I'll be there. You can bet your badge on that," Jim said. He scrawled his signature across the ticket, and handed it back to Bradford.

"You'll come all the way from Austin back here, merely to fight this ticket?" Bradford asked. "It would be far cheaper to just send a check to pay the fine."

He gave Jim his copy of the citation.

"I have no intention of being blackmailed into enriching Marfa's coffers by paying a fine for a bogus charge," Jim snapped. "Now, if we're finished here, and as far as I'm concerned we are, my boy needs to use the bathroom. You've also awakened by baby daughter. That means she'll need to be fed and changed. I'll see you in court. Have a nice day."

"Drive carefully," Bradford said, with a smirk. He went back to his car, and watched while Jim and his family went into Uncle's Convenience Store.

The Marfa City Hall was directly across the street from the store. It had a carport to shelter a single vehicle.

"Jim, that cop is now parked under the roof in front of the city hall," Betty said, when they exited the store. "I think he's still watching us."

"Let him watch," Jim said. He turned, looked directly at Bradford, and gave the Marfa officer a mock salute.

"Time to get outta this town."

Later that night, Jim slipped into bed alongside his wife.

"Are they finally asleep?" Kim asked.

"The kids, or the dogs?"

"Both."

"Yes," Jim answered. "Josh went down right away. Katerina took a little longer. I know she's only three months old, but I think she misses her own crib. I sang her to sleep."

"Poor baby," Kim whispered.

"What was that you just said?"

"I said 'lucky baby,' to have a father willing to sing to her."

"Nice save," Jim answered. He leaned over to kiss Kim. She turned away from him.

"Don't you try and kiss me, Mister," she said, angrily.

"What? Why not? What did I do?" Jim asked.

"You know damn well what you did."

"No, I don't. I swear, honey, I don't have a clue what you're upset about," Jim protested.

"Don't even try to wiggle out of it. I caught you looking at those pretty girls, who were ogling you by the pool today."

"What? I've been *ogled? Ogled?*" Jim

exclaimed. "I didn't notice anyone giving me the once-over. I feel so cheap, so tawdry, so, so *used*. I guess I'm just a boy toy to all you females. A mere sex object. I'll have you know I'm not just a great body and handsome face. I've got a brain to go along with them."

"Don't flatter yourself, cowboy," Kim retorted. "I'm not buying that line you didn't see those girls, either."

"Which girls? You mean the blonde, with light blue eyes, eighteen to twenty years old, about five foot eight, weight around one hundred fifteen to one hundred twenty pounds, measurements approximately thirty-eight by twenty-seven by thirty-six, wearing a blue string bikini. She had a ladybug tattoo on her left ankle, and a Monarch butterfly tattoo on her right breast. And her friend, light brunette hair, hazel eyes, about the same age, height around five foot six, weight close to one hundred ten pounds, measurements thirty-five by twenty-four by thirty-three, wearing a tie-dyed bikini. She had a diamond or rhinestone stud in the pierced right side of her nose. A daisy tattoo around her belly button, which formed the center of the flower. The daisy's stem, which had two leaves, went down from the flower, and disappeared behind the bikini bottom. You can imagine where it ended. Her belly button was an innie. Are those the girls you mean?"

"So you *were* looking at them! You admit it."

"No, I wasn't *looking* at them. I was *observing* them. I also studied their boyfriends. One had wavy red hair, green eyes, and a smattering of freckles across his nose and cheeks. His skin was sunburned, which most likely indicates he hasn't been in this area for long. Age about twenty-two to twenty-five. He was between five foot ten and six feet tall, weight around one hundred ninety. Waist around thirty inches, broad chest and shoulders. Wore red Speedo type swimming trunks. Had three teardrops tattooed under his left eye, a typical gang tat. Also had a long knife scar on his upper right arm. The other man was Hispanic, probably Mexican lineage if he's from this area. Medium brown complexion, black hair cut or shaved short, very dark brown eyes, height six foot two to six foot four, weight about two twenty. Muscular, but had a very slight paunch. Waist probably thirty-eight or forty inches. Age late twenties-early thirties. Bullet scar on the left side of his chest, just below the collarbone. Wore green and white striped Speedo type trunks. Tattoos covering both arms, which included several known gang images. Black rose inked around and over his belly button, with the stem extending down from the blossom, and disappearing behind his trunks, much like the brunette woman's daisy, so she's probably his girlfriend. Again, you can imagine where the stem ended. Several thorns on the stem dripping

3

After spending the morning exploring Alpine and its environs, Jim and his family stopped for lunch at Guzzi Up, a pizza and pasta place located in downtown Alpine, next to the AMTRAK station and across the street from the historic Holland Hotel. The building itself was a converted gas station, an open, family friendly space. Jim had chosen it because they wouldn't have to worry anyone would complain about Josh making a ruckus, or little Katerina fussing or crying. The owners assured Jim he and his family would also be able to remain and talk as long as they liked. They wouldn't have to be concerned about being rushed out to make room for other customers. They even allowed them to bring in Frostie and Fritz, since it was far too hot to leave any animal in a car.

As always, Jim requested, and was granted, a corner table in the back of the room, where he could see everyone who entered, and where no one could get behind him without being seen. A Ranger made plenty of enemies, and even out here, where Jim's identity wasn't generally known, you could never be certain one wouldn't turn up, looking for the chance for an ambush revenge.

"There will be one more person joining us, in about half an hour," Jim told Honey, their server. "We'll order our meal then."

"That's quite all right," she answered. "Would any of you care for something to drink in the meantime?"

"I'll have a long neck Lone Star," Jim answered.

"Dr Pepper for me," Kim said.

"Me too, Mommy," Josh piped up.

"I'll have the same," Betty said.

"And I'll just bet the little cutie patootie smiling at me doesn't want anything," Honey said. "What's her name?"

"Katerina," Kim answered.

"Well, ain't she just the cutest little doll."

"She's not a doll. She's my baby sister," Josh said. He had a scowl on his face.

"Of course she is, darlin'," Honey replied. "And she's lucky to have a handsome big brother like you to take care of her. You watch her while I go get your soda pop."

Honey bustled off. She returned shortly, and set the beverages in front of the Blawcyzks.

"Let me know if y'all need anythin' else, y'hear?"

"We'll do that," Jim assured her.

"We might as well take a vote while we wait for Leon to arrive," Jim said. He took a long swig of his beer, then set the bottle down.

"Kim, Ma, you've seen pretty much what there is to see of Alpine, Marfa, and this area. We've already talked a lot in the car. What are your final thoughts? Do we make the move, or stay put?"

"Jim, clearly there are drawbacks to leaving Austin for west Texas," Kim said. "It's more isolated out here than I imagined. Traveling for work will be more difficult than I first believed. However, that will only be for two years, unless I decide not to exercise the option to end my contract, so it's not a deal breaker. It will also take some getting used to, being so far away from a major city. On the other hand, this is almost exactly what I pictured as the place to raise our family. Having a university here is certainly a major plus. I might think about applying for a teaching position there. I believe I could love it here. Additionally, won't it be at least a bit less dangerous for you?"

"*Quien sabe*?" Jim said, with a shrug. "There's drugs everywhere, of course, even in the smallest towns. There's smugglers and human traffickers out here, that there aren't many of in Austin. But with fewer people, not quite so many violent crimes, so I guess perhaps."

"I understand, Jim."

"Ma?" Jim asked.

"I hate the thought of leaving your father behind, but I feel he wants us to make this change.

He's buried with his kinfolk, so I'm certain he's at peace. While we were driving around, I swear I could hear him whispering to me it was time to let go of the past, and start a new chapter in my life."

"He's with you all the time anyway, Ma. Both of us. His spirit isn't in his grave."

"I don't believe we need to ask your opinion, Jim," Kim said. "This is your place. You were meant to be out here."

"Oh, I don't know," Jim answered. "I've got lots of friends back in Austin. And like Ma, I'm a bit sad over the thought of leaving the family homestead. There's over one hundred and fifty years of Blawcyzk family history in that little patch of Texas soil. But it will always be there, if we decide we want to move back. And the land out here calls to me."

"So do we really need to vote?" Betty said.

"Just to say out loud what we all seem to be agreed on," Jim answered.

"Then I vote yes."

"Kim?"

"Once we find the right house, I'm certain everything else will fall into place. Yes."

"Then I'm outvoted," Jim said. "I planned on voting no."

"What?" Betty and Kim both exclaimed.

"Oh. You're talking about the move," Jim said. "I thought we were voting on toppings for our pizza. Y'all know I can't stand mushrooms. Yes on the move."

"Betty, I might end up killing your son and burying his body so deep in the desert no one will ever find it, if he keeps up his antics," Kim said.

"I'll help you," Jim's mother offered. "It would be justifiable homicide. No jury would ever convict us."

A man's deep voice boomed through the restaurant. It belonged to a burly individual, in his late fifties or early sixties, who stood about six foot six, and weighed about two hundred fifty pounds. A broad brimmed Stetson covered his graying hair. The hat shaded piercing gray eyes, set deep in a weather-beaten face. A wide smile played across the newcomer's lips.

"Jim, am I hearing a conspiracy to commit murder being plotted?"

"Howdy, Leon. It seems as if, and I'm the intended victim," Jim said. He stood up to shake the new arrival's hand. "It's sure good to see you again. I'd like to introduce my mother, Betty, and my wife, Kim. The little *hombre* in the booster seat is our son, Josh. That's Katerina, our new baby, in the carrier. Ma, Kim, this is Ranger Leon DaSilva."

"Ladies."

Leon doffed his hat.

"Leon's the Ranger who's worked out of Alpine the last what, fifteen years, Leon?"

"Closer to twenty. I was glad to see y'all are already here. I'm a few minutes earlier than planned."

"No problem, Leon," Jim said. "I'm plumb starved. Now that you're here, we can order lunch. Have a seat."

"As I recall, Jim, your father claimed you were always starved. Said he was gonna have to take a second job just to keep your belly filled," Leon said, laughing, as he pulled up a chair.

"As his mother, I can attest Jim hasn't changed one bit, Ranger DaSilva," Betty said. "I swear sometimes he needs one refrigerator all to himself."

"Leon, please, Ma'am."

"Of course."

"Your husband and I were accepted into the Rangers just about the same time," Leon continued. "He stayed near San Antonio, while I came out here. He was a terrific man, and a fine Ranger. I'll miss him until the day I die."

"That's very kind. Thank you."

"Jim, I couldn't help but overhear," Leon said. "It sounds like you've made your decision about taking the transfer to Alpine."

"We pretty much have," Jim answered. "It's just a matter of finding a place to live."

"Boy howdy, that's certainly good news. Especially for me. I was afraid you'd turn down the transfer, which would delay my being able to retire. Molly's worried half to death I'll change my mind."

"I had to make certain my transferring to Alpine would be the best thing for my family, Leon," Jim answered. "It wasn't an easy decision. If Kim or my mother hadn't agreed, I wouldn't have made the move. And of course it's not official until I sign the papers. I plan on doing that Monday."

"Ladies, I'm sure you won't regret moving west," Leon said. "The Big Bend's a fine place to raise a family. Me'n Molly raised six kids here. They've all turned out fine."

"That's why we're doing it. I don't want to have my children grow up in a big city," Kim said. "We're going to do some house hunting while we're here."

"That's an excellent idea."

"Would you happen to know a real estate agent you could recommend, Leon?" Jim asked.

"As a matter of fact, I do. See Mary Dobson over at Alpine Mountain Vista Realty. She's fantastic at finding exactly what a client is looking for. Tell her I sent you. The office is a couple of blocks down the street."

"Thanks, Leon. We'll stop there soon as we have lunch."

Leon started laughing.

"What's so funny?" Jim asked.

"I just thought of your last name. I have enough trouble around here with mine. Everybody thinks

DaSilva is Spanish, but it's not. It's Portuguese. If folks can't even figure that out, they'll damn certain never be able to handle Blawcyzk."

"They'll figure it out. I'll make certain of it," Jim said. "Here comes our waitress. Let's order."

After finishing their meal, and saying goodbye to Leon, the Blawcyzks made the short drive to Alpine Mountain Vista Realty. There was only one person in the office, a pleasingly plump woman in her mid-fifties, who had auburn hair piled high on her head. Her hazel eyes peered out from behind a pair of red-framed glasses, which were trimmed with rhinestones.

"Howdy, folks," she greeted, getting up from her chair. "Welcome to Alpine Mountain Vista Realty. How might I help y'all?"

"We're looking for Mary Dobson," Jim said. "Leon DaSilva recommended her."

"Well, bless Leon's heart. I'm Mary Dobson."

"James Blawcyzk, my wife Kimberly, and my mother, Elizabeth. The little ones are Joshua and Katerina."

"Why, aren't they just cute as a button," Dobson said. "And who are these two darling puppies?"

"Frostie and Fritz," Jim said.

"Let me get you boys a treat. And a lollipop for Josh."

She took two chew bones from one jar on her desk, a grape lollipop from another. She gave the bones to the dogs, the pop to Josh, who thanked her.

"There. Now, if you'll all take a seat, y'all can tell me what you need."

"We're moving to the Alpine area from just outside Austin, Mrs. Dobson," Jim said.

"Mary. And may I call you James?"

"Jim would be preferable."

"Jim it is. How about you ladies?"

"Kim."

"Betty."

"Excellent. You were saying, Jim?"

"We're looking for a home in this area, preferably not too far outside Alpine. Our needs are very specific. Leon told us you're quite good at matching your clients to the right property."

"That Leon. He's such a flatterer. I take it y'all are friends?"

"Me'n Leon are," Jim explained. "The rest of my family just met him."

"Well then. Describe what you require, and I'll go through my inventory. Are you interested in land, where you can build a new home, or would y'all prefer something already built and ready to move into?"

"Since we'll both be transferring, an already existing home would make the move much less stressful," Kim answered.

"That will narrow the possibilities down considerably," Dobson said. "Could you give me a basic idea of what you would want? The size of the house, style, rooms for entertaining, anything else you can think of."

"Kim, that's your department," Jim said. "I'm not all that fussy about my living space."

"We don't do a lot of entertaining, Mary," Kim answered. "We'd like something with at least four bedrooms, and a room I can use for an office, since I work from home. Jim will also need one of those. Because I do work from home, reliable internet access is a must. A good-sized kitchen. We also like having a fireplace. Two full baths, plus a bath with whirlpool tub and separate shower stall as part of the master suite. Definitely a deck or patio. A yard for the children to play. The location should be close to town, but not necessarily right in town. After living in the city for so long, a view would be nice."

"We also need a guest house or smaller home on the same property, for my mother," Jim added. "Ma, tell her what you want."

"I don't need anything large, Mary. Three rooms, living room, kitchen, and bedroom, and an open room I can use for my studio. I work in stained glass. Plenty of natural light, especially in the studio, would be a plus."

"You haven't mentioned the style," Dobson said. "One floor or two? Wood, brick, or adobe? Open concept interior, or more traditional?"

"We're flexible on that," Kim answered. "However, there's one thing that's a must. Jim, get it over with. Go ahead and tell her."

"Oh, brother. Here we go," Betty said. "This could take a while, Mary. Jim's about to give you a long list, lots more than just *one* thing."

"I've got all afternoon."

"You'll probably need it," Betty answered. "Get started, Jim."

"Mary, we have several horses, so we'll need an eight-stall barn. It has to be in excellent condition. Each stall should have a run-in paddock. I'll want a minimum of two corrals. Also dependable water, whether that comes from a deeply drilled well, or a natural spring, which I know is rare in west Texas. We, or I should say my wife and mother, keep chickens, so a coop and pen is needed for them. Our dogs are used to running free on our land in San Leanna. That won't be practical here, so we'll need a large, fenced in area, preferably the back yard, where they can be let loose. Also important is access to riding trails. Parking for six vehicles is an absolute necessity, plus space for two horse trailers, a four horse and a two horse. One of the cars is a restored antique Chevrolet station wagon, so that one needs a garage, or a carport at the minimum. The barn will need a feed room, wash stall, and large tack room. Hay would preferably be stored in a separate shed, in case of fire. We also have several barn cats."

"Six cars?" Kim exclaimed.

"Yep. Your car, Ma's car, the old Chevy wagon, my state vehicle, and both of my pickups."

"Jim, you're not seriously thinking of bringing your old truck out here? It can barely make it out of the yard."

"I'm not thinking of it. I'm doing it. That old truck's still got lots of life left in her," Jim answered. "Mary, when you come up with some potential properties, my wife and mother will be considering the houses. I'll be looking over the barns and land. I'm very particular about my horses' living quarters. There also has to be some trees. We're not like some of those city folks, who move out to the desert, then the first thing they do is rip up the native vegetation and plant grass, which needs irrigation, wasting water. Truthfully, I'm looking forward to landscaping with cacti. But we do require a few trees for shade. Preferably two of them will be close enough to each other, and stout enough, that I'll be able to hang a hammock. One last thing. There *has* to be access to riding trails. I realize I've already mentioned that, but that's the one thing which for me is non-negotiable. That's another of the reasons we're leaving Austin. Too much land is being bulldozed for development. We lose more space for riding and other outdoor recreation every day. That's about all I'm looking for."

"The house?"

"Whatever my wife likes is fine with me."

"You might find this hard to believe, but I have a property that's been on the market for quite some time, which I think would be perfect. It seems to be exactly what y'all are looking for. The price was recently reduced, once again. Would you like to hear more?"

"Yes," Kim answered.

"Wonderful. One of the old ranches, about three miles west of town on Highway 90, was subdivided into an equestrian community two years ago. While the roads are paved, there are horse trails in place of sidewalks. The minimum lot size is five acres. Homeowners have a choice of having a barn on their own property, with a maximum of two horses, or there's a community stable where they can board their horses, plus a riding arena and corrals. There's a professional stable manager who lives on site. Quite a few families live there, so it should be easy for you to make friends. Your children will also have plenty of playmates."

"That sounds like a stable environment for my family, all right," Jim said. Dobson winced, then forced a laugh.

"Jim, forget the bad jokes, and finish telling Mary what you require," Kim ordered.

"Yes, Ma'am! Mary, we'd need room for more than two horses, and I sure won't put our animals in a boarding stable. There are times when I need my horse in a hurry, so he has to be right in our back yard," Jim said. "And I for dang certain won't move into a subdivision where there's a homeowners' association. Not a chance. Too many rules and regulations. Plus the board members are usually fussy old women and persnickety old men, who send threatening letters if so much as a leaf is out of place. They'd drive me crazy, and me them."

"Jim, please, let Mary finish," Kim said.

"Thank you, Kim," Mary said. "I'm not suggesting you move into the subdivision. That wouldn't suit your needs at all. What I feel would be ideal for your family is the main part of the original *Tres Alamos Ranch.* That includes all the remaining original buildings, which date back to circa 1882. While the buildings retain many of their original features, they've been completely updated, with all the modern amenities. For some reason, although several people were interested in it, no one has ever made an offer. If you purchased the place, it would be like moving into a brand-new home. Well, actually, now that I recall, one couple from California did make an offer, but the amount was ridiculously low. The property includes a hundred acres of land, plus access to a thousand protected acres of open space and conservation easements on two still working ranches. You'll have lots of room to roam, on horseback or hiking. There are spectacular views of the mountains in all directions, including the Twin Peaks. That part of the ranch was kept separate from the subdivision. None of the subdivision regulations apply to it. Interested?"

Dobson couldn't help but notice the eager gleam in Jim's eyes. It was obvious she already had him nibbling at the bait, and soon would have him, hook, line, and sinker.

"It sounds like it has possibilities," Kim said.

"I have a binder with all the details, and photos of the property right here. I also have a virtual tour. Would you like to see either?"

"I sure would. The binder, please," Jim said. "Kim?"

"Yes. If we like what we see, then we'll go look at the place. If not, it will save us all a trip for nothing," Kim said. "Mary, I'm afraid Jim's not a big fan of computers, or virtual tours. Otherwise, the video would have been lovely."

"All right."

Dobson took a thick three ring binder from her desk drawer. The cover had a logo for *Tres Alamos Ranch*, underneath which was a watercolor illustration of three large cottonwoods. She opened the binder, to reveal a photograph of a rambling, red tile roofed adobe and cypress log structure.

"This is the main house," she said. "It has five

bedrooms, any of which could be used as an office. There are two full baths, and a half bath off the kitchen, in addition to the master bath. There's a den, living room, dining room, and large eat-in kitchen, which has all brand new appliances. The laundry room is off the kitchen. There's also a mud room before you enter the kitchen from outside. Not that we get a whole lot of mud out here, you understand. There's a fireplace in the living room and another in the master suite. As you can see, the home is constructed of adobe and cypress logs, which keeps it cooler in summer and warmer in winter. The original windows have been replaced with larger, energy efficient ones to let in more light. One feature I especially love is the veranda which stretches the entire length of the front. The arches supporting the roof are a lovely touch."

"Hold on just one minute, Mary, before you go any further," Jim said. He flipped the pages, until he found the one he wanted. "Is this here the barn?"

"Yes, it is. When we reached that page, I was going to mention the barn has a large office. That would probably be ideal for your personal use."

"Let's go take a look."

"Jim! We haven't even looked through all the photographs yet," Kim protested. "We don't know if there's a place for your mother. You haven't even asked the listing price. On top of that, we don't know if the property is available for showing today, or if Mary is free."

"It is, and I am," Dobson said. "I've got the combination to the lockboxes, and a key to the gate."

"Problem solved. Mary, you said most of the original buildings are still standing. Does that include the bunkhouse?" Jim asked.

"Yes, Jim, it does. It's been completely renovated, and is an ideal set-up for an in-law or guest house."

"There, Kim. Ma's all set. And if you don't like the bunkhouse, Ma, we can just build you a new home instead. Right?"

"We need to see the entire property first, Jim," Betty answered. "Not just the doggone stable."

"Just look at that beautiful barn. And an 1880s ranch house. I've seen all I need to see. Let's go."

"Jim, we won't be living in the barn. Although you might be," Kim threatened.

"No, but our horses will. And for that matter, I could handle staying in that barn. Copper and his buddies deserve a stable like this one."

"Jim . . ."

"We're burning daylight. Let's *go!*"

"Betty?" Kim asked, looking pleadingly at her mother-in-law.

"He won't be happy until he sees the place, Kim," Betty answered. "You know how stubborn Jim is when he gets something in his head. Let him get it out of his system. We don't have anything to lose but time."

"All right. But Jim, we're not making any commitment. Not today," Kim said. "Mary, it's time for Katerina's feeding. Will you please give us an hour?"

"Of course. My personal office is the first one on the left, if you'd like to use it. It will allow you privacy."

"I think I'll look through the rest of the pictures while you do that, Kim," Jim said. "Maybe take Josh for an ice cream. I know I could use one."

"I'll stay with Kim," Betty said.

"Thank you, Betty," Kim said. "I need a rational mind with me right now."

4

Mary Dobson owned a large Mercedes SUV, and insisted she drive everyone out to the *Tres Alamos Ranch.* That way, all the Blawcyzks could look at the area while she described it.

"We don't have all that far to go," she said, as she pulled out of her office's lot and turned west on 90. "The ranch is only a little way past the Quarter Circle 7 Hotel, and Spicewood Restaurant."

"We're staying there for the weekend," Jim said.

"Then you know it's owned by the same family who runs the Quarter Circle 7 Ranch. They've been ranching here for four generations. They own some land near the *Tres Alamos.* You'll be neighbors."

"*If* we buy the property," Kim said.

"Of course," Dobson agreed.

She pointed out a few landmarks as they neared their destination.

"We turn here," she said, indicating a large boulder with a brass plaque reading *Tres Alamos Ranch Estates*, in an old West style font, attached to it. She turned left, onto a recently paved road. New houses on large lots were scattered on both sides of the road. Some had small barns and corrals, many of which held horses, while others were unfenced. They were all brick and low slung, designed to blend in with the high desert landscape. Nearby mountains loomed against the horizon.

"These houses look nice, but they're not what I pictured," Jim said. "It seems we'd be hemmed in. This would be just like back in Austin."

"Don't fret about that," Dobson said. "It's still more than a half mile to the entrance to the ranch itself. I just wanted you to see the rest of the development, to make certain you'd be happy with the neighborhood."

She swung her vehicle into a cul de sac, which ended at a large complex of corrals, surrounding a good sized stable. She parked alongside the nearest corral, which held several horses. They were gathered under a corrugated green fiberglass shelter, keeping to the shade. In a large riding arena, several riders were exercising their mounts.

"This is the equestrian center. It's the center of the entire development. As I mentioned back at the office, there are no sidewalks here, just riding trails. The deed restrictions with each residence perpetually limit trails to horseback riding, walking or hiking, and bicycling. No motorized vehicles, on or off road. "

"I did notice there are hitching posts at each driveway," Kim said.

"That's so anyone who wishes to stop by their home, or to visit a friend, will be able to do so, with a place to leave their horse. There are stipulations they must clean up any deposits their horse or dog leaves behind," Dobson explained.

"It *is* quite a nice place," Betty said.

"The heirs to the property insisted on the subdivision being true to the history of the ranch, and the area, before selling this section and allowing building to proceed."

"Speaking of proceeding, may we please get to the ranch itself?" Jim said. "That's what we really want to look at."

"Of course. I know you're eager to see what I hope will be your new home," Dobson said.

She put her Mercedes in gear and drove back to the subdivision's main road. She took a right off that, drove by a few more houses, then through an undeveloped patch of land. She stopped at three giant old cottonwood trees. A wrought iron sign reading *Tres Alamos Ranch — Est. 1878* arched over the road. At the gate, the road went over a cattle guard, and changed from asphalt to caliche.

"This is the original ranch entrance," Dobson said. "The spot we just drove through is a buffer between it and the subdivision. The main compound is right ahead."

After unlocking and opening the gate, she drove under the trees and sign, and around a bend. All of the ranch's major buildings were spread out before them, with the Twin Peaks forming a dramatic backdrop.

"Stop right here!" Kim said.

Dobson complied.

"Look at that setting!" Kim then exclaimed.

"And the view," Betty added.

"It's even more spectacular once you're inside the house," Dobson said. "Shall we continue?"

"Don't ask me," Jim answered, with a grin. "I'm not the one with the rational mind."

"I guess that's a 'yes,' " Dobson said, when Kim and Betty remained silent.

The Blawcyzks' tour of *Tres Alamos Ranch* had concluded. They were back at Mary Dobson's office, seated at the conference table.

"Are you certain you don't want to look at any other properties?" Dobson asked, one final time.

"Absolutely not," Kim answered. "We've all fallen in love with the ranch."

Only Katerina, at three months old, had not been impressed by what would soon be her new home. Even Josh had loved exploring the place. He was fascinated by the cattle grazing, and antelopes running free in the distance. He laughed when Jim called them "cantaloupes."

The house had been completely updated. Its original small, narrow, and high up windows, meant as a defense against raiders, had been replaced with large, triple glazed solar ray blocking glass panes. The wide walls allowed eighteen-inch frames around each window, creating deep sills for potted plants, knick-knacks, or *objets d'art.* All the rooms were spacious, most with the original cypress logs that supported the roof exposed. Ceiling fans in each room would cut down on the need for air conditioning. Kim and Betty "oohed" and "aahed" over almost every feature. For Jim, the clincher, in addition to the barn, was the large glass windows and sliding doors from the living room and kitchen, which opened onto a large patio and an acre of back yard, which was surrounded by a four-foot high and foot thick adobe brick wall. That wall would keep both animals and children safely confined, but with plenty of room to roam. Amazingly in this arid country, the thick wooden gate in the wall opened to a small pond, evidently spring fed. A shallow creek drained the pond, winding its way through the pastures toward the subdivision. In the main pasture, an antique windmill clanked away, pumping water from deep underground into a stock tank. With the exception of the security cameras and electric lighting, looking at the ranch from a distance felt like being transported back to the late nineteenth century.

"How soon would you like to start the paper-work?" Dobson asked.

"If you could have the preliminary documents ready before we head back home tomorrow, that would be helpful," Kim said.

"I can certainly have those prepared. What time would you like to meet?"

"We'll be going to the eight o'clock Mass at Our Lady of Peace, then having breakfast and checking out of our rooms," Jim answered. "Say ten-thirty?"

"You always like to cut things close, Jim, just like your father did," Betty said. "We need to allow a bit more time, rather than running around like *cucarachas.* Eleven would be better."

"Your mother's right, Jim," Kim agreed.

"Then we'll make it eleven," Jim said.

"Eleven is fine with me. I would like to point out I understand the eight o'clock service at the Catholic church is in Spanish," Dobson said.

Jim paused a moment before answering.

"*Eso no es un problema. Todos hablamos Espanol con fluidez. Incluso el pequeno Josh esta aprendiendo le idioma.*"

He couldn't resist adding, "*Mowie tez beigle po polsku.*"

Dobson looked confused.

"Of course," she stammered out. "There are a few things I need to know before I start working on the papers. Will the deed be in the names of James and Kimberly Blawcyzk, or James or Kimberly Blawcyzk?"

"And," Jim answered immediately.

"Excellent. Will the purchase be contingent upon the sale of your present home?"

"No. We're keeping our place in Austin. It's been in my family for even longer than *Tres Alamos Ranch* has existed. The family cemetery is on the property," Jim explained. "We may move back there when we retire. We'll rent out the main house, but probably keep my mother's to use for visits back to the city."

"Down payment? The standard twenty percent?"

"Now you're in Kim's area of expertise," Jim said. "She handles all the family finances. She's much more intelligent about money than I am."

"Mary, I'm planning on thirty percent down, with a fifteen-year mortgage," Kim answered. "I'll have a five-thousand-dollar deposit transferred from my account to yours this evening."

"That's more than satisfactory," Dobson answered. "Do you have a particular lender in mind?"

"We'll use our current bank, unless one of the local lenders around here can provide a better interest rate. We'll have to move our accounts in any event."

"I'll check around, and find the best rate. Do you have a particular closing date in mind?"

"Jim's transfer won't be effective until Monday,

when he officially accepts it," Kim explained. "It will take me some time to complete the transaction for my business. Jim will be moving here a few weeks ahead of the rest of the family. If the closing can be done in two weeks, that will be fine. No more than sixty days. One thing I do need to tell you, except for the necessary parties, no one, and I mean absolutely no one, is to know who we are, or our occupations, until we give you permission. If that happens, the purchase will be cancelled."

"Even if that means forfeiting your deposit?"

"Yes. Everything has to be kept strictly confidential, until the closing. After that, it's a matter of public record, so our information will be available anyway."

"I understand. This will be done exactly as you request. The closing date shouldn't be a problem."

"We all appreciate that," Kim answered.

"I have one last question for now," Dobson said. "Who will be your attorney?"

"We'll get back to you on that," Jim said. "I'll check with Leon for a recommendation."

"He'll give you the names of several reliable ones," Dobson answered.

"I know," Jim said, with a smile. "Unless there's anything else you need, we'd like to head back to our hotel, and get some rest. We've got a long drive home tomorrow. If you should think of anything, you have our phone numbers, or you can always reach us at the hotel."

"I should have all the information I need to get started," Dobson said. "I'll see you at eleven tomorrow. Thank you. And congratulations on your new home. I'm sure you'll love it, and Alpine."

"We're counting on that. I'm certain we will," Kim answered. "Goodbye for now."

"Goodbye."

The next afternoon, after filling out all the forms and signing the necessary documents to begin the process of purchasing *Tres Alamos Ranch*, Jim and his family were on the way home.

"Soon as we reach Fort Stockton, we'll stop for lunch, and to fill the tank," he said. "Would you like to drive from there the rest of the way home, Kim?"

"If you wouldn't mind, I would," Kim answered. "That will give you a break."

"It has been a long, busy weekend, hasn't it?" Betty said.

"It sure has been," Jim agreed. "And what happened to 'we're not making a commitment today'?"

"All I can say is I couldn't let the opportunity to buy a beautiful place like that get away," Kim answered. "We could never afford a home like that in Travis County, if we could somehow even find one with only a quarter of the acreage. I know, I'm supposed to be the level-headed one in this marriage. But sometimes you just have to take a chance. This is one of those times."

"Do you think you'll have any regrets?" Jim asked.

"I'm certain there will be some buyer's remorse. There always is, in just about any major life change," Kim answered.

"Oh, now you tell me," Jim said. "You had buyer's regret about making me your husband. Now I see."

"Jim, *eres un payaso*," Kim retorted. "There's always an exception to every rule. You're one. I never once had second thoughts about marrying you. None at all."

"Well, if I'd been you, I sure would have," Jim answered.

"Will you two just stop your bickering? Honestly," Betty said. "I'm going to change the subject, at least a bit. Jim, what do you like most about our new home?"

"That's a tough question to answer, Ma," he answered. "There's so much to like. The land, of course. We won't be cramped into a corner. The horses will have a lot more room to stretch their legs. The house is gorgeous, especially the huge bathroom in the master suite. A sunken marble whirlpool tub, a shower with about six different options, including steam. And a sauna. Not even mentioning the floor to ceiling glass windows, which look out on the mountains."

"I am a little worried about those windows in the master bath, of all places," Kim said. "I'm not certain the potted palms and other plants will provide enough privacy."

"They'll provide more than enough," Jim said. "Talk about a place where plants can be happy. All that sunlight, and the moisture from the tub and shower. The foliage is already so thick it's almost like a jungle in front of the windows. Don't forget, the tub is enclosed on three sides by glass brick walls. Besides, no one should be snooping around behind the house anyway. The only one peeking through those plants to look at you will be me. We can play Stanley and Livingstone. I'll hunt through the undergrowth until I find you. When I do, I'll say, 'Mrs. Tavares-Blawcyzk, I presume.' When you say 'Yes,' I'll ask for proof. I'll let you imagine what kind."

"Jim!"

"Don't worry, honey. I won't cook you for supper."

"That's not what I meant. The kids."

"Josh is sleeping, and Katerina's too young to care."

"Jim, there must be something else," Betty broke in.

"Having a garage to keep our vehicles in will

be handy. They'll be much cooler to get in, since they'll be shaded, rather'n in the hot sun all day. However, I think the most useful feature, for me, is the so-called 'office' in the barn. It turned out to be a small apartment. Instead of one of the extra bedrooms, I'll use that for my office. That way, I won't be traipsing through the house in muddy boots or filthy clothes. I can take a shower in the barn. And when I get home too late, I'll sleep out there, rather than disturbing the entire household."

"What *I* love about having your office in the barn is that you won't need to put any pieces of evidence in the freezer in my kitchen," Kim said. "I still want to scream every time I think about the day when I found the package in the freezer marked 'liver.' I thought you'd bought some for supper, until you told me it was a human liver."

"Well, as Simon and Garfunkel sing in their old song, 'There must be fifty ways to love your liver.' "

Jim looked at Kim and laughed.

"I think we'd better move on to you, Kim. Right now, we're only encouraging him. What caught your eye?" Betty asked.

"The view of the mountains. It's unbelievable. The brilliant flowers planted along the veranda. And the kitchen, as long as I can keep your son out of it, except when he's eating."

"I'll help you with that project. It's a two-woman job, full time," Betty said. "Anything else?"

"The skylights in the living room, and the patio. Those will allow for some wonderful stargazing on clear nights. Also, the watercolor of the *Tres Alamos* over the living room fireplace. I'm amazed it was part of the sale."

"Mary explained the family wanted it to remain with the house," Jim said. "I'm surprised you aren't worried about the skylight in the master bath. You never know when some helicopter might be flying overhead, and hover right over the house to watch while you're taking a shower."

"I never thought of that. Good thing the skylight has a shade. I can close it when I'm in the shower, or the tub."

"How about you, Ma?" Jim asked.

"Do you even have to ask that question? My bunkhouse."

"You can't even tell it was a bunkhouse, except from the outside, Betty," Kim said.

"I know. The renovations were perfect. The light in the room which will be my studio is just wonderful. I also fell in love with the bougainvilleas planted around the building, with the hummingbirds flitting about, darting in and out of the blooms, searching for nectar. I'm going to call the house 'Hummingbird Bunkhouse Studio.' "

"You should hang some feeders. That might

attract even more of them," Kim suggested.

"That's a great idea, Ma," Jim said. "You can hang little bells from the feeders. When they're empty, the little hummers will tap the bells with their beaks to let you know they're hungry. We can call them humdingers."

"Betty, how much farther to Fort Stockton?" Kim asked.

"I'm not certain. However, even if it's only a couple of miles, that's a couple of miles too far," Betty answered. "Jim, I love you, but please, just shut the hell up and drive."

"Daddy, will you ride in the back with me . . . *please?*" Josh pleaded, when they were getting back in the car after their Fort Stockton lunch and fuel stop.

"Of course I will," Jim answered. "It'll be a mite crowded, what with Frostie and Fritz back there too, but we'll manage."

"Daddy may want to get some rest," Kim said. "If he falls asleep, don't you wake him, Josh."

"All right, Mommy. I won't."

Once they were back on the interstate, Jim took off his Stetson, and placed it on the floor next to his seat. He leaned his head against the side window. Within two miles, he was drifting off to sleep. One final thought went through his head.

Boy howdy, I've dodged some bullets in my time, but this was the closest one yet. I don't know what I would have done if I'd had to tell Kim my transfer wasn't an option. It was make the move, or get fired. Thanks, Lord, for getting me out of that jam.

He shifted to a more comfortable position.

"Did you say something, Jim?" Betty asked. "I thought I heard you mumbling."

Jim didn't answer.

"Shh, Gramma. Daddy's sleeping," Josh said.

"I'll be quiet. You be, too. Daddy needs to nap. I hope he sleeps all the way home."

5

THREE WEEKS LATER

Late in the afternoon, Jim pulled into the parking lot of the Texas Department of Public Safety's Alpine Area Office Building. Leon DaSilva's office, in a week to be Jim's, was in the complex. The building itself was on Texas 118 just past the municipal airport, a short distance north of town.

Jim parked his truck and horse trailer in front. He opened the trailer's escape door to allow Copper more air in the heat. He offered the horse a drink. Copper sucked down the entire bucket.

"I figured you were thirsty, pal," he said, as he gave the paint a carrot. "The air's a lot drier out here in the high desert than back in our old stompin' grounds. We're both gonna have to get used to it. The entire family is. You just take it easy. I know it's been a long trip, but I won't be but a short while. Then I'll take you to your new home."

Jim opened the tailgate of the Tahoe and removed three large boxes. He carried those into the building.

"May I help you, Sir?" the woman behind the bullet-proof glass at the reception area asked, when he walked in.

"Howdy. You sure may. Jim Blawcyzk, the Ranger who's takin' over for Ranger DaSilva. Would you please buzz me in?"

"I hate to ask you this, since you're carrying those boxes, but I really do need to see your identification."

"Not a problem."

Jim put down the boxes, and reached for his wallet.

"Never mind, Ranger. I see your badge. I'm Miriam Colter. Welcome to Alpine."

"Thank you," Jim answered. "Since I've already got my wallet out, we might as well finish up."

He slid his Ranger identification card under the window. Miriam glanced at it, then slid it back.

"I'll let you in," she said. "Do you need any help with those boxes?"

"Nah. It's just some of my personal stuff," Jim answered. "I know the way to Leon's office."

"I'm sorry I didn't know who you were, but I've just returned from vacation, so we've never met."

"That's okay," Jim said. He smiled his crooked smile. "We'll have plenty of time to get to know each other."

Miriam buzzed him through the door. He headed down the hallway to Leon's office.

"You in here, Leon?" he called. "I can't see a damn thing over these boxes."

"What the hell?" Leon answered. "It's a live

stack of cardboard. Zombie boxes. Don't move, or I'll have to shoot you."

"If I have to keep holdin' these much longer, that'd be a kindness," Jim answered. "They're doggone heavy."

"Put 'em in the corner, Jim," Leon said.

Jim set the boxes on the floor.

"What in the blue blazes?" Leon exclaimed. "You planning on movin' in here? Did Kim finally come to her senses, and toss you out on your ear?"

"No, nothing like that," Jim answered. "This is only some of my personal stuff, and files I'll still need. I just figured I'd drop them off on my way by."

He stretched to ease a kink in his back.

"Boy howdy, I know one thing for certain. I'm sure not gonna miss bouncing back and forth between Buda and Alpine."

"I can sympathize with you there. It's a long haul," Leon said. "And they still haven't chosen your replacement?"

"Not yet. They've narrowed it down to three people, but still haven't picked one. The Rangers from Austin will be coverin' my old territory for now."

"You're gonna stay in that big old ranch house at *Tres Alamos* all by your lonesome? When'd you close on it?"

"No. I'll be living in the barn apartment until the rest of the family moves in. Closing was the day before yesterday. All via computer. I just picked up the keys. And I've got to thank you again for hooking us up with Mary Dobson."

"*Por nada*. Any idea when your wife and kids will be able to get here?"

"And my mother. Probably another four to six weeks. There's a lot of paperwork involved before the sale of Kim's business is finalized. But I'll tell you one thing. I'll sure be happy when they finally make the move."

"I can imagine. You got a few minutes to have a cup of coffee and palaver?"

"Only a few. I've got my horse outside, in his trailer. It's been a long, hot trip for him. I don't want to leave him out there too long."

Leon threw back his head and laughed.

"It figures, Jim. You left your wife and kids behind, but brought your horse. Only you."

He shook his head.

"I didn't have a choice. I had to be here by tomorrow. You know that, Leon. Major Voitek made that plain enough. Even Lieutenant Stoker couldn't change his mind. And you know Stoker and me didn't exactly see eye to eye. But we respected each other. Even had a few laughs together."

Leon grew somber.

"I know. But Major Trujillo's been pushin' for

a long time to get you transferred out here. This country is where you belong, Jim. Not back in a big city like Austin. You'll be a much better fit. Hell, you know that as much as I do. Just about every man and woman in the outfit does. And I'll still be around to lend a hand, if you need one."

"*Gracias*, Leon."

Leon poured two mugs full of black coffee. He handed one to Jim.

"I realize it's been a helluva rough stretch for you, pardner," he said. "The Rangers would have been damn fools to force you out. Plumb *loco*. Six generations of accumulated Ranger history and experience in your family, and they wanted to toss you aside like a sack of trash. Dunno what the organization's comin' to. I reckon it *is* really time for me to retire, much as I hate the thought. I don't belong in the outfit any longer, neither. But Molly'll certainly be happy."

"Kim would've been happy as a pig in mud if I'd quit," Jim said. "I got lucky. Turned out she wanted to leave Austin too. Wants to raise our kids away from that whole section of Texas. So things worked out."

"You didn't tell her you had no choice?"

Jim shook his head.

"Nope. She brought up movin' out here first. Mebbe I should've. I just don't know. I probably will, someday. After we've been out here awhile."

He downed the last of his coffee.

"Your coffee's still kinda weak, Leon. I'd better get movin'. I need to pick up some groceries before I go to the ranch. I'll see you tomorrow. Soon's I get back from Marfa."

"That's right. You said somethin' about a traffic ticket when you called?"

"Yeah, when we were here looking at houses. Damn fool Marfa cop nearly ran into us. But he gave me a ticket. Two, actually. Failure to stop at a controlled intersection, and failure to yield to an emergency vehicle."

"What was the son of a bitch's name, Jim?"

"Bradford."

"Ah, so you've had a run-in with Marfa's Money Machine," Leon said.

"Huh?"

"That's what everyone around here calls Nolan Bradford. He has a habit of lyin' in wait for cars with out of state plates, or those that look like they're from out of town. Issues a lot of citations. Helps fill the city coffers, since very few folks have the time, or the inclination, to come back and fight the ticket. They just mail in the fine."

"Well, this is one *hombre* who's dang for certain gonna fight him. Got all the evidence I need, captured on Kim's car's dashcam. I'm goin' to let him testify as to why he stopped me, then spring the video on him."

"About damn time someone did. I take it he's not aware you're a Ranger?"

"Not yet, least not that I know of. But he will be when I show up in court tomorrow. One time I'm grateful for the damn dress code."

"You might be stirrin' the pot here, already, Jim, before you even start work," Leon warned.

"This area's gonna have to get used to me sooner or later, Leon. I figure it might as well be sooner."

"Y'know, if I weren't so doggone busy, I'd take a drive over to Marfa, just to see the look on Bradford's face. Boy howdy, I can picture it now."

"I'll tell you all about it. See you tomorrow, Leon. I'll make the coffee. Like I said, yours is too dang weak."

"I've heard about yours. We'll see. *Adios*, *Jim*."

"*Adios.*"

Jim stopped at a livestock supply shop called The Feed Store, which was just down the street from the D.P.S. building, where he purchased a bag of grain, a bale of hay, and a bag of shavings. Those would last Copper the next two days. He also placed an order for a large delivery of those same items to be brought to the ranch the next day. He paid for the order, explaining to the clerk he'd leave the main gate open, and where to put the supplies if he wasn't home. Once that was done, he stopped at Porter's, the largest, actually the only true grocery store in Alpine, to pick up some ground beef, hamburger rolls, potato chips, a coconut layer cake, and Dr Pepper for his own supper, along with bacon, eggs, and coffee for breakfast. He'd pick up a full supply of foodstuffs the next day, after returning from Marfa. Chores completed, he headed for home.

Jim didn't bother to close the *Tres Alamos*' gate after he drove through it. He went straight to the barn, and unloaded Copper.

"Don't want to appear un-neighborly, Copper," Jim said to the horse, who had his head lifted high as he scanned the surrounding land. The gelding's nostrils flared as he keened the desert air. He gave a sharp whinny. "I figure to only close the gate when none of us are home."

Copper whinnied again.

"You're goin' to have the entire spread to yourself for a few weeks, pal," Jim said, "I'm gonna keep you confined to your stall and paddock for a couple of days, until you're used to the place. Let's see if everything's all set."

He led Copper inside the barn and put him in the stall closest to the office. After spreading shavings over the stall floor, he took the grain and hay he'd purchased from the trailer's front compartment. He poured a half full bucket of grain into Copper's manger, tossed him three flakes of hay, and filled his water bucket. He groomed the big paint while Copper ate.

"You're all set for tonight, buddy," he said,

giving the horse a peppermint horse treat and a pat on the shoulder. "It's high time I fill my own belly, then take a shower and hit the sack. I'll see you in the morning. G'night."

Copper whickered, nuzzled Jim's shoulder, then went back to munching his hay. Jim went into the office/apartment, where the furniture he'd ordered from Mitchell's had been delivered, set up, and placed right where he wanted it.

"Sure was nice of Mary Dobson to agree to meet the delivery guys," he said to himself. "Of course, she made a nice fat commission on the sale of this place. She was probably more than happy to do me that favor. Reckon I'll unpack before I eat. Make the bed, too."

Jim took an hour to unpack and put away his clothes, get the sheets and bedspread in place, hang the towels and curtains, and lastly stock the supplies in the cabinets. Once that was done, he made his supper on the charcoal grill he'd brought from home. After eating, he decided to check on Copper one final time, and give the horse his nightly oatmeal raisin cookie. Copper whinnied eagerly when he saw Jim approaching.

"You missin' your friends, pard?" Jim asked, as he gave Copper his treat. "You don't have to worry. I'll be with you all night. Tell you what. I'll leave the door to the office open. Maybe you won't feel quite so lonesome."

Copper nuzzled Jim's cheek. Jim gave him

an extra cookie, and a pat on the nose. Thunder rumbled in the distance.

"Sounds like a storm rollin' in, boy. I'd better take my shower before it arrives. G'night."

Late afternoon or evening thunderstorms were not uncommon in west Texas during the summer months. Quite often they dropped little rain, despite having strong winds, along with considerable lightning and thunder. Jim was fond of calling them Shakespearean storms, *Much Ado about Nothing*, or "Full of sound and fury, signifying nothing." This one, however, did have copious amounts of rain. The huge drops pounded on the roof, accompanied by vivid lightning and deep-throated thunderclaps. It blew in quickly, right after Jim had begun his shower.

"You can huff and puff and try to blow this barn down all you want, storm, but you ain't chasin' me outta here," Jim muttered. "I'm tired, dirty, sore, and I need to clean up real bad. You just go ahead and make as much of a ruckus as you want."

The storm continued unabated. Over its noise, Jim didn't hear a person come into the office, until they walked into the bathroom.

"Brewster County Deputy Sheriff! Who's in here?"

Jim was in the midst of washing his hair. Some of the shampoo ran into his eyes, burning them and blurring his vision. Through the steam coated glass of the shower stall, Jim could make out only the vague silhouette of the person, who appeared to have his right hand on the butt of a pistol.

"The owner of this ranch," Jim answered, as he turned off the water.

"This place is still owned by the Harrison estate."

"Not any longer. My wife and I recently bought it."

Jim could hardly see the deputy lift his gun from its holster, and point it at him.

"Raise your hands and get on out here," the deputy ordered. "Don't make any sudden moves."

"Do you honestly think I've got a gun in the shower with me?" Jim answered. "Where the hell would you think I could hide one?"

"You can never tell what anyone might do. Get those hands up and come out of there . . . *now!*"

"Would you mind tossin' me a towel so I don't have to come out there buck naked?"

"Yeah, I suppose that's not a bad idea."

The deputy pulled a towel from off the rack and threw it over the top of the shower door. Jim caught it, wrapped it around his waist, and tied it in place.

"Now raise your hands, and step out."

Jim complied. The deputy centered his gun at the middle of Jim's chest when he emerged. He was about Jim's age, height, and weight, but with dark brown hair and light brown eyes.

"Hold it right there. You've got some explaining to do, *hombre.* What's your name?"

"James C. Blawcyzk, Texas Ranger. I'm taking over the post in Alpine, as of next week. Soon as Ranger DaSilva retires."

"You got any identification?"

Jim glanced down at his dripping wet body, clad only in the towel, then back at the deputy.

"On me? Exactly where do you imagine I would keep it?"

"Just answer my question."

"My identifications card's in my wallet, in my pants pocket. My badge is still pinned to my shirt. They're both on the bed, where I left 'em."

"Let's go look. You first."

Jim edged his way past the deputy, who kept his gun pointed at Jim's back while they went into the bedroom. Jim nodded at his shirt.

"See, there's my badge, like I said."

"I can see it. Get your I.D., but stay away from that pistol lyin' there."

"I'm just goin' to take out my papers," Jim answered. He removed his wallet from his pants pocket and handed it to the deputy, who flipped open the wallet and studied Jim's Ranger identification card.

"Well, the picture seems to match your face. And I reckon I've seen a whole lot more of you than it shows," he said, with a chuckle.

"Seems as if," Jim agreed. "But if you'd

walked in a few minutes later you'd have seen a lot more."

"Sure glad *that* didn't happen. I guess you're who you say you are all right, Ranger," he said. "My apologies. I'm Deputy Gene Molson."

He handed Jim's wallet back.

"No apologies needed," Jim answered. "It's good to know the local law keeps an eye on things. Reminds me to keep the doors locked, too. You mind if I towel off and get dressed? Then we can palaver. Coffee's keeping hot in the pot on the stove. Pour yourself a cup. I'll only be a minute."

"*Gracias.* I'll call in that everything's clear here while you do that."

Jim hurriedly dried and dressed, in a faded pair of jeans, and a neon green *Keep Austin Weird* T-shirt. Still barefoot, he padded his way into the kitchen. Molson was seated at the table, scowling at his coffee.

"Damn, Ranger, how do you drink this stuff?" he asked. "I think it curled my toenails. Never seen a pot like that one, neither."

Jim poured a cup of coffee for himself and sat down before answering.

"Name's Jim. A lot easier to wrap your tongue around than BLUH-zhik. There's milk in the fridge if the coffee's too strong. I like it that way. Far as the pot, it's an old electric percolator. I've got one for here, and one for my office. My wife won't let me put one in the kitchen. The rest of my family'll be movin' here in four or five weeks. When they do, I'll move up to the main house with 'em. For now, it's just me and my horse here. No need to open the whole house for just one person. I am kind of curious about one thing. What made you decide to check on my place?"

"I saw the gate open. Never seen that before, so I figured I'd better check things out. There's been rumors the place was sold, but nothing more than that. With a big place like this, empty for so long, there's bound to be trespassers or vandals. I was on my way home from my shift. I live over in the *Estates*. Have a wife, Melody, a boy, Terry, who's a little more'n four years old, and a new baby daughter, Virginia, born a month ago today. You mentioned your family?"

"Yup. My wife's Kimberly. My kids are almost the same age as yours. Josh is also a bit more'n four, and Katerina is three months. I keep tryin' to call her Katy, but Kim won't stand for it."

"My wife's the same way. If someone calls the baby Ginny, she gives 'em what for."

"My mother's also coming with us. She's had a little place of her own right next to ours, ever since my Pa died."

"Wait a minute! Blawcyzk. Your father's the man who stopped the attempted attack on the

Alamo. He lost his own life, but saved a lot of others. I'm sure sorry, Jim."

"I appreciate that, Gene."

"Listen, I'd better get goin', before my wife starts wondering where the hell I'm at," Gene said. "We'll be seein' each other, I'm sure. Once your family arrives, we'll have to get together. Y'all got horses?"

"Yup. Copper's here with me. The others will come with the family."

"Then we'll go riding, first chance we get. Me'n Melody can show you some of the trails."

He hesitated before continuing.

"Jim, I hate to bring this up, since it's really none of my business, and if you don't want to answer my question just say so, but I am curious about one thing."

"What's that?"

"How did you manage to scrape up enough money to afford *this* place, on a Ranger's pay?"

Jim laughed.

"I didn't. My wife came up with most of it. She started a successful business, before we even met. She just sold it, but will be staying on as an independent consultant. That, and this ranch has been for sale so long the price was reduced several times. So it was barely within what we could afford. But it was a helluva lot cheaper than it would have been back around Austin."

"Understood. Sorry if I was pryin'."

"That's what law officers do, Gene. I'll be stopping by the Sheriff's Office to introduce myself in the next day or two. Mebbe I'll run into you there. If not, long as the gate's open, I'm home, so you can stop in anytime it is. Have a good night."

"You too, Jim."

As soon as the deputy left, Jim said his evening prayers, pulled back the bedspread, and slid under the sheet. At this altitude, the heat of the day would dissipate quickly, leading to a cool, dry night, perfect for sleeping. The storm had blown itself out. Only a slight breeze was stirring the curtains at the windows.

No need for air conditioning like back in San Leanna.

That was Jim's last thought before he fell into a deep sleep.

The next morning, Jim, in clothing that met the exact specifications of the Texas Ranger dress code, arrived at the Presidio County Courthouse, a few minutes before traffic court opened. He was wearing a light blue dress shirt, to which his silver star in silver circle badge was pinned above the left breast pocket, subtly striped dark blue tie, pressed tan khaki pants, and tan leather western boots, which were polished to a high shine. His white Stetson was freshly brushed. In addition to the tooled leather belt with silver Texas Ranger insignia buckle and initialed keepers encircling his waist, he wore his gun belt and holster, his Sturm, Ruger Model 1911 service pistol at his left hip. He joined the line of people conferring with the Marfa city prosecutor, who was attempting to clear as many cases as possible before they actually went to trial. The prosecutor glanced at Jim questioningly. Jim returned his look with a shake of his head.

When Jim reached the head of the line, the prosecutor introduced himself, then asked Jim for his name.

"I'm Harold Boyle, representing the city of Marfa. May I have your name please, Sir?"

Jim couldn't resist a touch of sarcasm.

"*Texas Ranger* James C. Blawcyzk, recently placed in charge of the Ranger post at Alpine."

"You're here on official business?"

"Only with the city of Marfa. I was issued a summons for an alleged traffic violation."

"I see. Let me find it."

Boyle thumbed through the cases on the table, until he came up with Jim's. He read through the complaint.

"Ranger, rather than going through trial, the city would be willing to reduce the charge to a simple failing to obey a traffic control device. You could pay the fine, and be on your way."

"Prosecutor, even if the city was willing to drop the charges entirely, I would insist on taking this matter before a judge. From my own experience, and from other statements I have received, it appears there is an egregious abuse of police powers in Marfa, targeting out of towners. I intend to prove that."

"You believe you can?"

"I know I can."

"Then I'll leave your case on the docket. It's the fourth one. It will probably be about an hour before we reach it."

"I've got all day."

Jim waited until Nolan Bradford arrived. The officer stared at Jim, startled. When he did, Boyle called him over.

Jim could hear the prosecutor berating Bradford.

"What the hell is wrong with you?" Boyle hissed. "You ticketed a damn Texas Ranger, of all people. Not only a Ranger, but the Ranger who's taking Leon DaSilva's place. And he's fighting the charges. Wouldn't even think of pleading guilty to a lesser offense."

"How the hell was I supposed to know he was a Ranger?" Bradford protested. "It doesn't matter who he is anyway. He broke the law."

"Are you certain of that?"

"Of course I am."

"You'd damn well better be, Bradford. Because I have the feeling he knows exactly what he's up to. And that's making you look like a damn fool."

• • •

"All rise. Court is now in session. The Honorable Marion Yolanda Cummings, presiding."

"Please be seated," Cummings said, once she had taken the bench. "Bailiff, what is the first case?"

It was fifty-five minutes later when Jim's case was called.

"The City of Marfa versus James C. Blawcyzk."

The bailiff then read the charges, then continued.

"Will the defendant please rise?" he called.

Jim stood up, holding his hat.

"*You* are James C. Blawcyzk?" the judge questioned, staring at Jim.

"Yes, Your Honor, I am."

"Very well. How do you plead?"

"Not guilty, Your Honor."

"Not guilty. Prosecutor, is the arresting officer present?"

"Yes, Your Honor, he is. Marfa Police Officer Nolan Bradford."

"You may present your case."

The prosecutor repeated the charges, the date, time, and place where they occurred. He called Bradford to the stand. After the officer testified, Jim was called to the stand, and sworn in.

"Please be seated," the judge said.

"Thank you, Your Honor."

"Proceed with your statement."

"Yes, Your Honor. My name, again, is James C. Blawcyzk. I have just been transferred from Buda to Alpine. On the date in question, my family and I were in Alpine for the weekend, touring the area and looking for a house to purchase. We were westbound on U.S. 90. When we reached the center of Marfa, I stopped at the red blinking traffic signal and stop sign at 90, U.S. 67 South, and Texas 17 North. I waited for a semi-trailer rig to clear the intersection, then proceeded. I was already under the traffic signal when a Marfa police car, which I learned after being pulled over was driven by Officer Bradford, came into the intersection from Texas 17. I had to swerve my vehicle to avoid a collision. Officer Bradford waited until I drove past his vehicle, then made a traffic stop. I tried to explain to him that he was the party in error, but he would have none of that. If it pleases the court, I have an SD card from my wife's vehicle, which I was driving that day, in my camera. It shows the entire incident, and is date and time stamped. If you would be willing to view it, it will clarify what happened."

"I would be quite interested in seeing that video," Cummings said. "Please, give your evidence to the bailiff."

Jim handed his camera to the bailiff, already set to play the video. The bailiff in turn handed it to the judge. She watched the video without comment, until it concluded.

"Prosecutor Boyle, Officer Bradford, please approach the bench," she said.

When they reached it, she replayed the video.

"As both of you can clearly see, Ranger Blawcyzk is correct in his testimony before this court. Officer Bradford, not only did you make an illegal traffic stop, you have also presented false testimony here in my courtroom. I am sorely tempted to charge you with perjury. However, I will hold that decision in abeyance at this time. Nonetheless, Ranger Blawcyzk, if you wish to press charges, you certainly have the right to do so."

"I'm not interested in that, Your Honor," Jim answered. "However, I have been informed by a reliable source, and of course this is hearsay, the city of Marfa, and in particular certain of its police officers, have been using traffic violations, legitimate or not, as a revenue stream for the city, targeting out of state or out of area motorists. If that is true, I would hope today will put an end to that practice."

"Officer Bradford, consider yourself warned . . . and lucky. Prosecutor, if you bring another case based on falsified or unsubstantiated evidence in front of my court in the future, I will have you cited for contempt. Case dismissed."

"Thank you, Your Honor," Jim said.

A murmur rippled through the spectators as Jim walked out.

6

Jim spent the next week being brought by Leon to meet the law enforcement officials in the three counties, Brewster, Presidio, and Jeff Davis, which Jim would be taking over. He had brief interviews with, and photographs taken for, the area newspapers, as well as a live session on the morning show on KVLF, Alpine's AM radio station. The rest of his time was taken up going over Leon's few still open cases.

Today was the day Leon officially retired. Major Alejandro Trujillo, commanding officer of Company E, had come from El Paso to Alpine, along with Lieutenants Brian Foster, from Midland, and Francisco Castellon from El Paso. There was no formal retirement ceremony per se, just a short meeting at the Ranger office in Alpine, then dinner at the Reata Restaurant. They were at the restaurant, having drinks, before ordering their meal.

"Leon, I hope you enjoy your retirement, and taking life easy," Trujillo said. "At the same time, I'm really sorry you've decided to hang up your spurs. However, you're making way for a fine man. It's no secret I've been pushing to get Jim transferred to Company E for a long time. He's exactly the kind of Ranger we need out here."

"You're not gonna get rid of me that easily, Major," Leon said. "I told Jim to call me if he ever needs a hand."

"I'd wager Molly is going to have something to say about that," Castellon said.

"And I'm counting on him for just that," Jim added. "I also appreciate your confidence in me, Major."

"That's fine, as long as you both realize Leon will no longer have law enforcement authority. And Jim, take all the advice Leon can give you. He knows every inch of your new territory."

"I'll give him the first piece right now," Leon said. "Jim, you're well aware west Texas ain't anythin' like your old area. Yeah, there's plenty of isolated spots in the Hill Country, but in most of it help is still just a cell phone call or radio transmission away. You're never all that far from a big city or good-sized town. Out here, there's plenty of places where you'll be miles from any phone or radio service. You won't be able to call 9-1-1 if you get in trouble, either. You *ARE* 9-1-1. The only help you'll have to rely on in the back country is yourself. That means your wits, your brain, your instincts, your rifle and your sidearm."

"And my horse," Jim added.

"In many cases, yes," Leon agreed. "You make one mistake, and it might not only cost you your life, but your body will probably never be found. The *mal hombres* who smuggle drugs and humans across the border would have no compunction about chopping you to bits, and leaving you for the scavengers. Or else dropping you into a deep canyon or throwing you into the Rio."

"Not to mention the ordinary criminal types," Foster added.

"Jim, I know you had some issues at Company F, particularly over the last few months," Trujillo said.

" 'Some' is an understatement."

"Possibly. However, Jim, that's all in the past. Lieutenant Stoker and Major Voitek stood up for you when it counted. I'm aware Voitek really didn't want to, but he still did."

"I know that, Major, and I'm beholden to both of 'em."

"So am I, because their support enabled me to have you sent to Company E. Out here, while we go by the same rules and regulations as all the other companies, sometimes a Ranger has to make a decision before being able to call in for instructions. Hell, like Leon just said, there will be plenty of situations where you won't even be able to reach help. It's a little more like the old West days in these parts. That's not saying any man or woman under my command has *carte blanche* to take matters into their own hands. What I do mean is, if you're in a tight spot, and need to do whatever has to be done to save your life, the lives of others, or bring in a murderous *coyote* or drug mule, do it, as long as it's legal. The politicians and lawyers be hanged. We can always deal with them later."

"Literally?"

"Jim, you didn't hear this, but sometimes I sure wish that could happen," Trujillo said, laughing.

"At least ninety percent of the population would agree with you, Major," Leon said. "Especially about the politicians."

Trujillo glanced at his watch.

"We'd better order dinner, since you and Jim are the only ones who don't have long drives back home tonight. But first let's toast Leon's retirement, and to many happy years of it."

The four Rangers raised their glasses.

"To Leon, one of the finest Rangers to ever work for Company E," Trujillo said.

"To Leon!"

The men clinked their glasses together.

"*Muchas gracias*, Major," Leon said. "And to all of you. Now I'm going to propose a toast of my own. To Jim Blawcyzk, who I predict will be another of the finest men in Company E's long and storied history. *If* he doesn't raise too much hell."

"Boy howdy, Leon, you hit that target dead center," Trujillo said. Again, glasses were raised.

"To Jim Blawcyzk," Leon said. He grinned.

"Here's hoping the Big Bend can survive him."
"To Jim!"

It was full dark when Jim rolled up to his gate. It was wide open.

"I could swear I locked that gate when I left this mornin'," he said to himself. "Mebbe I forgot, but I doubt it. I'll go in slow and careful."

He turned off the Tahoe's lights, and cut the switch to its interior lights, before driving through the gate. He stopped, got out, and swung the gate shut.

"Someone busted the gate's lock open. I knew damn well I locked it," he muttered. "Let's hope whoever it was is still here."

He drove slowly toward the house. A mule deer jumped out of the brush, bounded across the road in front of Jim's truck, and dove back into the scrub.

"Somethin' besides me could've spooked that fella," Jim said. "And my gut tells me it was."

When he came into view of the buildings, he could see a large flatbed truck backed up to the barn. It was stacked with bags of grain and bales of hay, with room for still more. Copper was pacing in his paddock, whinnying nervously.

"Looks like someone's decided to help themselves to my horse's feed," he spoke, half-aloud. "Let's hope I can get down there while they're still inside."

He put the Tahoe in neutral, letting it coast down the slope until the ground leveled off. He put it back in gear, and stopped it up against the flatbed's front bumper, effectively blocking the truck between his vehicle and the barn.

"I'm not in the mood for playin' games tonight," he said, lifting his shotgun from its bracket. He got out of his truck, leaving the door open so as not to make any noise, then stood alongside it, waiting. It wasn't long until two men came from the barn, each with a bale of hay on his shoulders.

"Howdy, fellers," Jim said, his voice soft, but threatening. "I sure hope you weren't plannin' on goin' anywhere with my hay. Texas Ranger. You're under arrest."

The men both stopped dead in their tracks, frozen in shock. Jim eased back the hammer on his shotgun. The ominous click sounded loud as a cannon blast in the silence.

"Just put those bales down, and lie on your bellies right alongside 'em. *Do it!*"

One of the pair started to make a move as if to throw the bale he carried at the tall Ranger. Jim shifted his shotgun slightly, aiming it straight at the man's stomach.

"I wouldn't, if I were you."

Both men dropped the bales, then lay face down in the dirt.

"Hands behind your backs," Jim ordered. He

handcuffed one, and bound the other's wrists with baling twine. Once they were secured, he dialed the Brewster County Sheriff's Office.

"Brewster County Sheriff's Department. How may I help you?"

"Brewster County, Texas Ranger Jim Blawcyzk, Ranger Unit 810. I require an officer at my place for transport of two prisoners. It's the *Tres Alamos* Ranch, off U.S. 90, four miles west of Alpine. Also will need a heavy duty hook for a large flatbed truck."

"10-4, Ranger. Stand by for an ETA."

Jim could hear the dispatcher calling one of the deputy sheriffs. In a moment, she got back on the phone.

"Ranger, ETA is approximately five minutes."

"10-4. Advise your officer my gate is shut, but not locked. Also advise to meet me at the barn."

"10-4. Will advise. Out."

Jim hung up, then spoke to his captives.

"You're both under arrest for trespassing, breaking and entering, burglary, and theft of property or goods worth more than five thousand dollars. That's a felony, boys. You have the right to remain silent . . ."

By the time Jim finished reading his prisoners their Miranda rights, a Brewster County Sheriff's Department Dodge Durango SUV, lights flashing, rolled up. Gene Molson stepped out of it.

"Boy howdy, Jim, I didn't expect to see you

again this soon," he said. "What've you got here?"

Jim nodded at the two men still lying secured on the ground.

"I came home to find these two *hombres* cleaning out my feed room and hay loft. They must've thought I'd be gone longer. Haven't I.D.'d them yet."

"You don't have to," Gene answered. "Bobby Jack Curtis and Tucker Gibson. Howdy, boys. Up to your old tricks once more, eh? Well, I reckon it's time to haul your sorry butts into the county jail . . . again. You know the drill. I see you've already met Alpine's new resident Texas Ranger. Neither of you has ever been the sharpest tool in the shed. Dammit, won't you ever learn?"

"I take it you know these two," Jim said, as they lifted the prisoners to their feet.

"I sure do. They just got out of the county prison less than a year ago, for the same thing. Stealin' anything that isn't nailed down from barns and sheds, all over the county. Watch your head, Tucker," he said, as he opened the right rear door of his truck, then helped Gibson into the back seat. "Slide on over for your buddy. Bobby Jack, get on in there."

Once Curtis was settled, Gene slammed the door shut.

"You gonna follow me and file the charges, Jim?" he asked.

"Yep. Otherwise those two might get some sharp lawyer to claim this wasn't a legal arrest."

Gene snorted.

"These jackasses? They'll be assigned a public defender. Not that the two we have in this county aren't crackerjack lawyers."

"So why take chances?" Jim said. "I've gotta wait here for the hook comin' to take their rig to the D.P.S. impound lot. I'll be along soon as that's done."

"I'll be waitin' for you. The hook's coming from Maldonado's. It'll be here in thirty minutes or so."

After calming his horse with some carrots and oatmeal raisin cookies, Jim took photos of the suspects' truck and gathered evidence from it, while he waited for the hook. It took forty-five minutes for the tow truck from Maldonado's Truck and Towing Service to arrive. The wrecker driver greeted Jim warmly when he jumped out of the big Western Star's cab.

"Howdy, Ranger. Jesse Maldonado. Pleased to meet ya. *Mis disculpas.* I would have been here sooner, but I had to fuel up my truck."

"*No hay problema,*" Jim answered. "Jim Blawcyzk *es el nombre.* I need this truck towed to the D.P.S. impound lot. It's evidence in a theft case. You'll have to strap the load down before you hook it up. I'll also need the load tarped, to keep it dry until I can get a release for it from the court."

Maldonado laughed.

"I can tell you're new here, Ranger. We hardly get any rain in these parts a'tall."

"Tell that to the storm we had the other night."

"*Si.* We do indeed get our *verano* frog-stranglers," Maldonado admitted. "I'll wrap everything up good and tight."

"I'd appreciate that," Jim said. "I just paid a small fortune for that load of feed."

"You tellin' me the *hombres* who tried stealin' this feed took it from your barn?"

"Seems as if," Jim answered.

"*Tan estupido*. Don't fret none, Ranger. I do tows for the county and D.P.S. all the time. I know what's required."

Maldonado went to work, efficiently securing and tarping the hay and grain, then hooking up the would-be thieves' truck.

"I'm all set, Ranger," he said. "I'll drop this thing off. You goin' to the impound with me?"

"I don't think that'll be necessary, Jesse. I've got to get to the sheriff's office and book the *malditos tontos*."

"That'll be fine, Ranger. *Te atrapo mas tarde*."

"*Muchas gracias*, Jesse. *Buenas noches*."

Jim and Gene were having coffee in the sheriff's office break room after Curtis and Gibson were booked, and ensconced in their cell.

"Mebbe this time those two clowns will finally learn their lesson, but I doubt it," Gene said. "At least they should spend more time behind bars. That might help."

"They've been doin' this for a while, I take it," Jim said.

Gene took a swallow of coffee before replying.

"Yeah. A few years now. They stake out a business, watch for them to make a delivery, follow the truck to the delivery address, then wait until no one's home and make their move. They've stolen everything from electronics and furniture to construction supplies."

"And now livestock feed."

"That's a first for 'em, far as I know, Jim. But with the cost of hay and grain goin' sky high, I'm not surprised. I expect we'll see more such thefts. It is kind of ironic, though, your first arrest bein' made at your own place."

Gene looked at his watch.

"Break time's over. I'd better get back out there."

"And I'm gonna head on home and turn in," Jim said. "My first full day in charge tomorrow. I want to go in a little early."

Both men drank the last of their coffee, washed out the cups and put them away. Gene resumed his patrol, while half an hour later, Jim was sound asleep.

7

Jim went home for the weekend, to the good news the sale of Kim's company would be consummated sooner than anticipated. His family would be able to move to Alpine in three weeks. While the movers would be doing most of the packing, boxes for items Kim wanted to pack herself were stacked in the living room.

Before leaving, Jim loaded his fourteen-year-old Silverado with most of the things from his home office, then hooked it up to the Tahoe's trailer hitch. Kim and his mother shook their heads when he pulled out of the yard. They had thought this move would finally force Jim to scrap that old Chevy. They were wrong.

The trip back to Alpine was uneventful . . . until Jim pulled into the yard. Gene Molson had promised to care for Copper while Jim was away. Copper was in his paddock, but he wasn't alone. The paint was nuzzling another horse, which stood outside the paddock's fence.

"What the heck?" Jim exclaimed, as he got out of his truck. Copper whinnied when he saw Jim. The strange horse added a loud nicker of his own.

"Who's your new friend, Copper? I hope he's not a surprise from Gene," Jim said. Expecting his usual treat, Copper nuzzled Jim's chin. The new horse pushed his muzzle into Jim's shoulder, still nickering.

"All right, all right. I'll go get you fellas some treats."

Jim went into the barn's apartment. He took two apples from the refrigerator, and a bag of Mrs. Pastures Horse Treats from a shelf. When he went back outside, both horses looked at him eagerly. He gave each an apple. Copper took his, as did the newcomer. Jim then gave each a handful of treats. The new horse kept nickering, loudly.

"Enough. Don't you ever shut up?" Jim said to him.

"You're a handsome fella," he continued to the horse. It was a light tan buckskin gelding, about 15.2 hands high, his muzzle black, all four legs black from the hooves to the knees and hocks. The horse had a buckskin's jet-black mane and tail. The only white on him was a small white snip on his nose. He was not underweight, his hooves were trimmed, and his coat was clean, indicating someone had been caring for him.

Jim stepped back and put his hands on his hips as he looked at the horse.

"Now, what the devil am I supposed to do with you? Reckon I'd better put you inside and give you some hay and water, first off."

Once again, the horse nickered.

Jim got a lead rope and Copper's spare halter.

The buckskin readily slid his head into the halter and allowed Jim to buckle it in place. He followed along docilely when Jim put him in the stall next to Copper's. Copper trotted inside. He and the newcomer nuzzled each other through the bars.

"Copper, I'll leave your paddock door open, but your pal's gonna have to stay inside. I can't chance him busting down the fence and running off. Looks like you get some extra hay tonight. Soon as I do that, I'll take a drive over to the subdivision's stable. Hopefully somebody there can tell me who owns this big fella."

Jim gave both horses two flakes of hay and filled their water buckets. Once that was done, he unhitched his old truck, and drove over to the *Tres Alamos Ranch Estates* community stable. When he walked into the barn, a woman filling mangers with grain looked up at him. She was in her middle thirties, about five foot seven and trim. Shoulder length auburn hair hung loosely from under the Texas A & M baseball cap which shaded her hazel eyes. She was dressed in a dark red T-shirt, jeans, and rubber muck boots.

"Howdy, Sir. I'm Doris McDonaugh, the stable manager. How may I help you?"

Since Jim was off duty, he was dressed in a light blue Luckenbach, Texas T-shirt, well-worn jeans, and scuffed boots. A red bandanna hung loosely around his neck. A battered straw Stetson covered his thatch of unruly blond hair. He had his antique Colt Peacemaker, which had been passed down through six generations of Blawcyzks, in the holster on his left hip. The sight of the heavy revolver didn't faze the woman one bit. This *was* west Texas after all, where guns were as common as jackrabbits, armadillos, and roadrunners.

"Howdy yourself," he said. "I'm Jim Blawcyzk. My family just bought the main ranch. Sorry I haven't dropped by sooner, but I've been travelin' back and forth between here and Austin. My family's still back there. They'll be moving over in about three weeks."

"You're the new Ranger. Deputy Molson told me about you."

"Yes, Ma'am, I am. Would you like to see my identification?"

"Doris. And you just made a rhyme. No, seeing your I.D. won't be necessary."

"I reckon I did, at that," Jim said. "I'm hoping you can solve a mystery for me."

"I'll try."

"I just got back home a few minutes ago. It seems like another horse wandered over to visit mine while I was gone. A buckskin quarter horse gelding, who never shuts up."

"So *that's* where he got himself to this time," Doris exclaimed.

"Seems so," Jim said. "I'm hoping you can tell me who he belongs to."

"His name's Mr. Sandman, although he's generally called just plain Sandman, or Sandy. And you're right, he is a talker. Gentle as a kitten, though. He doesn't really belong to anyone."

"I think you need to tell me what you mean."

"Sandy belonged to an old ranch hand named Cowboy Dave. He was a gift to Dave from a friend," Doris explained. "Dave hadn't owned a horse for quite some time. He had terminal cancer. His final wish was to have another horse of his own before he passed. So his friend gave him Sandy. When Dave died, she asked me to look after Sandy. She didn't have the time or room to take him back. Of course I said yes. I've been trying to find him a new home, but without success. He somehow got out of his stall today, and wandered off. He does that once in a while. I would imagine one of the kids didn't close his door all the way. This is the first time he's been gone this long, though. There's a few folks out looking for him. I'll call them back in. Sandy must have heard or scented your horse, and went for a visit. I don't suppose you'd take him? There'd be no money involved."

"Kim'll kill me."

"What was that you just said, Jim?"

"I said I'll take him, Doris. Copper, my horse, has already taken a shine to him. And Sandman's taken a shine to me."

"Doesn't sound like what I heard."

"Sometimes I think out loud. Mumble a lot. But I'll keep Sandman. He's already followin' me around like a lovesick puppy dog."

"I don't suppose the half-empty package of horse treats I see sticking out of your back pocket has anything to do with that."

Jim gave a rueful smile.

"I'll admit I spoil my horses. My dogs, too. Heck, even the barn cats are spoiled."

"Then this is a perfect match. I've got Sandy's tack here. Would you like to take it along?"

"If it's not a problem, I'd rather wait a day or so. I literally just got home, to find this strange horse in my yard. I got Sandman in a stall, gave him and Copper some hay and water, then headed straight over here. I've got a bunch of stuff in my truck to unload, before I can take a shower and call it a night."

"There's no hurry. His things will be here whenever you want them. And if you ever need a hand caring for your animals, just let me know."

"I appreciate that, Doris. I'm gonna say goodnight. Don't worry about Sandman. I have a feeling my little boy and him will be best friends, the minute they lay eyes on each other."

"I'm certain they will. Have a good night. Now I'd better call in the search party. They'll be so relieved to know Sandy's been found."

• • •

"Jim Blawcyzk, you're just plain crazy," Jim scolded himself, as he drove back to his place. "The last thing you need is another horse to feed. And Kim's gonna have your hide."

He shook his head. When he reached the barn, Copper was still inside his stall. He went inside, and both horses hung their heads over their stall doors, whinnying.

"Last treats for tonight, you beggars," Jim said. "Looks like you two won't be separated. You'd better hope Kim feels the same way about me'n her, once she finds out about Sandman. I'll be damn lucky if filin' for divorce is all she does, rather'n gettin' her gun and shootin' me dead."

He gave the horses the rest of the treats, then shut the door to Copper's paddock.

"Sorry, pard, but I want you to stay inside tonight. I'll let both of you out in the morning."

Copper snorted a protest, and shoved Jim in the back. Sandman gave out with a loud neigh, sounding much like a horse laugh.

"That's enough out of the both of you," Jim said. "Go to sleep."

8

Jim spent most of the morning putting away files, and fixing up his new office with the prints and decorative items he'd brought from home. He'd started, of course, by unpacking his old electric percolator and brewing a pot of strong black coffee. He'd also filled the office's small refrigerator with cans of Dr Pepper, and put half a dozen cans of cashews in the cabinet. He'd just hung the last of his Andy Thomas western paintings when his phone rang.

"Better see who that is," he said. He crossed the room and picked up the receiver.

"Texas Ranger Company E, Alpine office. Ranger James Blawcyzk."

"Ranger, it's Miriam. You must have forgotten to un-forward your phone."

"I apologize. I did," Jim admitted. "My old office was in a sheriff's substation, so the calls came directly to me. If I wasn't there, the caller had a choice of leaving a message, or calling D.P.S. directly. I'm not used to having someone to take a call when I'm not in."

"Don't worry. It was no trouble. I have a caller on the line, who insists on speaking with you. She refuses to give me her name."

"Put her through."

"Of course."

Jim waited for the connection to be made.

"This is Ranger James Blawcyzk. With whom am I speaking?"

A woman's voice came over the receiver.

"Ranger Blawcyzk?"

"Yes."

"I'm sorry. I just had to be certain I was speaking with you. Are you alone?"

"Yes."

"You don't have the phone on speaker?"

"No."

"Good. I have to be careful. My name is Georgina Delehanty. I'm the former police chief for Marfa. I was fired several months ago. So were the two officers I hired, when I was given the chief's job. I hope Leon DaSilva mentioned you'd be hearing from me."

"He did, briefly. I'm certain you understand we had a lot of things to go over."

"As long as he told you. We need to talk, Ranger Blawcyzk. As soon as possible."

"Of course. I'll be spending most of my time in the office the rest of the week, bringing myself up to speed. Just give me a time."

"No. I can't take a chance someone would see me meeting you. You can't come to my home, either."

"Then where? You're still more familiar with the area than I am," Jim said.

"The Marfa Lights viewing area. You know where that is, right?"

"Of course."

"That's the place. Usually, there aren't many people around. Even if some do happen to be there, they'll be too busy looking for the lights to pay any attention to us. We can strike up a casual conversation, like two strangers who just happened to come looking for the lights on the same night. I've got plenty you need to hear, Ranger. Can you meet me tonight?"

"What time?"

"About nine o'clock. I'll get there shortly before that, so we don't both pull in at the same time. I drive a red F250."

"You won't be able to miss my vehicle. That's all I'm gonna say about it," Jim said. "I figure it's better if you don't know what to look for. It'll appear less suspicious to not have you watching all the cars coming in. I'll park close to yours, but far enough away it won't appear as if we're meeting."

"Okay. I appreciate you taking the time to listen to my story, Ranger."

"Well, I have to admit, you've got me intrigued. So does the little bit of information Leon gave me. The only thing that would prevent me from being there is if my presence was needed at a crime scene."

"I understand that. See you tonight."

"I'll see you then."

Delehanty clicked off.

"Hmpfh. I wonder what she has that's so all-fired important," Jim said to himself. "Leon didn't indicate there was any urgency for me to get in touch with her. Well, I guess I'll find out tonight. Might as well finish gettin' this office together."

He took the big wooden Texas Ranger badge replica that had his name emblazoned across the star from a box. That would hang behind his desk, as it had in Buda. Just about every Ranger in the outfit owned one of those plaques.

"Soon as this is hung, it'll be time to get some lunch."

Jim pulled into the Marfa Lights viewing area shortly after nine. There were only two other vehicles in the lot. One was a red Ford F250, Delehanty's truck. The other was a bright blue Subaru WRX. It was evident the teenage couple inside the small car was at the site for a purpose completely unrelated to looking for ghostly lights.

Jim parked several yards away from either of the other vehicles. He took his binoculars off the seat of his truck, got out, and leaned against the hood. First with his naked eyes, then with the binoculars, he scanned the horizon, ostensibly looking for any sign of the elusive Marfa lights.

Delehanty was closer to the observation building. She waited for a few minutes before calling to Jim.

"Mister, you won't see anything from the parking lot. You'll need to go onto the viewing platform."

"*Gracias*. Out that way?"

Jim pointed in the direction of the viewing area's open-roofed, offset rotunda.

"Yeah. Your first time here?"

"It is."

"Let me show you the best spot to see the lights," Delehanty answered.

"I'm obliged. Spot the spotlights. That's funny," Jim said.

Delehanty gave him a crosswise look.

"If you say so. Just follow me."

She led Jim around the building, to the slightly elevated viewing platform.

"You want to look west-southwest. Kind of follow the same direction as the power poles. The lights aren't usually too far above the horizon. Sometimes they're steady, other times all over the place. If they appear at all. I'm Georgina, but I go by just plain George. Call me that."

"Jim. Pleased to meet you."

"Same here. By the way, you weren't kidding about your truck. Where the hell did you find that heap? From some damn desert rat?"

Jim shook his head. He laughed.

"Nope. I bought it brand new, fourteen years ago."

"Looks more like four hundred and fourteen years ago."

"Well, I must admit we've had a few adventures."

"More like a few demolition derbies."

They kept scanning the horizon while they continued their conversation.

"George, we don't want to spend too much time here," Jim said. "Why'd you need this meeting?"

"I'll keep it brief. As I told you, I was fired, along with two other officers, from the Marfa Police Department. The original department was disbanded quite a few years back, and law enforcement turned over to the county and state. It's only been a couple of years since the city decided to have its own police department again, rather than relying on the county sheriff's department and the Texas Highway Patrol. I was hired after the previous chief moved on. He was only there a year. Some people weren't too happy a woman was given the job. That's a bit of background."

"Understood."

"The city came up with all sorts of reasons for my firing. Incompetence, failure to maintain proper records, improper supervision, more. But the real reason is I ruffled too many feathers. I'm certain Leon informed you there's a problem out here."

"There's problems everywhere, no matter how large or small the town. You can't get away from 'em," Jim said. "Wait. Look over there."

He pointed at a dim light, which was slowly moving in a northerly direction.

"That's just a car's headlights," George said.

"I know, but we *are* supposed to be looking for lights," Jim answered. "Continue with your story."

"There's a place in Marfa that provides all sorts of entertainment for those willing to pay for it, and know how to keep their mouths shut. I tried to go after the so called private 'club.' I was told in no uncertain terms to stop my investigation. I was fired after I refused."

"What kinds of entertainment?" Jim questioned.

"There ain't any of it legal, that's for damn sure," George answered. "Gambling of all kinds, mostly for high rollers, after hours liquor, prostitution, probably drugs. I do have to say the people behind the club aren't sexist, racist, homophobic, misogynistic, or any other damn 'ist' or 'ic' you can name. They have male prostitutes for women, gays or lesbians for those so inclined. Even arrangements for, what's that French phrase, *ménage à trois* encounters can be made. Swingers' parties, also. There's even a couple of special rooms, from what I've uncovered. You can imagine what goes on in those."

"I can, but I'd rather not. How do they stay in business? You'd think someone would blow the whistle."

"No one would dare. The backers are some of the most influential people in this here Presidio County."

"Did you go to the Sheriff's Department?"

"No. I just don't trust any of the county officials, either. I'm certain at least some of them are in the operation up to their *keisters*. I went to Leon DaSilva."

"What did Leon have to say?"

"He informed me that he'd begin an investigation, but was getting ready to retire. After a long discussion, we decided I should wait until the new Ranger came on, since it was only a matter of a month or so, and no one in Marfa was going anywhere. Well, you're the new Ranger, so here we are."

"I trust you have some proof, or at least evidence, to back up your accusations," Jim said. "And names."

"Ranger, I wouldn't have gone to Leon if I didn't. I've got plenty. Here's the key to locker A18 at Alpine Safe and Secure Storage. You'll find the club's address, names, dates, photographs, the whole nine yards. Everything except someone who is willing to put the evidence together cohesively, so that it will be enough to obtain a probable cause warrant. That's where you come in. Leon will lend a hand if you need his help. My home address and my phone numbers are in the top box."

George dropped a key to the concrete.

"Let me get that for you," Jim said.

He picked up the key, made the motion of handing it back to her, then slid it into his own pocket.

"You'll find everything I have in that locker, Ranger. And before you ask, everything I obtained was obtained legally. There's documentation along with the files. Are you goin' to help me?"

"I'll look everything over first, to make certain it's all kosher. Two quick questions, though. One, why didn't you just move on?"

"Because there's no possible way I can get another police job anywhere in the country until this blot on my record is expunged. That, and I'm damn mad."

"I can understand that. Two, have there been any threats against your life? Or those of the other two officers who were fired?"

"Not directly. But there's been plenty of hints dropped I should get the hell out of town, without looking back."

"I'm not surprised. I just thought of one more question, then we'd better scoot."

"What's that?"

"Have you seen anyone around who match the following descriptions? Two males, one red-haired, green-eyed. Has a three-teardrop tattoo under his left eye, and a knife scar on his upper right arm. Skin burned red as a beet. Other one Hispanic, probably Mexican. Tall, hair shaved close. Both arms covered with tattoos. Black rose tattoo on his belly. Bullet scar on his chest. Both in their twenties. Might've been two women with them. One blonde, one brunette. Both in their late teens to early twenties. The blonde has a lady-bug tattooed on her left ankle, and a Monarch butterfly on her right breast. The brunette has a daisy tattooed around her belly button. She's also got a pierced nose, with a diamond or rhinestone stud in its right side."

"I have seen them around town, although I can't say about the belly tattoos, nor the chest scar on the Mexican *hombre*. I don't know their names. They opened a bicycle rental and touring shop in Marfa about eight or nine months back. It's the Big Bend Bicycling Adventures Company. Why do you ask?"

"No particular reason, except they were stayin' at the same hotel in Alpine as my family, when we were house hunting. Something about 'em didn't strike me as quite right. With that sunburn, the redhead sure looked like he hadn't been here more'n a week."

"You must know the Big Bend attracts all sorts

of crazies, Jim," George answered. "As far as the redhead's sunburn, I'll wager he's got skin like yours. Unless I miss my guess, you never tan, just burn."

"Sadly, you're right, George. Twenty minutes in the sun and I look like a ripe chili pepper. We'd better get goin'. I'll be back in touch first chance I have. Doesn't seem to be any lights tonight anyway."

"Hold on just a minute. Look!"

George pointed at a pair of flickering lights, which were moving erratically, just above the horizon. Another pair was not far behind, and closing the gap. Jim put his binoculars to his eyes, and focused in on the glowing orbs. They continued southward for a few hundred yards. The lights were now practically on top of each other. The front pair jerked, once, twice, then they suddenly swerved, pointed upward, and flipped over. A brilliant orange flare took their place, then settled to a dull glow. The other pair took off at a much greater speed.

"What the hell?" George exclaimed. "I've never seen the lights act like that before."

"Those weren't anything from out of this world," Jim said. "Those were car headlights. Unless I miss my guess, somebody just crashed their car, and it's burning. I'd better get on over there."

"Want some help?"

“No, but thanks for the offer. People might wonder how we both happened to be at the same place at the same time. I’ll get those papers first chance I have. And I believe your story.”

Jim ran to his truck. As always, the old Silverado fired right up when he turned the key, the clutch screaming like a Comanche warrior when he punched it to the floor, the transmission grinding when he changed gears. But the battered pickup’s engine accelerated quickly. Jim left the parking area, then jammed the gas pedal to the floor.

“Bet you thought you were done chasin’ folks around, didn’t ya, ol’ gal? Well, I’m countin’ on you for just one more run.”

He dialed Presidio County Dispatch as he raced west.

Jim had to drive through the center of Marfa to reach the site of the apparent crash. His old pickup had no emergency lights or siren, so the only caution signal he could use was his four-way emergency flashers. Sure enough, when he passed the Marfa City Hall and wrestled his pickup through the intersection and left on U.S. 67, the truck’s tires squealing and smoking, a Marfa Police unit shot out of the building’s carport, its warning lights flashing and siren screaming. Jim flashed his headlights, hoping the officer chasing him saw the acknowledgement, then increased his speed. He hit the redial on his phone.

"Presidio County Dispatch."

"Dispatch, it's Ranger Blawcyzk. Updated location is south on 67. Approximate arrival at suspected accident site is less than three minutes, depending on the exact location. Being pursued by a Marfa police officer. I have no radio in this vehicle. Please contact Marfa and advise them of situation. Have them instruct the officer to follow me to the scene."

"10-4, Ranger. We cover Marfa's calls at night. Will advise officer."

I sure hope I find the wreck before that Marfa cop decides to try'n shove me off the road. If he does, I know how to counteract a PIT maneuver, but I don't want to have that happen.

In his rear view mirror, Jim could see red flashing lights, far in the background.

Looks like the fire department volunteers got out fast. Mebbe that'll help the cop figure out what I'm doin'.

The orange glow Jim had seen from the viewing area now shone more brightly ahead. It grew rapidly in size as he approached, soon becoming a column of flame and smoke. Just beyond Ranch Road 169, he came upon an overturned vehicle, which had gone off the road, spun, and went up a small embankment before landing on its roof. Flames were shooting from the engine compartment, but had not yet reached the passenger cabin.

"Presidio County, Ranger 810 on scene. Location is just south of Ranch 169."

Jim slammed on the brakes, skidding to a stop. The Marfa officer stopped right behind him. Both men jumped from their vehicles. Jim recognized his pursuer instantly.

"Officer Bradford! We've gotta see if anyone's still in that wreck."

The Marfa officer recognized Jim's voice.

"I'm right with you, Ranger. Let me grab my fire extinguisher. It might buy us a couple of minutes."

"Fast as you can," Jim answered.

Jim ran to the overturned vehicle, while Bradford raced for his extinguisher. Two people were trapped inside the car. The driver's neck was broken, his scalp half torn off. He was plainly beyond help. Jim checked him for a pulse, confirming he was indeed dead, then went to the passenger's side. The man in that seat was unconscious, but still breathing. He was pinned in place.

Bradford hurried up. Besides the fire extinguisher, he also carried a pry bar.

"Anyone still alive in there?"

"This *hombre*. The driver's dead. We've got to try and get this one out before the fire spreads."

"I'll hit the flames with my extinguisher,"

Bradford answered. "It won't stop 'em, but it'll buy us a few minutes."

"*Bueno*."

Bradford emptied the extinguisher at the base of the flames, then tossed it aside and rejoined Jim.

"What's got him stuck, Ranger?"

"Look like his left leg's caught between the seat and the center console."

Bradford dropped to his knees and peered inside the vehicle.

"He's tangled in his seatbelt, too. If we can cut that, I should be able to pry the seat and console apart enough to yank him outta there."

Jim pulled a jackknife from his pocket and opened it. He slashed at the belt, separating it with three strokes.

"Go ahead," he said to Bradford. "See if you can get his leg loose, then we'll pull him out."

The Marfa officer crawled as far as possible into the overturned car. He inserted the pry bar between the seat and console, then pushed down on it as hard as he could. He managed to bend the console by a few millimeters.

"I think you've got it," Jim said. He slid his hands under the injured man's shoulders and pulled him free. Bradford backed out of the car. Together, they dragged the man a safe distance from the burning vehicle.

"Let's try'n get the driver's body out of that car," Jim said.

"We're too late, Ranger."

A tongue of flame shot from beneath the car's dashboard. Within seconds, the interior was a raging inferno.

"I reckon so," Jim said. Both men watched as a Marfa fire truck and ambulance rolled up. They waved the paramedics over to the injured man.

"This the only one who was in that wreck?" one of them asked.

Jim shook his head.

"There were two. The driver was already dead. We managed to get this *hombre* out before the flames got to him."

"We'll get to work on him."

"Bradford, I want this road closed at 169, and also a quarter mile south of here." Jim ordered. "No one gets through, except for Presidio County deputies, or any more firefighters who might show up."

"Ranger, that'll shut down the only road from here to the Mexican border. There's no other way between Presidio and Marfa, except some old dirt desert roads that ain't passable in places."

"That doesn't matter. Folks'll just have to wait, or turn around and detour by way of Terlingua and up to Alpine."

"That's one helluva detour," Bradford protested.

"I'm well aware of that, but this here's a crime scene," Jim explained. "Until some Presidio County deputies arrive, I need you to make certain no one drives past 169. And for damn certain no one gets out of their vehicles, and starts takin' pictures or snoopin' around. You block the intersection with 169. Send one of the firefighters to stop traffic south of here. Soon as the deputies arrive, they can take over. I want you here with me once they're on scene."

"Me? Why me? I'm out of my jurisdiction."

"Because you were the first law officer on scene, along with me. I want you to assist me when I go through that vehicle. Don't worry about jurisdiction. My asking you for help makes it legal. Unless you have a reason you'd rather not."

Bradford gave Jim a puzzled look.

"I can't think of any. Sure, I'll give you a hand, Ranger."

"I'm obliged."

Jim had to wait until the fire was extinguished and the vehicle cooled off before he could begin processing it. While he waited, he took some measurements of the scene, and as many photographs, with his phone, as would come out sufficiently to be used as evidence. He had Nolan Bradford assisting him, taking notes when necessary. Now, only he, Bradford, Marco Pena, the county coroner, Presidio County Sheriff Jacob Marlin, and three deputies were still on location, along with a fire truck and three volunteer firefighters. Marfa was so far off the beaten track the media hadn't even shown up.

"Unfortunately, we can't do much more until daylight," he told Bradford. "The fire department's lights aren't strong enough. It's gonna be hard enough gathering evidence in any event. Between the fire, the water and foam used to extinguish it, and the firefighters trampling all over the scene, the majority of the evidence will be damaged or destroyed. What's left of the driver will have to go to the coroner, to see what he can come up with. I've got a thermos of coffee in my truck. Want some? We can palaver while we take a break."

"I could use some," Bradford said. "I'm also a mite curious, if you don't mind me askin' a few questions."

"Not at all," Jim said. "Let me just tell the sheriff what we're up to. I'll meet you at my truck."

After speaking with Sheriff Marlin, Jim rejoined Bradford. He took his thermos from the floor of his truck, along with a tin mug. He filled the mug, handed it to Bradford, then filled the thermos's cap for himself. He lowered the Silverado's tailgate.

"Might as well take a load off our feet," he said, as he sat on the tailgate.

"I reckon that's a good idea."

Bradford sat alongside the Ranger.

"Sorry the coffee's not real hot, but I didn't plan on being out all night," Jim said.

"No problem. At least it's coffee."

Bradford took a large gulp from his mug, then winced.

"At least I thought it was coffee. Tastes more like used motor oil. How old is this stuff?"

"Brewed it day before yesterday. It should be just about right," Jim answered.

"It'll keep you awake all night, that's for damn certain. Believe it or not, I've had worse. But even that was nowhere near this strong."

Bradford took another swig. He shook his head, then nodded at Jim's old pickup.

"I still don't know how you managed to keep in front of me with this thing. I would've thought anythin' faster'n twenty miles an hour would shake it to pieces. Yet I could barely keep up with you."

"She's taken a lot of abuse, that's for certain," Jim said. "But she takes a lickin' and keeps on tickin'. Look, I know you've got to have a whole passel of questions for me. Why don't you get started?"

"Sure. First off, how'd you know this wreck wasn't an accident?"

"If I hadn't sorta seen it happen, I wouldn't have. Unless the responding officers looked real close, they probably wouldn't have either. It would've been chalked up as just another accident caused by drivin' too fast, bein' drunk, or fallin' asleep at the wheel."

"You saw it happen?"

"From a distance. I was over at the Marfa Lights viewing area. Thought I might see something unusual. Well, I sure did, but not what I expected. I saw a few lights that were obviously mere reflections from cars' headlights. Just as I was getting ready to call it a night, I noticed two sets of lights. One set was gainin' on the other fast. I trained my binoculars on 'em. When the second pair caught up to the first, they almost disappeared. The first set bounced around, then flipped over. Soon as they did, a ball of fire rose into the air. The other lights took off real fast, still goin' south. I realized I'd just seen someone deliberately run off the road. So I called it in, then headed over here. Sorry I couldn't take the time to pull over just for a minute, to let you know why I was in such a hurry. And I don't have a two-way radio in this truck."

"You're kiddin'!" Bradford exclaimed. "I never would've guessed."

Both men chuckled.

"You might not've noticed, but the skid marks on the road show there were two vehicles involved in the wreck. This one, and the one that shoved it off the road. Soon as it's light enough, I'll photograph those, then take measurements. I doubt there'll be any tread marks in the dirt that'll be good enough for casts, but I'll look." Jim glanced at his watch. "I can't do much without my evidence kit. There's enough time for me to go home and retrieve it before sunup. Take a walk with me while I speak with the sheriff."

They went over to where Marlin was leaning against his SUV. Pena, the coroner, was with him.

"Quite a mess you've started off with, Jim," the sheriff said.

"Tell me about it, Jake," Jim answered. "Listen, I've got to swing by my place to pick up my evidence collection kit and equipment. Change clothes, also. That won't take me more'n an hour, tops. Keep this site secured until I return."

"You've got it. Is there anything we can do to help while you're gone?"

"Sure. You can have a deputy mark any evidence along the road. That'll save some time. Run the plate on that car. Call the hospital and get the identification on the passenger, and see if they have any information on his condition. Order up a hook to remove the wreck. I want it standing by when I return, or as soon afterwards as possible. I don't want anything here moved, though. Not until I can go over the scene in daylight."

"How about removing the driver's remains from that car?" Pena asked.

Jim shook his head.

"I want to take a closer look inside before he's moved. I've also got to get my camera. The pictures I took with my phone won't show the detail I'll need."

"I suppose waiting a while longer won't matter," Pena said. "There's not much left of him to work with."

"Nope. He's definitely toast . . . burnt toast," Jim said. "See you in a little while."

"You're not comin' back in that old pickup, are you, Ranger?" Bradford asked.

"No. My supervisor would frown on that. I'll be back in my state vehicle. One more thing. If someone from the media shows up, none of you say a thing to 'em. Tell 'em I'll give them a statement when I return."

Marlin snorted.

"You don't have to worry about that, Jim. The reporters for the *Big Bend Sentinel* and *Alpine Avalanche* are snug in their beds. They always call first thing in the morning to see if anything happened overnight. No one from the El Paso papers or television stations will come all the way out here just for a possibly double fatal accident. If they learn it's something more'n that, then they might show up . . . maybe."

"*Bueno*. Be back quick as I can."

• • •

The sun was just topping the eastern horizon by the time Jim returned. He'd replaced the jeans, denim shirt, scuffed boots, and old Stetson he'd been wearing with a dress shirt, khaki slacks, kelly green tie, polished boots, and new straw Stetson, dyed white, which met the Texas Rangers dress code for hot weather. He now wore his Sturm, Ruger 1911 service pistol in the holster at his left hip. He had pulled his BDU over his clothing. He parked next to Marlin's black and white Presidio County Sheriff's Department Tahoe. Next to Marlin's SUV was a black Chevy Express van, its only windows, the windshield and the doors, tinted dark gray. Nolan Bradford was with Marlin, along with the coroner, Pena. Jesse Maldonado had also arrived. With him was his son and partner, Jose. He was parked on the side of the road, waiting in his Western Star flatbed tow truck.

"You made good time, Jim," Marlin said, when Jim got out of his truck.

"I usually do," Jim answered. "Stripes was just opening when I went by there, so I swung in and bought a box of coffee and a couple dozen doughnuts. Plenty of paper cups, too. They're on the front floor of my truck, if you want to have one of your people get them and pass 'em around. What'd you find out while I was gone?"

"Enough for a start. The registration came

back to a Lemuel T. Jackson, 219 South Cebada Street, El Paso. Matches the vehicle, a black 2015 Infiniti Q50 sedan. Obviously, confirmation it was actually Jackson driving the vehicle will have to wait until the deceased's identity can be confirmed, from dental records or through DNA testing."

"Anything on the passenger?"

"The hospital got his identity from his driver's license. DeQuawn X. Trainor, 454 South Raynor Street, also El Paso. He was still unconscious and undergoing evaluation in the E.R. when I spoke with the nurse. I haven't had the chance to run either man's records yet."

"That can wait for now," Jim answered. "Anything else?"

"A few vehicles came by. We questioned their occupants whether they'd been by here last night, and seen anything. None of 'em had."

"Any complaints about the road being closed?"

"A few folks grumbled, then went on their way. Also, there wasn't much for evidence along the road. We marked a few items, but I'm not certain they'll be useful."

"Then I guess it's time for me to get to work. Jake, I'll want you with me. You too, Officer Bradford."

Jim pulled on two pairs of nitrile gloves, and a pair of nitrile booties over his boots. Before starting to gather evidence from the wrecked car, he turned on his digital recorder, entering a case number, date, location, and approximate time of the incident.

"Vehicle is at approximately the same location where I observed it crash from the Marfa Lights viewing area. From visual evidence at scene, it appears vehicle was shoved off the pavement by another one. Upon impact, subject vehicle, a black 2015 Infiniti Q50 four door sedan, bearing Texas license plate George X-Ray Yankee-2586, then spun approximately one hundred and eighty degrees, struck an embankment, overturned onto its roof, and caught fire. The other vehicle involved apparently continued south on U.S. 67.

"Myself and Officer Nolan Bradford of the Marfa Police Department were the first responders to arrive. Two males were in the vehicle, the apparent driver and a passenger. The driver was already deceased, ostensibly from a fractured neck, head injuries, and possibly others. Officer Bradford and I were able to pull the passenger from the vehicle before flames erupted in the passenger compartment. We were unable to remove the deceased occupant of the driver's seat. The passenger was transported by Marfa Volunteer EMS to Big Bend Regional Medical Center in Alpine. He was unconscious when removed. His condition at this time is still unknown.

"Vehicle was registered to one Lemuel T.

Jackson, residence of record 219 South Cebeda Street, El Paso. Passenger's driver's license is for DeQuawn X. Trainor, 454 South Raynor Street, also El Paso. Identities of both still need confirmation. As there are only skeletal remains of the vehicle's apparent driver, confirmation of his identity will need to be from dental records, or DNA testing. I am going to make a perfunctory examination of the remains *in situ*, then release them to Presidio County Coroner Mario Pena for autopsy and full forensic testing."

Jim switched off the recorder.

"I'm gonna go through this vehicle now. Jake, call Jesse Maldonado. Tell him in about thirty minutes I'll want him to turn this car back on its wheels."

"You've got it, Jim."

After taking photographs of the car from all angles, Jim got down on his hands and knees to look at the driver's remains. It only took a minute.

"Coroner, there's nothing I can do here," he said, as he got back to his feet, brushing dirt from his knees. "You might as well take the bones to the morgue. I'd like the autopsy results as soon as possible."

"I'll get started immediately," Pena answered. "Determining the cause of death shouldn't take long. The toxicology reports will require a few days."

"Understood," Jim answered. "Anyone else have a sudden craving for barbequed ribs?"

Pena groaned. Marlin shook his head. Bradford turned pale.

"Leon DaSilva warned me about your so-called sense of humor, Jim," Marlin said. "But he didn't give me an inkling just how twisted it was."

"You've got to be able to laugh in this business, or you'll go plumb out of your mind," Jim answered. "While I'm goin' through this car, could I ask you to have a couple of your deputies measure and photograph the skid marks?"

"Certainly. We'll get right on it. Soon as we help Marco remove the body."

"While he does that, I'll scour the area around it for any possible evidence. Bradford, I'll still want you with me."

Jim found no traces of evidence around the wrecked Infiniti.

"I'm a bit surprised there weren't any parts from the other vehicle involved, Ranger," Bradford said.

"It's a little unusual, but this isn't the first time," Jim answered. "It does tell me one thing."

"What's that?"

"Whoever ran this car off the road was drivin' something that didn't have plastic bumper covers. Probably little to no plastic trim, either. Otherwise, we'd have found at least a few small pieces. It looks like the coroner has finished removing the remains. Let's go through that vehicle. Wave Jesse over. It won't take long to examine it while it's still on its roof. I'll most likely learn more once it's upright."

Jim crawled into the burnt-out passenger compartment. Whatever evidence might have been inside had been consumed by the fire.

"Nothin' useful in there," he said, once he was out of the car and standing up. "Jesse, pull that thing back on its wheels. Careful with it. I'll process as much as I can here, then you'll haul it to the D.P.S. impound lot."

"Of course, Ranger."

Jesse shook his head and chuckled.

"Somethin' strike you funny?" Jim asked.

"Not funny, just a thought I had. You've only been here less'n a month, and you've already been good for business."

"That's not much of a compliment, Jesse."

"I reckon not," Maldonado admitted. "Jose, let's roll this sucker over."

Maldonado and his son attached a cable and hook to the underside of the Infiniti. Slowly, they pulled it onto its side, then dropped it onto its wheels. The trunk, which had appeared to be relatively undamaged except for some scorched paint and minor dents, popped open. It was crammed full of cardboard boxes.

"Whoa! What've we got here?" Jim exclaimed.

"Jesse, get your cable unhooked, so I can take a look."

"Yessir, Ranger."

As soon as the cable was removed, Jim took his knife, and sliced open one of the boxes.

"Fentanyl," he said. "Probably enough in here to kill the entire population of both Presidio and Brewster Counties. Maybe more."

He slammed the trunk shut.

"Now we know why two *hombres* from El Paso were out here in the middle of the night," Marlin said. "You think this was a drug deal gone wrong?"

Jim shrugged.

"*Quien sabe*? Could be that, or somethin' else entirely."

"What's your next step?"

"Those drugs will have to be inventoried back at the D.P.S. office, by two people, me and a state trooper, both wearing full Hazmat suits, in case any of the stuff broke open during the wreck. Jesse, I've got one thing to do before I let you take this car. You'll need to get your tarps, and wrap it up *tight*."

"Jose, you heard the Ranger. Get what we need."

"*Enseguida, Papa*."

"Officer Bradford, I want you to bring your car over here."

Bradford gave Jim a quizzical look.

"My car? Sure Ranger. But why?"

"You'll know in a minute," Jim answered.

"Okay. Be right back."

While Bradford went for his Explorer, Jim got out his tape measure. He waited until the Marfa officer parked near the burned-out Infiniti.

"All right, let's see if my hunch is right," Jim said. "We might've gotten lucky. Since the fire never got beyond the passenger compartment, it didn't completely destroy all the evidence. The firefighters did a good job of stopping the blaze before it devoured the whole car. I'll have to stop by and thank 'em when I get the chance."

"You mean the drugs," Marlin said.

"More than just the drugs," Jim answered.

He walked behind the Infiniti. Two narrow vertical dents, almost identical, about three feet apart, were apparent in the back bumper's plastic cover. He measured the distance between those.

"Now to see if we have a match."

He went over to Bradford's cruiser and measured the distance between the vertical rods of its push bar, then the bar's height from the ground.

"It's almost exact, allowing for other damage to the Infiniti from the wreck."

"You're not accusing me of running those men off the road, are you, Ranger?" Bradford asked.

"Not at all. Your location at the time the incident occurred alone clears you of any involvement. But whoever did shove this car off the road was using a vehicle equipped with a push bar, almost certainly a Ford Explorer, according to my measurements. It was probably a decommissioned police vehicle they picked up at auction. There are probably hundreds, if not thousands, of those on the streets of Texas alone. Jake, get word out for all local and county law enforcement agencies between Fort Stockton and El Paso to be on the lookout for any Explorers, or similar type vehicles, with push bars and possible front-end damage. I'll notify D.P.S. Jesse, wrap up the car and load it up. Soon as you do, I'll check the area under it for anything relevant. Jake, I'll be leading you back, and the evidence you collected. I also need you, or one of your deputies, to help escort Jesse to Alpine. Soon as everything's gathered, we can clear the scene."

"Is there anything else you need me for, Ranger?" Bradford asked. "If not, I should get back to town."

"Not at the moment. But if your chief can spare you, I would like you to return to Alpine with me. I'll have a few more questions for you."

"I'll let him know."

"*Bueno*."

Jim took out his phone, and hit the speed dial for the Alpine D.P.S. office. He pushed zero to bypass the menu.

"Texas Department of Public Safety Dispatch, Alpine."

"Dispatch, this is Ranger unit 810. I should be clearing the scene here in approximately thirty to forty-five minutes. I need all Rangers and State Troopers in the triangle from Fort Stockton to El Paso, down along the Mexican border to Presidio, then back up to Fort Stockton through Marfa and Alpine, to be watching for a late model Ford Explorer or similar vehicle, with a push bar and probable front end damage. Vehicle is possibly a decommissioned police patrol car. Occupant or occupants are suspects in an apparent homicide in Presidio County, just outside Marfa. Last seen heading south on U.S. 67 toward Presidio. They should be considered armed and dangerous, and approached with extreme caution. Presidio County Sheriff has already notified all county and local authorities."

"10-4, Ranger 810. Do you also want the Border Patrol notified?"

"You read my mind, Dispatch."

"10-4. Dispatch, out."

"Ranger 810, out."

Jim next called Company E Headquarters in El Paso. A woman answered the phone.

"Texas Ranger Company E, El Paso, Administrative Assistant Eileen Brady. How may I direct your call?"

"Good morning. This is Ranger Blawcyzk, out of Alpine. Is Lieutenant Castellon in?"

"He just arrived a few minutes ago, Ranger. Would you like to speak with him?"

"Please."

"I'll put you right through."

"Much obliged."

After a brief pause, the lieutenant's voice came over Jim's receiver.

"Ranger Blawcyzk, good morning."

"Good mornin', Lieutenant. Sorry to bother you so early, but I'm gonna need some assistance from one of the Rangers assigned to El Paso."

"What've you got?"

"An apparent homicide, just outside Marfa. Vehicle with two men inside, run off the road. Trunk was jam-packed with fentanyl. Possibly other drugs also. I'm still on scene. Will be leaving shortly for Alpine. I'll inventory the drugs there."

"Any suspects?"

"Not yet. The only lead I've got is the vehicle whose driver was responsible for the wreck is possibly a decommissioned police Explorer. Word's out to all authorities from Fort Stockton to El Paso to look for it. I'll send you a full report later today."

"Good. Keep me posted on any developments. What else do you need?"

"The victims, whose identities haven't been confirmed yet, had El Paso addresses. First was a Lemuel T. Jackson, 219 South Cebeda Street.

Second was a DeQuawn X. Trainor, 454 South Raynor Street. I'll need search warrants issued for their apartments, and any of their vehicles. Background checks. Families and friends questioned. Jackson died in the wreck. His body was burned beyond recognition. Trainor was transported to Big Bend Medical Center in Alpine. Last word I received is he's still unconscious. From what I saw of his injuries, odds are he won't pull through."

"I'll get those warrants issued as quickly as possible," Castellon promised. "I'll assign Javier Perez to assist you. He's the most knowledgeable *hombre* in the company about gangs. He'll know where to poke around, ask the right questions, and the right people to ask 'em from. Sounds like some of the bad boys from El Paso might be involved."

"I wouldn't bet my hat against that, Lieutenant."

"Anything else, Jim?"

"Not at the moment. I'm about ready to leave the scene. I'll call you with an update once I get back to my office, and process the evidence I've got, which is damn little."

"Except for the drugs," Castellon said.

"Except for the drugs. Talk to you later, Lieutenant."

"Later, Jim."

9

"Jesse, I need those tarps left in place. Bill them to the state," Jim said.

Maldonado had just dropped the Infiniti in the D.P.S. impound yard.

"Sure thing, Ranger. If you'll just sign the papers, I'll be on my way."

"Of course."

Jim scrawled his almost illegible signature on Maldonado's bill and release.

"Thanks, Jesse, Jose. You too, Deputy Moreno. Appreciate the assistance."

"Anytime, Ranger."

"Officer Bradford, I don't want to keep you any longer than necessary," Jim said. "It's been a long night for all of us. I'll ask you my questions before I finish processing that car. Come on into my office."

"All right."

"Have a seat. Coffee?" Jim said, once they were inside.

"I don't think I could handle two cups of your coffee in one day, Ranger," Bradford responded. Now that the work at the accident scene was complete, he was feeling nervous, unsure what questions Jim might have for him.

"How about a Dr Pepper, or a Coke? I've got both in the fridge."

"A Dr Pepper sounds good."

"Comin' right up."

Jim rummaged in the refrigerator and came up with two cans of Dr Pepper. He handed one to Bradford.

"You can work on that while I ask my questions. You mind if I record our conversation?"

"Not at all."

"Obliged."

Jim put his recorder on the desk and switched it on.

"Continuing the investigation into the apparent homicide by motor vehicle on U.S. Route 67, just south of Marfa. I am about to interview Marfa Police Officer Nolan Bradford. He was the first officer to arrive on scene, along with myself. Officer Bradford, if you would please state your name and official title for the record."

"Of course. Nolan R. Bradford, senior patrol officer with the Marfa, Texas, Police Department."

"Officer, we know the vehicle in which one person died, and another critically injured, was a 2015 black Infiniti Q50 four door sedan. Have you ever seen that vehicle, or a similar one, in Marfa or its surroundings prior to last night?"

"No, Ranger, I have not."

"Evidence indicates the other vehicle involved in the crash had a push bar, and was possibly a Ford Explorer or similar SUV, perhaps a decommissioned police vehicle. Have you observed any of those in the area?"

"Ford Explorers, yes. With push bars, only on police department patrol vehicles that are currently in service."

"All right. Last night, as you are aware, I observed the incident occur from the Marfa Lights viewing area. To reach the scene, I had to pass through the center of Marfa. As I was in my personal vehicle, I had no lights or siren. When I turned from 90 onto 67 South, you immediately began a pursuit, from where you were parked at the Marfa City Hall. The two vehicles involved in the incident were southbound on 67, meaning they had to also go through the same intersection. Can you explain why you apparently did not observe those vehicles at that point?"

"I stopped to take a bathroom break. I had only returned to my vehicle a moment before you went by. Since Presidio County receives and dispatches all calls for Marfa after eighteen hundred hours, I checked in with them before leaving my vehicle, and notified them when I returned. They will have the times on record. The suspect vehicles must have gone by while I was still inside the building. Since I had no way of knowing you were behind the wheel of the old pickup I observed going through town at a high rate of speed, I started a pursuit. When advised by Presidio County of the situation, I accepted their instructions to follow you and assist at the scene."

"Please describe what you saw, and your actions, for the rest of the night."

"Certainly, Ranger."

Bradford went into a detailed account of his recollections of the previous night. Jim turned off his recorder when Bradford concluded his statement.

"Thank you, Officer," he said. "I'll be in touch with you if I need anything more. Right now, I'd suggest you head for home and get some sleep."

"That's exactly what I'm planning on doing. However, I'd like to ask for a few more minutes of your time, before I go."

"Of course. What's on your mind?"

"I want to speak with you about the traffic ticket I issued you last month, when you were driving through Marfa with your family."

"I thought you might," Jim answered. "We can't today, though. I've still got to inventory the drugs we found, then go through the car for evidence, put a preliminary report together, and talk with Company E Headquarters over in El Paso. I'll contact you in a day or so, and we can arrange a meeting."

"Not at the department," Bradford said. "I don't want anyone there to know we had this conversation."

"I understand."

Jim took a business card from the holder on his desk and handed it to Bradford.

"Here you go. All my phone numbers, including home, are on there. Call me whenever you wish."

"I'll do that, Ranger. Let me give you my numbers. And *gracias*."

"*Por nada*."

Jim spent the rest of the afternoon with State Trooper Judy Donavan, inventorying the drugs, making certain they were logged in correctly, and secured in the evidence locker. After processing the burned-out car for any further evidence, he made a quick call to Lieutenant Castellon, then went home for a much needed meal, shower, and night's sleep.

Now, the next morning, he was going through some of the files of unsolved cases Leon DaSilva had left him, while he waited for a call from El Paso. He had just poured himself another cup of coffee when his phone rang. He picked it up after two rings.

"Texas Rangers, Alpine Office. Ranger James Blawcyzk."

"Jim, it's Lieutenant Castellon. Ranger Perez is also on the line. We've both read over your report. Javier has more information to add to what you forwarded. Before we start, has the hospital indicated when you might be able to question Trainor?"

"Not yet, Lieutenant. It appears he's at least partially paralyzed. He suffered extensive head injuries, and second and third degree burns over forty percent of his body. The doctor treating him told me there could be permanent brain damage. How serious is unknown. I've already got a request in for a search warrant, so I can obtain blood and bodily fluid samples. That should be ready by the time we're finished with this call. The hospital's plan right now is to get Trainor stabilized, then transfer him to a larger facility in El Paso or Midland."

"Let's hope he recovers enough to provide us more information. Javier, if you would proceed."

"Of course, Lieutenant. Good morning, Jim."

"Mornin', Javier."

"Jim, as you probably already found out, both Jackson and Trainor have long criminal records."

"I checked those earlier," Jim said. "Two altar boys they sure weren't."

"I won't argue with you there. They both belonged to the Black Wolves gang in El Paso. Over the past year or so, the Black Wolves have been in a turf war with the *Diablos de la Frontera* gang out of Del Rio. That outfit works hand in glove with the *Mano de la Muerte* Mexican drug cartel out of Ciudad Acuna."

"You have any idea why Jackson and Trainor would've been carryin' a boatload of opioids through this area? You've seen the inventory, right?"

"I sure have. Ten kilos of heroin, enough Oxycodone and Oxycontin to supply every damn pharmacy in El Paso for a week, not to mention the fentanyl."

"You have a clue why they were so far off the main drug trafficking routes?"

"One reason comes to mind. Both outfits want to expand into the Big Bend. The markets in their home territories are pretty well saturated. They need to find new buyers for their product."

"Alpine? Marfa? Hell, there's nowhere near enough potential customers over this way," Jim said.

"No, but there are always some, and with that area so isolated the markup on illicit drugs is tremendous," Javier answered. "However, what we believe both gangs are up to is attempting to find new routes to use to avoid detection. Rather than taking the interstates, they're trying out the back roads. For example, if a shipment's going east out of El Paso, the mules might get off I10 in Van Horn, swing around on 90, then take any of the U.S. or state highways back up to I10, say like 118 through Fort Davis. Coming west out of Del Rio, they could do the same. Follow 90 to any of the roads that head north to I10. From Fort Davis, it's an easy shot up 17 to I10 or I20. After that, our *malos amigos* could head in almost any direction, into New Mexico and Albuquerque, over to the Dallas-Fort Worth metroplex, even up to Oklahoma City and Tulsa. They know all the law enforcement agencies in this region combined don't have enough man-power to cover all those roads. And I'm not even talkin' about the dirt ones through the *malpais*."

"Makes sense, but I was kind of hopin' I left the big drug problems back in Austin when I transferred out here."

"Jim, you know there's no escaping drugs, unless maybe you move to Antarctica," Castellon interjected.

"Yeah, you're right, Lieutenant. Javier, have you dug up anything on who might've run Jackson and Trainor off the road?"

"I'm working my sources. With luck, I'll know something in a few days. I can tell you right now, though, I'd wager it was a hit ordered by the *La Muerte* cartel."

"Jim, Javier, I've got to get to a meeting with Major Trujillo. I want you both to work closely with each other on this case. I don't know why I'm even saying that. I know you will. Unless there's something more to add right now, we'll end the call."

"I've got nothing at the moment, Lieutenant," Jim said.

"Me either," Javier added. "Don't worry,

Lieutenant. We'll keep you posted, and apprised of any developments."

"Good. Let's try'n stop this turf war before it really starts."

10

Two days later, Jim had just finished his breakfast at Judy's Bread and Breakfast Bakery Café in downtown Alpine. The waitress was handing him his check when his phone rang.

"Ranger Blawcyzk."

"Ranger Blawcyzk, Brewster County Dispatch. Please hold for Sheriff Zuniga."

"10-4."

A moment later, Sheriff Maximilian Zuniga's voice came over the speaker.

"Ranger, one of my deputies was murdered last night. We need your assistance at the scene. The killing seems to be tied in with the homicide outside of Marfa."

"What's the location?"

"U.S. 90, about twenty-four miles east of Marathon. I'm already there."

"Leaving Alpine now. Will be on scene in approximately thirty minutes."

Jim pulled out his wallet, threw a twenty dollar bill on the table, and walked quickly out the door, leaving the waitress and customers staring slack-jawed at his back. Once his Tahoe started, Jim hit the switch for its lights and siren, threw it in gear, then jammed the accelerator to the floor.

• • •

Slightly over thirty minutes and fifty-four miles later, Jim rolled up to a cluster of emergency vehicles. In addition to a number of Brewster County Sheriff's Office patrol cars and pickups, there were two fire trucks from the Marathon Volunteer Fire Department, and an ambulance from the Marathon Volunteer Emergency Medical Services. There were also several civilian vehicles belonging to some of the fire personnel. Sheriff Zuniga waved Jim to a stop.

"You made good time, Ranger. Appreciate that."

"You helped by closing the road at 385, Sheriff. Kept the curious outta the way."

"I had Terrell County close it at Sanderson, too. My deputy's body is just ahead, in a shallow draw. Follow me."

"Any idea what happened?"

"Not yet. A trucker passing by called it in. He remained here until we arrived. My chief deputy is interviewing him now. It appears Jolene Matheson saw something suspicious. But she never radioed in she had stopped. Her body's next to an SUV near the bottom of a draw. The vehicle matches the description of the one you're looking for from Marfa. Right here."

Zuniga pointed over the guardrail, which was damaged from a vehicle crashing through it. A black Ford Explorer Police Interceptor lay on its passenger side at the bottom of the draw. It had been repainted, but still had a police searchlight and push bar. The back tailgate was open. Ten yards behind the SUV lay the body of the deputy. A large blotch of scarlet spread across the back of her shirt.

"The damage to the rail didn't come from that vehicle down below," Jim noted. "You can see the tracks where it was driven into the draw, then tipped over. Plus the damage isn't new."

"No, that railing was torn up over a month ago, from another wreck," Zuniga said. "It stopped the car in that one from goin' over the side. The DOT just hasn't gotten around to repairing it yet."

"Anybody go down there yet?" Jim asked.

"No. I hated leaving Jolene like that, but I knew you wouldn't want anything disturbed until you arrived."

"Let me gather my equipment, and I'll get started. I'm sure sorry about your deputy, Mack."

"I appreciate that. But the time for mourning'll be after we determine exactly what happened here."

"Come with me. I'll get some basic information while we walk. What time did your office receive the call?"

"About six-thirty."

"What was the last time Deputy Matheson checked in?"

"Around four o'clock."

"Long time between her last transmission and her bein' found," Jim noted.

"I know. But radio and cell service are spotty out here, at best. Plus it was a busy night. It's not unusual for an hour or more, maybe even a couple of hours, to go by without an officer havin' the chance to call in. As far as her not bein' found quicker, well, you can see for yourself, in the dark a hundred cars could drive by this spot and not see a thing. That car's pretty well hidden from the road. Hell, it could have been there since the night of the first killing. Whoever ran those other *hombres* off the road could've doubled back or circled around through the back country and dumped it, then taken off in another vehicle. Of course, until we get a closer look, it's not possible to determine if Jolene came up on 'em while they were dumpin' the car, or she saw it and believed she had just come up on an accident."

"Well, we're about to find out."

Jim removed his evidence kit from the back of his truck.

"Mack, just from takin' a quick look at the road's shoulder, I can see there was a second vehicle stopped here. Can you have photos of the tire tracks taken, and casts of the treads? It'll save time. Check for footprints, too."

"Sure. You want one of my people to go through Jolene's car?"

"Okay, go ahead. I doubt you'll find anythin', but you never know. If it's still running, it can be turned off."

"It's not. Either Jolene shut it off, or it ran out of gas and stalled. You want someone to go down into that draw with you?"

"In a bit. I'd like to take a look around first. Has the medical examiner been notified?"

"He has. Should be here in about an hour."

"How about a hook? I hope you called for two, one for the vehicle in the ditch, another for your deputy's car. Both will have to go to the D.P.S. impound."

"Jesse Maldonado's been called. He's bringing his flatbed, and a heavy duty conventional wrecker. I figure we'll need that to reach the car in the draw. It's pretty far from the road."

"*Bueno*. Lemme get on down there. Stay on your phone."

Jim donned his nitrile gloves and booties. After dictating the basics into his recorder, he descended into the draw, following Matheson's footsteps, taking photographs and commenting along the way. She had taken the only safe path to the wrecked SUV, other than tying off a rope to the guardrail and lowering herself into the draw.

Some instinct warned Jim to stop before he reached the dead deputy.

"Somethin's not quite right here," he muttered. He took a closer look at Matheson's body, then the back of the Explorer. The menacing twin barrels of a twelve-gauge shotgun peered from the open tailgate. A tripwire, connected to the shotgun's triggers, was run from the truck and hidden under the sand. It reappeared, crossing the path, tangled around Matheson's right boot.

Jim spoke into his phone.

"Sheriff!"

"Sheriff Zuniga. What have you found, Ranger?"

"Your deputy walked into a booby trap. Move everyone back at least a hundred yards, until I sweep this vehicle and the ground around it. The sons of bitches might have left us a few more surprises."

"Roger. Need any assistance?"

"No point in putting anyone else at risk. I'll call you soon's everything's clear."

"You be careful, Jim."

"You know it."

Jim knew, if he followed Matheson's exact path, he would be relatively safe. What he had no idea of now was how many more deadly traps might have been set up in or around the Explorer. He got as near the truck as he dared, took photographs, then dropped to his belly. He studied the contours of the ground, and peered into the interior of the overturned Explorer.

"Rotten bastards!" he exclaimed. He took more photos, then crawled back away from the wrecked SUV. Once certain he was clear, he took out his phone.

"Sheriff, you still there?"

"I am. Everyone's moved back, like you ordered."

"Move 'em back another hundred yards, except for you, one of your deputies, and the firefighters and EMTs. You and that group, meet me at my truck."

"Will do."

When Jim got back to his truck, the only persons still within two hundred yards of the wrecked Explorer were Sheriff Zuniga, Deputy Sheriff Thomas Bascomb, half a dozen volunteer firefighters and the two EMTs from Marathon.

"Everyone listen close," he said. "Sheriff, it's a dang good thing you didn't have anyone go down into that draw. The *hombres* who dumped that SUV wanted to kill as many people as possible, once it was discovered. Mack, Deputy Matheson was killed by shots from a double-barreled shotgun, which was hidden in the back of the car. It was activated by a tripwire. That's still wrapped around her right ankle. The vehicle is surrounded by land mines."

"Land mines?" Zuniga echoed. "I didn't see any signs of those."

"Whoever planted 'em knew what they were doin'. They covered 'em real good. I had to lay down on my belly to look real close at the ground. Even then I could barely see where it had been dug up, then brushed back into place. I don't dare go down there again. No one will. That's an order."

"So we'll have to clear those before we can do anythin'," Zuniga said.

"That's just the start. The vehicle's also wired to explode if anyone touches it. There's at least one bundle of dynamite inside, probably more. My guess is the blasting caps are attached to motion sensors. If anyone rocks that vehicle just a bit too hard, or opens a door, they'll be blasted to pieces. There won't be anything left to pick up except a few bits of bone."

"So what do we do now, Ranger?" Zuniga asked.

"There's a few options. None very good. The simplest, and safest thing to do would be set off those explosives. That's the way of taking the least risk, and the least chance of losing any more lives."

Jim paused, then continued.

"We could call in the Highway Patrol bomb squad. They would attempt to disable the mines and dynamite. That's awful dicey. First, it'd take 'em a minimum of two hours to get here. That's two hours with the sun beatin' down on that vehicle and the soil, heatin' things up. I'm not too worried about the land mines, but it'll get awful hot in that car, awful fast. It shouldn't get hot enough to set off the dynamite, but you can never be certain with explosives. If that dynamite's old, and starting to deteriorate, it'll be unstable. In addition, the wind'll pick up as the day gets hotter. If it blows hard enough to rock that vehicle, it could trigger the sensors, then boom! I hate risking lives on a trap in the middle of the desert. I'd rather render the damn thing safe by blowing it up."

"How would you do that, Ranger?" Bascomb asked. "Pardon my breakin' in."

"No need to beg pardon," Jim answered. "Everyone here has the right to ask questions. There's a couple of ways I can set off those explosives. If that's what I settle on, I'll want everyone else far back. The only person who might get hurt'll be me."

"Ranger, you haven't mentioned Jolene Matheson," Zuniga said. "I damn for certain don't want her body to be blasted clean down to Mexico. That's not right. It's gonna be hard enough telling her family what happened. I sure as hell am not gonna tell 'em they can't say goodbye to her, and give her a proper burial."

"I know, Sheriff. I'm hoping things don't have to come to that, but they just might. I've got a plan I need to run by everyone first. If we can pull it off. But it has to be done as safely as possible. I'd say the *hombres* who planted that car did it long before it was discovered. However, there's no way of knowing how close your deputy came to a mine when she fell. Or if there's another trip wire attached to the one she caught, which will go off when her body is moved."

"So what's our next step?"

"We try'n lift her outta there," Jim said. He turned to Marathon Fire Chief Tad Jones.

"Chief, does your department have a hook and ladder truck?"

Jones shook his head.

"No, Ranger, we don't. But Alpine has a tower truck."

"Good. Call mutual aid and have it sent down here. Get an ETA. We'll need that truck, and possibly Maldonado's heavy duty. Deputy Bascomb, call Maldonado. Get an ETA from him."

"Ranger, what do we do in the meantime?" Zuniga asked.

"While we're waitin', gather as much evidence as we can. First I'll explain the procedure we'll attempt to retrieve Deputy Matheson's body, so everyone here knows exactly what we're up against. If anyone doesn't feel up to the task, they can back out, with no repercussions, and no hard feelings. It's one thing to go into a blazing building. But forcing a person into maybe getting blown sky high is something I won't do. Especially since the firefighters and EMTs here are all volunteers. They're trained to fight fires, not defuse explosives. Also, I want any media people who turn up kept way back. We don't need them underfoot until the situation is stabilized."

"Ranger, I believe I can speak for every one of my people here, that we'll be with you all the way," Jones said.

"The same goes for me and my deputies," Zuniga added. "I'll radio the ones at the road-blocks to warn them to watch out for reporters. They know how to deal with them."

"*Muchas gracias.* I'm obliged," Jim answered. "There's one other thing we can do until Alpine arrives."

"What's that?" Jones asked.

"Pray."

Sheriff Zuniga gave Jim a hard look. They were still waiting for the arrival of Alpine's tower truck. Jim had gathered all the evidence, including some casts of footprints and tread marks, he possibly could, without returning too deeply into the draw.

"Ranger, I don't know you all that well yet, but I've known Leon DaSilva for years. I know how you Rangers operate. And I can damn for certain tell what you're thinkin'. You're trying to figure out some way to get back into that draw and pull Jolene's body outta there, without gettin' yourself killed."

Jim had been staring at the wrecked vehicle and deputy's body for the last several minutes.

Jim sighed.

"You're right, Sheriff," he admitted. "I'm thinking if I tie a rope to the guardrail and wrap it around my waist, I can lower myself down there without steppin' on any mines."

"And just what do you imagine you can do once you reach the bottom? You said yourself the sons of bitches who laid this trap did a good job of it. My deputy already sprang part of it, and it got her killed. You want to end up the same way? Just forget it. You hear me? Forget it. Alpine Fire will arrive any minute now. Just be patient, and wait for them."

"Unlike a doctor, I've never had any patients, or patience," Jim answered. "But I've got to admit you're right, Sheriff. I can't see any possible way of reaching that vehicle without tripping some kind of hidden trap. But dammit. If I could only just read the license plate, that would be a big help. Being able to decipher the VIN would be even better."

"Ranger, I know how frustrated you are. Hell, seeing poor Jolene lyin' there dead in the hot sun, slowly being roasted, and not being able to do anything about it, has got me just about plumb *loco*. It's all I can do to keep myself from goin' down there and pulling her out, the hell with the mines and tripwires. But gettin' yourself, or myself, or anyone else killed ain't gonna bring her back. It'll just mean more kinfolk grieving the loss of a loved one."

Jim sighed again.

"I know."

"There's Alpine rolling up now," Zuniga said. "It appears like Jesse Maldonado and his crew are right behind 'em."

"Good. The waiting's always the hardest part," Jim said. "Let's get back to work."

After going over his plan for the hazardous attempt to recover the body of Deputy Sheriff Jolene Matheson, making certain everyone who would be taking part in the effort understood exactly his or her role, and triple-checking for any possible thing which might go awry, Jim returned to his vehicle, while the Alpine firefighters maneuvered their tower truck into position. He changed out of his everyday dress clothes, replacing them with his BDU and combat boots. He also pulled on his bullet resistant vest, and replaced his hat with a riot helmet and protective face shield. His camera, hanging from a strap around his neck, was tucked into his BDU's right breast pocket. By the time he was finished, the tower truck was in place, the outriggers extended to support the truck, and prevent it from tipping once the ladder was extended.

"I'm ready. Do I need to go over anything again?" Jim asked.

"Not from my end," Sheriff Zuniga answered.

"Our truck's in place," Alpine Fire Chief John

Golden said. “Larry, are you, Marianne, and Bert ready?”

“We are,” Larry Montrose said. “Just waiting for the Ranger to give the go-ahead.”

“Let’s git ’r done,” Jim said. “Just remember, we’ve all got to move real slow and easy-like. I don’t need to remind any of y’all what will happen if we ain’t real careful.”

“You sure don’t, Ranger,” Marianne Bosley answered. “I’ll be working the ladder, along with Bert Manwaring, here. Soon as we have it in position, you can climb on up.”

“Okay.”

Jim waited while the firefighters swung the truck’s ladder perpendicular to its chassis, raised it at a slight angle, and extended it over the draw, stopping it directly over the wrecked Explorer and deputy’s body.

“Is that about where you want it positioned, Ranger?” Chief Golden asked.

“It looks like it,” Jim answered. “The ladder’ll probably need to be moved just a tad once I get out there.”

“*Bueno.* Here’s your two-way and the grappling line.”

Golden handed Jim one of the department’s walkie-talkies, and a coiled rope with a heavy, three pronged hook on one end.

“This ain’t gonna be exactly like ropin’ cows,” Jim said, with a grim chuckle. “Not bass fishin’, neither. Chief, I'm givin' you and your people one last chance to back out of this here situation."

"We take an oath to protect our community, and this is one of the things that come with that oath," Golden answered. "Besides, you're the one who's got the most to lose. We're far enough back we should be safe. If anything goes wrong the worst that could happen is we'll end up with a damaged ladder on our truck. But you, well . . ."

"I know. You'll be pickin' up chunks of me from here clear over to Sanderson, and back to Marathon," Jim said. "Wish me luck."

He blessed himself, then climbed onto the truck, stepped onto the ladder, and began edging up the rungs.

"Don't forget it'll be more bouncy, the farther out you get," Bosley warned him. "I'll be handling the radio. Once you're ready, let me know if you need any adjustments to where the ladder's sittin'."

"I'm not worried about the bounce, just the fall," Jim shot back. He continued slowly up the ladder, until he reached its top few rungs. He fastened his safety harness in place, lay down, then pressed the talk button on his two-way.

"Firefighter Bosley."

"I'm listening, Ranger."

"Swing the ladder about twelve feet to the left. I want to try'n get photos of the license plate on that wreck, and with even more luck the VIN."

"10-4. Holler when it's where you want it."

"10-4."

Jim braced himself while the ladder was swung.

"Hold it right there," he yelled into the radio, once it was about two feet beyond the front of the Explorer.

The ladder came to an abrupt halt. Bosley's voice crackled over the radio.

"You all right, Ranger?"

"I am. Gonna snap some photos, then have you move me slowly back to the original spot. I'll take some video while you do. Got that?"

"10-4, Ranger."

Jim got to his knees, and pulled his camera from his pocket. Leaning over the edge of the ladder, he took numerous photos of the scene, zooming in on the SUV's front license plate and VIN number.

"Dunno if that VIN'll come out clear enough to read or not," he muttered. "If it doesn't, the lab techs should be able to enhance the image enough to be readable."

He slid the camera back into his pocket, then called Bosley.

"Firefighter?"

"I'm listening, Ranger."

"Swing the ladder back to just a little way past where you first stopped it, about a foot or so.

Keep it as steady as you can. I'm gonna shoot some more video while you do that."

"10-4, Ranger."

Jim kept his camera running while Bosley moved the ladder over the Explorer.

"Hold it right there," he spoke into the two-way, when the ladder was directly over the deputy's body.

Bosley eased the ladder to a stop.

"Is that where you need it?" she asked.

"10-4. Listen carefully. No matter what I do, the deputy's corpse is gonna drag a bit through the dirt, before you can lift it off the ground. We have to keep that lateral motion to a minimum. If we don't, it might hit one of the mines and set it off. Soon as I tell you I've got it hooked, you need to lift the ladder straight up, as quickly as possible. As soon as the corpse clears the car, keep raising the ladder while you swing it back over the road. Just be positive you've got enough height to clear everything underneath."

"Understood. Fingers crossed and lips praying."

"And hands steady."

Jim uncoiled the grappling line. He slowly lowered it until the hook touched Matheson's body. He let out a little more slack, then tied off the rope.

"Here's hoping I can latch onto that deputy without too much trouble," he whispered to himself. "It'd be easier if I just hooked her wherever I could, but I'd rather not cause any more trauma to the corpse. The buckshot she took already tore her up. What happened to her is gonna be hard for her family to hear as it is. I don't want to make it any worse if I can help it."

He decided to attempt working one of the grappling hook's prongs underneath Matheson's gun belt. He believed the thick leather belt would be sufficient to support the deputy's weight long enough to bring her to the road. It took three tries, and a lot of cursing, before he managed to slide one of the prongs under the gun belt. The only apparent new damage to Matheson's body was a tear in her already bullet riddled uniform shirt.

Jim took up as much slack in the rope as he could, then called Bosley.

"Firefighter?"

"I'm here, Ranger."

"I've got the deputy's body secured. Lift me up as straight and quick as you can."

"Be ready when the ladder jerks. I'd hate to see you fall."

"I've got my safety harness in place, and I'll be hangin' on for dear life. Just get me outta here."

"10-4."

When the ladder lifted and the rope tightened, it dragged the deputy's rigor mortis stiffened body along the ground for over a yard before it lifted clear. The corpse came within a foot of where Jim believed one of the land mines was buried, then rose into the air. Bosley continued raising the ladder until the corpse was high enough to clear the guardrail. Once it was over the road, she lowered the ladder until the deputy's body was within reach of Montrose and Manwaring. Her partners held the murdered Matheson steady until she was placed on the road. Bosley let the rope go slack, so they could remove the grappling hook from beneath Matheson's gun belt. Once that was done, Jim climbed back down the ladder, and off the fire truck. He was trembling, and drenched with sweat.

"Are you okay, Ranger?" the sheriff asked.

"I am. Sheriff, you can have the medical examiner come take the body now," he told Zuniga. "I'll just make a perfunctory examination here, since the cause of death is obvious, and the time pretty well determined. Your deputy took two full loads of buckshot in her chest. Some of the shot went clean through her. The M.E. won't need to wait for me to observe the autopsy. As soon as he's on his way back to Alpine, I want all of you to go back with the others, then move back at least another hundred yards."

"What're you planning on doin' next?" Zuniga asked.

"I'll explain that once I'm done with my examination."

• • •

After examining Matheson's body, taking more photographs, and dictating some notes into his recorder, Jim allowed Brewster County Medical Examiner Tomas Calderon to remove the remains for autopsy. He removed his helmet and face shield to wipe away sweat running down his face, then opened the tailgate of his Tahoe.

"Time to move everybody back, Sheriff," he said. "I've got to finish things up here on my own. That way, whatever happens will be my responsibility. And if something goes wrong, my fault."

"You're in charge, Ranger. Anything else you need before I shove everyone back?"

"Nope."

Jim unlocked and opened an armored metal case in the back of his truck. He removed two concussion grenades. He also took his rifle from its mount.

"What the hell are you gonna do with those?" Zuniga asked.

"I'll use the grenades to blow up the land mines. The shock waves should set those off. I'm hoping it also sets off the dynamite in that SUV. If it doesn't, I'll use a bullet to explode it."

"You're liable to blow *yourself* up. Sky high," Zuniga pointed out.

"Nah. I should be all right. I'll have time to duck and cover before the mines go off. In addition, the soil's mostly sand and gravel, so there aren't any big rocks to worry about, and the sides of the draw will direct most of the blasts away from where I'll be. And if I do have to use my rifle, it'll be from a good distance back. Soon as I feel it's safe, I'll want you and your deputies to help me collect evidence."

"You mean pick up the pieces," Zuniga said.

"As long as they ain't my pieces," Jim said. He laughed, then slid his helmet back in place. He waited until Zuniga had everyone else well back, then drove his truck closer to the draw, positioning the big SUV to help shield him from any flying debris. Leaving his rifle on the front passenger seat, he took the grenades. He walked around the front of his truck, and looked into the draw, calculating distance and the likely radius of shock waves and debris field.

He chuckled as he readied to toss the first grenade.

"At least if I mess up this truck, I won't have to listen to Jake Kearney complainin' about it. Maybe I'll take a minute to cover it with a tarp."

He reopened the Tahoe's tailgate, and removed a blue plastic tarp, along with four bungee cords. He tossed the tarp over the truck and pulled it into place, securing it as best he could with a bungee cord attached to each corner of the bumpers.

"That's for you, Jake," he said, laughing.

Kearney was the Department of Public Safety's

chief mechanic in Austin. He viewed each vehicle under his care as one of his children. Jim's tendency to pound his vehicles off the roads and through the brush in pursuit of outlaws, dinging and denting fenders, nicking and scratching the paint, sometimes shattering headlights, had brought Kearney's ire down on him many times.

"Here goes nothin'."

Jim pulled the pin on the first grenade, and threw it into the draw. He dove to his belly alongside his truck, covering his head with his hands. The grenade exploded, followed instantly by several other larger explosions. Geysers of sand and gravel spouted into the air, much of it raining down on Jim. He waited until the dust settled, then got to his feet.

"Ranger? Ranger?" came over his two-way. "Are you all right?"

"Ask me that when I'm done, Sheriff," Jim answered. "I've still got to launch another grenade."

Jim walked back to the edge of the draw. While the wrecked vehicle had taken some damage, it had barely moved. There was still some relatively undisturbed ground, where he believed several land mines still awaited their unsuspecting quarry.

"Dang! I can't reach that side of the car without movin' in closer. I'll have to make certain my throw puts the grenade on the other side of that

SUV, then run like hell, which ain't easy in this bulky BDU."

Jim made the Sign of the Cross, murmured a quick prayer, then stepped through the gap in the guardrail and walked about ten feet down the embankment.

"Here goes."

He lobbed the grenade in a high arc over the Explorer, then ran hell bent for leather back up the bank, diving through the gap in the rail and rolling up against his truck, sliding under it just as the grenade went off. With a thunderous roar, so did the remaining mines. The Tahoe shook from the force of the explosions, while more sand and gravel rained down. Jim waited until the air cleared, then crawled from under the Tahoe.

"Looks like that did the trick, at least as far as the mines are concerned," he muttered. "The damn dynamite didn't go off, though."

The concussion from the grenade set off the remaining mines. The explosions had ripped off the tailgate of the Explorer, and shattered all its windows. But the dynamite was still in place, seeming to Jim that it was mocking his attempts to explode it.

His two-way crackled to life.

"Ranger?"

"I'm here, Sheriff. And just fine. The rest of the mines are cleared."

"Are you certain of that?"

"As certain as I can be. I've still got to get rid of the dynamite. That'll take care of any remaining traps, including any mine that might not've gone off. It's just too bad blowing up that SUV will pretty much destroy any evidence it contains."

"Is there anything I can do to help?"

"As a matter of fact, Sheriff, there is. Have the fire department trucks ready to roll soon as I give the word. The blast is likely to start a brush fire. If it does, we don't want that to get outta hand."

"10-4."

Jim pulled the tarp off his truck and stuffed it in the back. The tarp had done its job, and protected the vehicle from any body damage or broken windows. He then got in, turned the Tahoe around, and drove it about three hundred yards up the road. He turned it perpendicular to the pavement, parked, and got out, carrying his rifle.

Jim mounted the Bushmaster on its tripod, then placed it on the Tahoe's hood to steady his shot. He adjusted the telescopic sight. After calculating the wind, and aiming above his target to allow for cartridge drop, he slowly squeezed the trigger. His bullet hit precisely where he had placed it, through the blasting cap on the dynamite inside the Explorer. The ensuing explosion sent shards of the vehicle high in the air, in all directions. Smoke rose from the draw. Jim waited a few moments to make certain there were no further blasts, then called Zuniga.

"Sheriff."

"I'm listening, Ranger."

"Send the firefighters down. You and your deputies, too. Soon as everything's soaked down, we'll start collecting whatever we can find."

"10-4."

While the firefighters doused a small brush fire caused by the explosion, also watering down the Explorer and surrounding ground, Jim instructed the sheriff and deputies on what he needed from them.

"We have to gather as much evidence as possible, no matter how small a piece. I'm especially looking for the VIN number, and a license plate. Also important are any parts the suspects might have touched. Examples would be the steering wheel or pieces of it, the ignition switch or keys, any buttons or knobs, handles, anything like that. Make certain you don't pick anything up unless you're wearing gloves. Everything has to be bagged and tagged, since it will be going to the D.P.S. forensics lab for analysis.

"When we're finished, I'll need a roadblock set up here for the next five days. Stop every vehicle that passes by. Question the occupants as to whether they might have seen anything here, anything at all. Any questions?"

He was answered with a mumble of "nos," and shaking of heads.

"Good."

Jim turned to Jesse Maldonado, and his son and daughter.

"Jesse, once we're finished, I'll need you, Jose, and Magdalena to haul that wreck to the Alpine impound lot."

"Calling it a 'wreck' is an understatement, Ranger," Jesse said.

"You think so?" Jim answered.

There was little left of the mangled Explorer but a twisted, charred hulk. The driver's side doors had been blown off, the hood hanging on by one hinge. All of its plastic and fabric components had been melted or burned away, the tires, except one, just smoldering blobs of melted rubber.

"I know so," Maldonado answered. "*No hay problema.* Me, Magdalena, and Jose know what we're doin'."

"*Bueno.* I'll also need you to meet me at the impound tomorrow. I want you to remove some parts, like the push bar, from that wreck, and the one from Marfa. I'll be taking those to the D.P.S. forensics lab in El Paso for testing. Can you be there by eight?"

"*Por supuesto*, Ranger. But how're you plannin' on fitting those pieces in your vehicle?"

"I'm not. Is there any place in town where I can buy a small utility trailer, real fast? I'm gonna need one for my ranch anyway."

"There's a truck rental place, but they don't

have any units for sale, as far as I know," Maldonado answered.

"Then I'll use my horse trailer."

"*Gracias a Dios pore eso*," Maldonado said. "*Por un minuto*, I thought you were going to say you'd use your old pickup."

"If I was off duty, I would," Jim answered.

"Jim, I've got something for you before we head back to the station," Alpine Fire Chief John Golden said. He handed Jim a form.

"This is an application to join our department. From what I saw today, you'd have no problem passing the training. In fact, as far as I'm concerned, you already have. I hope you'll consider signing on."

"I appreciate the offer," Jim said. "Once my family's moved in, and I'm more settled in my new post, I'd be proud to. Your people did fine work today."

"*Gracias*," Golden replied.

It took the rest of the day before all the evidence was gathered and catalogued, and the destroyed vehicle removed. After arriving back at his office, Jim dusted some of the pieces for fingerprints. One of the deputies had recovered the VIN plate, so the last thing Jim did before calling it a night was run the number.

It was well after midnight before he got home. Knowing he'd be late, he'd called Doris

McDonaugh to feed and water Copper and Sandman, so they'd already had their supper. Both nickered sleepily at him from their paddocks. He gave each a handful of treats, and good night pats to their muzzles. He then went into his office, took a quick shower, and tumbled into bed.

11

Jim had already been at his office for an hour when Jesse Maldonado arrived. Once Miriam informed him that the auto body man had arrived, Jim met him at the impound yard gate.

"*Buenos dias*, Jesse," Jim said. "You're right on time."

"*Buenos dias*, Ranger," Maldonado answered.

"Make that Jim. It's easier. I'll unlock the gate. You can drive right on in."

"*Bueno*."

Jesse parked his truck and got out.

"Which vehicle do you want me to work on first, Jim?"

"The Explorer. I need you to remove the push bar, what's left of the front bumper, and the remainder of the right front fender. Both passenger side doors. I also need the steering wheel cut off and removed. I've already dusted it for fingerprints, and wrapped it in plastic. Don't remove that covering. With any luck at all, the lab will be able to get some DNA samples off the wheel. I also want the tire and wheel we found. They're not too damaged for me to compare the treads to the photos of skid marks on the pavement and tracks in the dirt I took at the first scene."

"How about the Infiniti?"

"I need the rear bumper assembly off it. And the trunk lid."

"I'll get right to work," Jesse said.

"*Gracias*. How long do you think it will take?"

"Most of the morning, possibly a bit longer. Where do you want me to put those parts?"

"Inside my horse trailer. I'll be in my office, processing some other items and following up on some leads. If you need help, or have any questions, come get me."

While Maldonado began disassembling the wrecked vehicles, Jim went back to his office. He poured a cup of coffee, then began processing the evidence he had collected.

"Lemme see. I reckon I'll get started by dusting the ignition key for prints first. That's the most likely place I'll find any."

He opened his fingerprint testing kit. The key was still jammed in the ignition switch, which one of the deputies had found the day before, in a piece of dashboard ripped out by the explosion. When Jim dusted it, two clear prints were revealed on each side of the key, a thumbprint on the front and an index finger print on the reverse.

"Got 'em," Jim exclaimed. "The same prints as were on the steering wheel. Now to see if we have a match."

He took close up photos of the prints, then

lifted them and transferred the images to paper. He uploaded the images into his computer.

"Let's see what IAFIS comes up with," he said, referring to the Integrated Automated Fingerprint Identification System, which contained over one hundred million files of both criminals' and civilians' fingerprints. He downloaded the images to the database. A moment later, an image and profile of the fingerprints' owner appeared.

"Got ya!" Jim exclaimed, "Rafael Mendoza, last known address 106 West Dignowity Street, Del Rio. Let's take a look at your record."

Jim whistled when Mendoza's record came up.

"You've been a very naughty boy, Rafael. Why you're not already behind bars is sure a mystery to me."

Mendoza'a arrest history ran for over three pages. It included car theft, assault, breach of peace, witness tampering, extortion, possession of drugs, possession of drugs with intent to sell, and armed robbery, among others.

"These prints are the clincher. Along with what else I've got, I should be able to obtain an arrest warrant for this *mal hombre*.

"Let's see, I reckon I've got to make a couple of phone calls. Then I'll keep on working my samples."

His first call was to the Presidio County Attorney, Raymond Nelson. He made an appointment to meet with Nelson, to discuss the evidence he had against Rafael Mendoza, and if Nelson agreed, to request an arrest warrant. Nelson assured him, from what Jim told him over the phone, issuing that warrant would be no problem. He'd begin the preliminary papers while waiting for Jim to arrive.

Jim's next call, through his computer link, was to Ranger Company D Headquarters in Weslaco.

"Texas Ranger Company D, Administrative Assistant Maria Shostakovich. How may I help you?"

"Good morning. This is Ranger James Blawcyzk, Company E, out of Alpine. I need some assistance from Ranger McCoy down in Del Rio. Is Major Hardy in? If not, could you put me through to Lieutenant Montez in Laredo?"

"Major Hardy is in his office. I'll see if he's available."

"Thank you."

Jim waited until Maria came back on the line.

"Ranger Blawcyzk? Major Hardy will speak with you now."

The line clicked, and Major Thomas Hardy's voice came over the receiver.

"Ranger Blawcyzk. Good morning. How are things way out there in west Texas? How's Leon DaSilva?"

"Good morning, Major. I'm afraid things are as hectic out here as in the rest of the state. Leon's just fine. Taking life easy."

“Good for him. Maria tells me you need some assistance from my company.”

“That’s correct, Major. Specifically, from Bill McCoy in Del Rio.”

“The matter must be really important, since you’ve called me directly, before calling Bill.”

“It is. I need his assistance in arresting a murder suspect. The warrant is being readied as we speak. However, the one suspect is only the tip of the iceberg. If you could get Ranger McCoy and Lieutenant Montez on a video call with us, I can go over what we’re up against.”

“I will certainly do that. Just give me a moment, Ranger.”

“Thank you, Major. I’ll turn my computer’s camera on while I’m waiting.”

Shortly, Major Hardy was back on the phone.

“Ranger Blawcyzk, I have both Lieutenant Montez and Ranger McCoy on the line. We all seem to have decent video connections. Let’s make certain we can all hear each other. Ranger Blawcyzk, you first. Then you, Lieutenant.”

“Good morning, everyone,” Jim said.

“Good morning, Ranger,” Lieutenant Gabriel Montez said.

“*Buenos dias* from Del Rio,” Bill McCoy added.

“Everyone can hear? Excellent,” Hardy said. “Ranger Blawcyzk, please proceed.”

“Thank you, Major. All of you should be aware

of the double homicide case in Marfa that I'm investigating. To bring you up to date, yesterday a Brewster County deputy sheriff, while apparently checking on a supposed motor vehicle accident, was killed by a shotgun blast from the wrecked vehicle. The shotgun was triggered by a tripwire when the deputy stumbled over it. The same vehicle was also rigged with dynamite, and surrounded by hidden land mines. It was a trap, not an accident."

"We did get the departmental bulletin on that, Ranger," Hardy said. "I'm assuming you're about to provide us with further details."

"I am. Most importantly, the booby-trapped vehicle, a 2017 Ford Explorer, was the same one involved in the Marfa homicide. Despite having to render the Explorer, and the area around it, safe by detonating the explosives it contained, I was still able to obtain a good amount of useful evidence from it. The license plates came back as reported stolen out of Eagle Pass, three months ago. The VIN number indicates the Explorer was formerly a *Ciudad Acuna, Coahuila* police department vehicle. I was able to match collision damage from the Explorer's push bar to the rear of the fatality vehicle in the Marfa crash. I was also able to obtain clear finger and thumbprints off the steering wheel and ignition key. Those prints came back to Rafael Mendoza, address of record 106 West Dignowity Street, Del Rio."

A low whistle came over Jim's speaker. On his monitor, he could see Bill McCoy shaking his head.

"Rafael Mendoza. He's a damn bad one, Jim. A member of the *Diablos de la Frontera* gang. Allegedly, he's their top enforcer. He's suspected of several gang related killings, but so far no one's been able to pin any of those on him. You're positive those prints are his?"

"That's what IAFIS tells me. They were the only ones in the Explorer. And I'm ninety nine percent certain I can match the damage to the Infiniti in the Marfa wreck to the damage on the Explorer's front end. I'm having the relevant parts removed from both vehicles now. I'll be taking them to the lab in El Paso for more testing. If the paint matches up, that'll cinch things. I'm also hoping forensics can come up with some DNA samples. The Explorer was driven into the wash where it was found, then pushed onto its side. It took more than one person to do that. There was evidence of another vehicle at the scene, along with footprints from multiple persons. I'm still hoping to obtain either more prints or DNA samples from the wreckage, but that's not very likely."

"One question, Ranger Blawcyzk," Montez said. "Why are you having the vehicles dismantled, rather than taking them as a whole to forensics?"

"I know, it's rather unusual," Jim answered. "There's a couple of reasons. One, the explosives in the Explorer were so powerful some parts of it couldn't be recovered. Much of what was left is useless as evidence. Second, I've gone through both vehicles thoroughly. The damage to both is so extensive hauling them from here to El Paso would be of little use. Even wrapped as tightly as possible, there's still a good chance parts could fall off during transport, possibly creating hazards for other motorists, or even an accident. You know how rough stretches of I10 are. Hell, parts of that road could shake a Sherman tank to pieces. I can always have the rest of the vehicles hauled up to El Paso later, if it becomes necessary."

"So at the moment, you're looking for me to arrest Rafael Mendoza," McCoy said.

"As soon as I get the warrant to you. Once we're done with this call, I've got one more to make, to my supervising officer. Soon as that's done, I'll be driving over to the Presidio County Courthouse to meet with the County Attorney. As soon as a judge signs the warrant, I'll get it off to you, Bill. Any idea how long it might take you to track him down?"

"*Quien sabe*? If he's in town, it shouldn't take me long to locate him. How much of a fight he puts up is another matter. The odds are about even he's crossed the border and is holed up somewhere in *Acuna*. If he has, prying him out of Mexico will be well nigh impossible. We'd have to try'n get cooperation from the Mexican authorities, which isn't likely. Not even mentioning the *Mano de la Muerte* cartel will be protecting Mendoza. They'd be more'n happy to bushwhack a couple of *Yanqui gringos*. If those *gringos* just happened to be Texas Rangers that would only sweeten the pot. There'd be a price on our heads the minute we crossed into Mexico to pick him up."

"If not sooner," Hardy interjected. "Ranger Blawcyzk, this sounds as if we may need to contact Austin, to make certain they don't have any objections. Particularly given your reputation as somewhat of a, um, maverick."

"You're one step ahead of me, Major. You're absolutely correct. However, I'd like to request we hold off twenty-four hours before we do that."

"I'm assuming you have a good reason," Hardy answered.

"I do. It's going to take the rest of today for me to put everything together, and get a preliminary report done. That means I won't be going over to El Paso until tomorrow morning. Ranger Javier Perez out of El Paso has been assigned to assist me on this case, since there's a connection to the city. He's already advised me the Marfa homicide is most likely part of a drug cartel turf war, that's going to involve all of us. What I'm proposing is I'll stop at the forensics lab first, drop off the vehicle parts, then head over to Company E. I'll set up another conference call, with the four of us, plus Javier, Lieutenant Castellon, and Major Trujillo. We'll formulate a plan of action, then contact Austin."

"This will require some precise coordination between all three companies," Montez noted. "DEA, ATF, and the FBI might also need to become involved. Perhaps the Border Patrol."

"It's likely," Jim conceded. "However, let's not plan on that yet. We can bring them in later if we have to."

"What time do you want to set up the call?" Hardy asked.

"Let's say fourteen hundred hours. That will give me time to confer with Javier first, then the lieutenant and major. I'll confirm the time once I speak with them."

"That should be fine, Ranger Blawcyzk," Hardy agreed. "Is there anything else at the moment?"

"Not that I can think of. Bill, I'll call you as soon as the warrant is issued."

"That's fine. With any luck, by the time we have our conference tomorrow, Rafael Mendoza will be behind bars."

"Let's hope so," Hardy said. "Since we're done for now, we'll conclude this call. Ranger Blawcyzk, keep us informed of any new developments."

"Of course, Major. *Adios*."

"*Adios*."

Jim finished his call to Major Trujillo at Company E, then drove over to Marfa to meet with the Presidio County Attorney. There was no problem getting an arrest warrant issued for Rafael Mendoza. By the time his business in Marfa was complete, it was shortly before four in the afternoon.

"I wonder if Nolan Bradford would be available for a meeting, long as I'm over here," he murmured. "I reckon I'll give him a call and find out."

He dialed Bradford's personal cell number. The Marfa Money Machine answered on the fourth ring.

"Howdy."

"Howdy yourself, Officer Bradford. It's Ranger Blawcyzk. Can you talk?"

"Sure. I'm alone."

"I happen to be in town. Is there any chance we could get together?"

"I don't see why not. I rotated to days, so I'm just about finished with my shift. Give me, say half an hour. You got any place particular in mind?"

"Not really. I still haven't had much time to do any exploring."

"Then meet me at the Lost Horse Saloon. We

can grab a bite and a couple of beers. Might be best if you don't go in there wearin' your Ranger clothes. You'd be less noticeable. You know where it's at?"

"I can find it. As far as dressin' down, I'll manage that. You think anyone will bother us?"

"Nope. The place is kind of laid-back. Sort of a local hangout. Most folks mind their own business. A few might say 'howdy,' but that's all. We'll be able to palaver without anyone listenin' in."

"Sounds good. I'll see you in thirty minutes, give or take. I'll meet you in the lot. What'll you be drivin'?"

"I've got a blue Ford F150."

"Good. I'll be watchin' for you."

"See you then."

"Sometimes I could swear my truck's not a Ranger vehicle, it's a damn menswear's store on wheels," Jim muttered, as he pawed through the contents of the duffle bag he always carried in the back of his Tahoe. "Spare Ranger dress shirt, slacks, tie, and socks. BDU. Jeans, bandanna, denim shirt, extra boots to wear in the brush so I can keep the dress ones polished, and straw hat in case I need to take to the *brasada* on horseback in the heat. Couple of regular shirts and T-shirts just in case. I could make more money sellin' this stuff than on my Ranger pay."

He was parked in the dirt alley which ran behind the Lost Horse Saloon, hard up against the establishment's stockade fence. It was unlikely anyone would notice him changing his clothes between the truck and the fence. To make doubly certain, he was standing between the open driver's side doors of his truck.

He took off his shirt, tie, and slacks, exchanging them for a short-sleeve red and blue checked Western shirt, and a pair of faded jeans. He tied a green silk wild rag around his neck, replaced his white Stetson with a dusty and sweat-stained gray one, and switched out his polished boots for a pair of scuffed black ones. Instead of his distinctive Ranger belt, he slid a plain black one through the jeans' belt loops. He slid his Ruger 1911 service pistol behind the jeans' waistband, snugging it against his belly, hidden behind his shirt. He took his antique .45 Colt Peacemaker in its holster from its case, and buckled its gun belt around his waist, settling the revolver at his left hip. Once finished, he locked the truck, then waited until he saw Bradford's pickup pull into the dirt side lot.

"Howdy, Ranger," Bradford said, when Jim walked up.

"Howdy, Nolan. Call me Jim. Since it seems as if we're gonna be workin' together, we might as well use first names."

"That suits me fine," Bradford said. "Let's head

on inside. The place has an outdoor courtyard with a few tables. Might be best if we talk there."

"Okay. We can do that."

Jim looked around when they walked inside. There were pool tables, a bar fronted with 1950s style chrome legged and vinyl seated stools, and a number of tables. The décor could best be described as west Texas eclectic, or perhaps flea market. Or perhaps an antique dealer's truck had crashed into the building and emptied its contents willy-nilly into the room.

Bradford called a greeting to the man behind the bar.

"Hey Mike, you old son of a gun, how you doin'? Been behavin' yourself?"

"Sure have. Good to see you, Nolan. You ain't been by for a spell."

"Work's been nonstop," Bradford answered. "This here's my *amigo*, Jim. He's just moved over to Alpine from east Texas. I invited him for a couple of beers and some chuck. Jim, this is Mike Shaddox, owner of the place."

"Howdy, Jim," Shaddox said. If he recognized the Ranger, he gave no sign of it. Hopefully, he hadn't seen the article about the new Ranger posted to Alpine, or Jim's picture, in the local papers.

"Howdy, Mike. I'm right pleased to meet you," Jim answered.

"Mike, we're gonna sit outside, if the patio's open," Bradford said.

"It is, but you're crazy, sittin' out there in the hot sun, rather'n in here, where it's nice and cool."

"What can I say? Jim claims to be a desert rat. That's why he made the change and moved out here. Mike, give me a longneck Lone Star. Jim, what're you drinkin'?"

"I'd better make it a Dr Pepper," Jim answered. "I still have to drive back to Alpine later."

"One Lone Star and one Dr Pepper comin' right up," Shaddox said. He rummaged in the under bar refrigerator, took out two bottles each of the requested beverages, and popped the tops.

"I figure you'll both want more than one," he said, as he passed them the drinks.

"You figure right," Nolan said, with a grin. "Dunno about Jim, but I'm plumb starved."

"I could eat a bite," Jim admitted.

"Good. I'll send Eloise out with menus."

"Sounds great. This way, Jim."

Bradford led Jim through a side door, into a dusty courtyard. He chose a table under the overhanging roof.

"This'll be a little cooler than sittin' in the sun," he said.

They sat down, and took long swigs of their drinks.

"I'm a little surprised you didn't ask for a beer, Jim," Bradford said.

"I would have, but I'm still on duty. No alcohol allowed, even undercover. And technically I'm not even that. Just changed out of my good clothes to fit the setting."

"Understood. Here comes Eloise with the menus. We'll talk after we place our orders."

"Howdy, Nolan, you handsome dog," Eloise said. "Who's your new friend? He's even better lookin' than you are."

Eloise was young, in her mid-twenties at most. She had light brown hair, worn straight and about four inches below shoulder length. Her eyes were a darker shade of brown. She stood about five feet five, and weighed about one hundred ten pounds, Jim would estimate. She had a nice figure. The yellow cotton blouse, its top three buttons open to reveal her cleavage, and tight jeans she wore showed off that figure to full advantage.

"The name's Jim, Ma'am."

He gave her his crooked smile, the one women for some reason, which Jim never did figure out, couldn't ever resist. Eloise flushed, and her heart fluttered.

"Why, if you ain't so damn polite!" she exclaimed. "Nolan, you could take a lesson from him. But Jim, please don't call me ma'am. It's Eloise."

"Certainly."

Jim flashed her that smile again. Eloise smiled sweetly as she handed him the menu.

"Do you want a few minutes, or would you like me to wait?"

Jim glanced at the menu.

"I've already made up my mind," he said. "A bowl of chili. Contains Hatch chiles, right?"

"It damn sure does."

"Excellent. An order of your bacon wrapped chicken lollipops and waffles. Three Hatch chile and smoked chicken *empanadas.*"

"Are you certain you want all that? The portions are really large," Eloise asked.

"Yeah, Jim. You said you wanted just a bite," Bradford added.

"That *is* just a bite," Jim answered.

"All right, then. Nolan, how about you?"

"I'll have the Southwestern Chicken flatbread, Eloise. And you might as well bring out two more longnecks."

"Two more Dr Peppers for me," Jim added.

"Of course. I'll put your orders in now."

"We're in no hurry. Take your time," Jim said.

He waited until Eloise was back inside before speaking again.

"Nolan, tell me what you wanted to discuss. Let's try and get this done before our meals arrive, so we can enjoy them."

"Suits me fine. Jim, first, let me apologize for issuing you that ticket. I knew damn well you hadn't violated any traffic laws."

"But you did anyway."

"Yes, I did. You see, as you pointed out in court, Marfa makes a lot of money from traffic citations issued to out of towners, who usually don't have the time, inclination, or even money to fight them. But that's only part of the story. Some of the officials in town make a nice chunk of change gettin' their cuts from those tickets. That's one of the reasons they fired Georgina Delehanty. She was snooping around. You already know the other reason."

Jim raised his eyebrows in surprise.

"You speak with George?"

Bradford shrugged.

"We keep in touch. You must have some questions."

"Some? I should say so. First off, why weren't you fired, along with the rest of the force? Second, why didn't you quit?"

"I've been with the department since it was reestablished. Was hired by the city before they even found a new chief. I guess they figured I wasn't about to stir up trouble."

"Were they right?"

"You have to understand, Jim. I couldn't afford to. Still can't. Hell, I dunno for certain why I'm even here talkin' to you now, since if I'm found out it'll cost me my job, at the very least. I guess mebbe I knew all along sooner or later someone would get wise. Seems like you're the one who did. And also you're in a position to do something about it."

"Leon DaSilva didn't know?"

"Only for the last few weeks. George mentioned the situation to him. He told her if they could shut down 'The Club' it would solve the other problem at the same time."

"Does anyone else know you and George talk? She never mentioned you. I don't want to get sandbagged again."

"We've been careful. I don't believe anyone else besides Leon does."

"But you can't be certain."

"No."

Jim grunted in disgust. He took off his hat and ran his hand through his hair, then replaced the hat before replying.

"Damn. Ain't this just a fine how-de-do?"

"You worried about gettin' involved?"

"Me? A Texas Ranger? You should know better than that. Hell, no. But I've still got more questions."

"Ask 'em."

"I need to know why you can't afford to walk away from the department."

"Because I'm a single father, with five kids. Two girls and three boys. About a year after our youngest was born, my wife walked out. She moved to Dallas with her former boyfriend. She filed for divorce, but didn't want anything out of me. No alimony, no property, and most of all she didn't want custody of the kids. Luckily, my oldest is seventeen. She's able to watch the others when I'm at work. I shouldn't have to tell you how hard it is to raise five kids on a police officer's salary, especially in a small town. But this is our home. None of us want to leave it. Now you know."

"I can understand that. How about proof? Do you have any?"

"I have some notes. If you can get into the records, you should be able to find discrepancies between the fines that were issued in court, compared to what went into the city's account."

"That'll take a search warrant. To get that, I'll need a little more than just your word."

"I know. I can give you some names to start with."

"Go ahead."

"Barry Asher. He's the police chief. Slate Daniels, the mayor. You've already met two of the others, Judge Cummings and Harold Boyle, the prosecutor. Each of them also belongs to 'The Club.' "

"That would explain why they came down on you so hard in court. They wanted to make certain it appeared as if handing out all those tickets was only your idea."

"That's right. But you'll find every officer on the force issues a whole mess of tickets. Since the town gets a lot of revenue from those, most folks look the other way. Plus, it can be a big mistake to cross some of the more powerful people in this town. The county, for that matter. Why do you think nothing's been done about 'The Club'? People are too afraid."

"Nolan, you do realize if this comes out, you might be in danger?"

"I damn for certain do. But I reckon as long as I keep on writing tickets, I should be safe."

"You'd better hope so. After today, it'd be best if we communicate by phones, as much as possible. The less we are seen together, the better."

"Does that mean you'll work on this?"

"I can't say for certain quite yet. First, I'll want to look over the notes you have. I also still need to go through the files George has compiled. Even before that, I'll have to see if Austin, and my commanding officer, will make an exception to the rules for me. If I can get their okay, I still have to get permission, in writing, from the Presidio County Attorney. We'll have to dang sure hope he's not involved in any of this."

"Raymond Nelson? I doubt it. He's a straight shooter. But why's that?" Bradford asked.

"You see, the rules were changed some time back. A Ranger is no longer allowed to investigate government corruption in his own area. Leon knew that. Could be the reason he asked

George to wait. So close to retirement, he probably didn't want to touch this hot potato. He decided to drop it in my lap instead. Can't say as I blame him. And of course the murder case is still my top priority. Until that's solved, pretty much everything else will have to stay on the back burner. However, I'm used to working more'n one case at a time. Give me a day or two. Until I get back to you, I don't want you talking to anyone, not even Georgina Delehanty. As far as this conversation, it never took place. That's to protect both of us. *Comprende*?"

"*Comprende*."

"*Bueno*. Looks like Eloise is comin' with our grub."

"Here you are, boys," Eloise said. She carried a platter full of food.

"Sure smells and looks good," Jim said, as she placed his chili in front of him.

"Oh, it is, darlin'. You can count on that," Eloise said. "I just hope you can finish it all."

"And you can count on that," Jim said. "*Muchas gracias*."

After his meeting with Nolan Bradford, Jim went back to his office and worked until shortly after twenty hundred fifteen hours that evening. He then decided to stop on his way home at Georgina Delehanty's storage unit, to pick up the evidence she claimed it held.

Alpine Safe and Secure Storage was located on South 5th Street, alongside the railroad tracks and directly across the street from the AMTRAK station. Locker A18 was on the track side of the facility, like most self-storage places a low slung, corrugated metal building. He backed up to locker A18's rollup door and opened it. Several legal sized cardboard tote boxes were stacked inside.

AMTRAK's eastbound Texas Eagle, miraculously running on time, which AMTRAK trains seldom did, pulled into the station while Jim was loading the boxes. He paused in his work to watch the few passengers alighting from or boarding the long passenger train.

One person in particular caught his eye. It was the redhead he'd seen at the Quarter Circle 7's hotel.

"I wonder what he's doin' here?" Jim said to himself. "It doesn't look like he's gettin' on the train. Yet he's got two suitcases. Wish I could get a better look at him. I'll try'n get some photos."

Jim grabbed his camera from his Tahoe. While he watched and took pictures, another person emerged from one of the train's sleeper cars. He set two identical suitcases to the ones the redhead carried on the platform. He picked up the redhead's cases and carried them back onto the train. With the stop at Alpine being only ten minutes, the conductor soon shouted his "All

Aboard," the locomotive's whistle sounded, and the train pulled out of the station. The redhead picked up the new suitcases and sauntered off to the parking lot. He got into the passenger's side of a large red Nissan NV van with the Big Bend Bicycling Adventures logo painted in white on its side.

"Huh. Interesting. I guess I'd better lock up here and follow that *hombre*."

Jim hurriedly rolled the locker door shut, padlocked it, slammed the Tahoe's tailgate closed, and hopped behind the steering wheel. The Nissan was just exiting the station's parking lot. It turned west on U.S. 90, toward Marfa.

"Good. I won't have to follow too close. I'll hang back so as not to spook that *hombre.* Because I'd bet my hat whatever's in all those suitcases isn't just clothes."

There was virtually no traffic this time of night, so Jim had no trouble following the van into Marfa. The driver went past the center of Marfa, then turned left on South Plateau Street. Jim continued for another block, took a left on South Mesa, and parked alongside Porter's Groceries. Taking his Nikon D5 camera, he walked around Porter's, going half a block west on South Dallas Street. The van was pulled up behind a building at the corner of 90 and South Plateau, which was the location of the Big Bend Bicycling

Adventures Company. The driver had just gotten out, and was opening the van's back doors. Jim recognized him immediately, even in the only illumination, which spilled over from the lights in Porter's front lot.

"The Hispanic *hombre* from the hotel!" he hissed under his breath. Two women came from the building to join the two men emerging from the van. "And there's their girlfriends."

Jim snapped pictures of the men and women unloading the truck. They carried the two suitcases, along with a number of other packages, inside.

"I'd sure like to get a look around that place, and that van," he muttered, when the door closed behind the four. "But I've got no reason to do that. I'll need some bit of evidence before I can even think of applying for a search warrant. Damn probable cause. Well, I guess I've got some more digging to do. That can wait until I'm back from El Paso. Right now, it's time to head on home and grab some shut-eye."

12

It was around a three-and-one-half hour drive from Alpine to El Paso. Since El Paso was in the small part of far west Texas in the Mountain Time Zone, Jim would gain an hour en route. Of course, he would also lose it on the way back home. He left at five in the morning, allowing time for slow moving traffic. Once he reached I10 at Van Horn, before getting on the highway he stopped for a quick breakfast, fuel stop, and bathroom break. He arrived at his initial destination, the Texas Department of Public Safety forensics lab in El Paso, just before eight. He'd arranged to have the testing of his evidence expedited. He spent most of the morning observing the technicians examining the samples, or working with them. They were able to process much of the evidence he wanted to have ready so he could have an updated report for his meeting that afternoon. After eating lunch at the nearby Tarahumara Mexican Food Restaurant, he made the short drive to Company E Headquarters. He walked in and greeted the woman behind the front desk. She was protected by a thick pane of bulletproof glass.

"Good afternoon. I'm Ranger Jim Blawcyzk, out of Alpine."

“Good afternoon, Ranger. Major Trujillo and the others are expecting you. They’re waiting in Conference Room C. That’s straight down the corridor to the left. I’ll buzz you in.”

“I’m obliged. Thank you.”

Jim went to the indicated room. In addition to Major Trujillo, Lieutenant Castellon, and Ranger Perez, two other men, and a woman, were present.

“Good afternoon, Major, Lieutenant. I’m not late, am I?”

“Not at all, Ranger Blawcyzk,” Trujillo answered. “It’s good to see you again. After going over your reports, Lieutenant Castellon and I decided we should bring in some of the other law enforcement agencies in the county. Allow me to introduce John Sampano, Commander of the Drug Enforcement Division of the El Paso Police Department, along with Detective Marcus Barberry, one of his best undercover investigators.”

“Pleased to meet you both,” Jim said, as they shook hands. Sampano was in his early fifties, with a swarthy complexion, black hair thinning on top, and dark brown eyes. He had a burly build, and was slightly under five foot ten. Barberry was a Black man, solidly built but slim, in his late twenties, about six feet four inches tall. His head was shaved, but he had a thick beard. At the moment, he wore a long-sleeved shirt.

The sleeves partially covered the tattoos which extended from the backs of his hands and up his arms.

"And this is Captain Gayle Quinones, head of the US DEA's El Paso office," Trujillo added.

"I'm also pleased to meet you," Jim said.

"As am I you," Quinones answered. She was in her mid-thirties, with shoulder length blonde hair and blue eyes. Her height was about five foot six or seven, her weight about one twenty-five.

"Jim, I hope you don't mind having the others join us," Trujillo said. "I've also got Ranger McCoy from Del Rio on the phone. He's on speaker. I didn't want to chance a video hookup today."

"Not at all, Major. I do have another case which came up, that I had hoped to discuss while I'm here in El Paso. I trust that will still be possible."

"Of course. You can hold it until the end, correct?"

"That's correct, Major."

"Then that's what we'll do."

"If you're prepared to start, pour yourself a cup of coffee and begin," Trujillo ordered.

"Of course, Major. I just came from Forensics, and updated my report to include their findings. I happened to make some extra copies, so I have enough for everyone here. Give me a moment to pass them out."

Jim handed out the copies.

"Y'all can read the entire thing later, and contact me with any questions. As you know, this whole investigation started with a motor vehicle homicide in Marfa. I received word this morning that the second victim succumbed to his injuries last night, without ever regaining consciousness. That of course means we won't be able to obtain any information from him. Both men were members of the Black Wolves gang of El Paso. Per Ranger Perez, the Black Wolves and the *Diablos de la Frontera* gang out of Del Rio are fighting to control drug trafficking in the entire Big Bend region.

"The murder weapon in the Marfa killings was a 2017 Ford Explorer Police Interceptor. It was a decommissioned *Ciudad Acuna*, Mexico unit. The plates it bore were stolen in Eagle Pass. We've been unable to trace its path since the *Ciudad Acuna* police sold it at auction."

"Do you have a firm match placing that vehicle at the crime scene, Ranger?" Quinones asked.

"My measurements on scene indicated the type of vehicle. The same type of vehicle was found in a dry wash outside Marathon. It had been deliberately wrecked, and booby trapped. A passing truck driver reported the supposed accident. The Brewster County deputy who responded was killed by a shotgun blast from inside the vehicle. The gun was triggered by a tripwire. The vehicle was also rigged with dynamite, and surrounded by land mines. I don't need to tell you that kind of ordnance is not something your run of the mill criminal can get their hands on.

"The only way to render the vehicle and surrounding terrain safe was to detonate the explosives. Once that was done, I was able to obtain some evidence, despite the destruction. I obtained a clean thumb and fingerprint from the vehicle's ignition key. I also was able to lift more prints from the steering wheel. They belong to Rafael Mendoza, a member of the *La Fronteras*. There's an arrest warrant out for him, but so far he hasn't been located.

"I spent this morning at the DPS forensics lab. Their tests confirmed the Explorer is in fact the murder weapon. The dents in the rear of the victims' vehicle match up exactly with the scrapes on the Explorer's push bar. Paint flecks on both vehicles matched up with the other. There is no question the Explorer was used to shove the other car off the road."

"Was there evidence of anyone else on scene?" Barberry asked.

"I have evidence there was at the location of the wrecked Explorer. In addition, it would take more than one person to roll that SUV onto its side. But anything incriminating, such as fingerprints or DNA, no. I'm hoping forensics can come up with something."

"Ranger, do you believe the ambush outside

Marathon was specifically meant to kill a police officer?" Sampano questioned.

"It's possible, but I don't believe so," Jim answered. "Anyone, not just a police officer, who came across the wreck might've gone down to check for anyone still inside. My belief is the trap was set as a warning, to the Black Wolves, law enforcement, and the general public. The *La Fronteras* are sending a signal they intend to control the drug market in all of southwest Texas. Along with the *La Muertes*. And nobody better get in their way."

"Which means they're working hand in glove with the *La Muertes* to enforce that," McCoy said, over the phone. "I'd wager they've got Mendoza under their protection. I haven't been able to locate him. He's got to be hidden somewhere in *Acuna*."

"If I might interject my thoughts for just a moment," Trujillo said.

"You're the commanding officer, so I doubt anyone will tell you no, Major," Jim said.

"You forget how well I know you, Ranger Blawcyzk," Trujillo retorted. "You've never been one to keep your mouth shut, even when you should."

"I have to admit that," Jim conceded. "Go ahead, Major."

"This case is going to require close coordination and cooperation between the Rangers, specifically Companies E and D, the Highway Patrol, local, county, and federal authorities. Agent Quinones, do you believe the FBI should also be called in?"

"Perhaps later. If we can handle this with the agencies gathered here now, then I would say no. The more people involved, the more chance of slip-ups. And of course squabbling over command."

"I agree," Sampano said. "Ranger Blawcyzk, since this case started in your area, do you have any suggestions for a plan?"

"Something happened last night which gave me the germ of an idea. If the rest of you agree, it means Detective Barberry will need to take on a crucial role. I have to ask you first, Detective, how long have you been undercover? And how deeply have you worked your way into the Black Wolves?"

"You can tell, Ranger?"

"You wouldn't be here today if you weren't undercover with the gang," Jim answered.

"Fair enough," Barberry said. "I don't want to get too specific. Let's just say I've been working undercover for more than six years. The last two and a half worming my way into the Black Wolves gang. I'm in good enough with the outfit to be one of the chief aides and bodyguard to the head honcho, Rolando DeJesus. I know their operations pretty damn well."

"Good. Let me run my plan by the group, then I'll ask everyone's opinion. I'll just need a moment to hook up my phone to the projector."

Once Jim had his phone's USB cable hooked to the digital projector, he began his presentation.

"I'd love to be able to say what I'm about to show you is the result of dogged investigative work, but the truth is I just happened to be in the right place at the right time.

"These photos were taken at approximately twenty hundred forty hours. This is AMTRAK's Texas Eagle, making its regular eastbound stop at Alpine. Note the redheaded man carrying two suitcases to the train. Do any of you recognize him?"

"I sure do," Barberry said.

"Me also," Javier Perez said. "That's Seamus O'Toole. He's a *capitan* in the Black Wolves. He's been arrested plenty of times, but except for a few minor convictions, none of the charges ever stick. Any witnesses either refuse to testify, recant their statements on the stand, or disappear."

"Or end up dead," Barberry concluded.

"Good. Watch for a man who's about to step off the train. Observe closely what he and O'Toole do next. And if any of you recognize the other *hombre*, speak up."

Everyone watched while O'Toole and the other man exchanged suitcases.

"That's Thomas 'The White Shark' Moore,"

Barberry said. "He got the nickname because he's so fair skinned and light-haired he's almost as white as an albino. His eyes are a real pale blue. That's where the 'White' comes from, The 'Shark' refers to his penchant for using a knife to cut up anyone who crosses him, leaving that person a bloody mess. He's another 'officer' in the Black Wolves. Moore's one real bad damn son of a bitch. What're he and O'Toole up to?"

"Keep watching," Jim said. "You noticed, of course, that they switched suitcases. The one you said is Moore got back on the train. I followed O'Toole. I'll skip over the dashcam video, and pick up where he arrived at his destination. You'll see some more of his friends."

Jim advanced the images until his arrival at the rear of the Big Bend Bicycling Adventures Company. He stopped when he got to the photo showing all four of his suspects.

"Raymundo Carillo," Perez said. "Another member of the Black Wolves."

"The women are Julie Ann Huntress and Juanita Ortiz," Barberry said. "O'Toole's and Carillo's respective girlfriends. What the hell are two of the top men in the gang's hierarchy doin' in Alpine, of all places?"

"Watch and learn, my son," Jim said, in his best preacher's voice. He clicked through the rest of his pictures.

"The first time I saw those four was at the

hotel where my family and I were staying while we were looking for a house to buy," he said. "Somethin' about 'em didn't look quite right. Later, I was told they opened a bicycle touring company in Marfa. That's its location where they're unloading the truck. I'd bet my hat the place is a front for distributing drugs."

"Knowing those bastards, they're probably also involved in human trafficking," Barberry said.

"Jim, you said you've come up with a plan to take this bunch down?" Trujillo said.

"The start of one," Jim answered. "It has to be finessed before we can put it into operation. AMTRAK's police will also need to be involved."

"Run it by us, and we can hash out the details. See if it's workable," Quinones said.

"You'll have all the help you need from my department," Sampano added.

"Excellent. Right now, it wouldn't be much of a problem to arrest this lot the next time they make an exchange. Since AMTRAK personnel have the right to inspect any baggage at any time, we wouldn't even need a warrant. TSA regulations would cover us. The two steps we'd have to take would be making certain we knew when the next exchange would take place. Then, we'd have to notify AMTRAK. They'd need to be part of this, preferably by having one of their railroad detectives on board. That's where you'd come in, Detective. Could you get word to us with the next transfer date?"

"I could find out, sure."

"Any chance you could make the trip along with whoever's making the delivery?"

Barberry shook his head.

"It'd be too big a risk. Perhaps another person from the department."

"Or a detective from the Highway Patrol," Trujillo suggested. "I'm not too certain about doing this without a warrant, though. A sharp lawyer might manage to get the charges tossed for an illegal search. Perhaps even claim entrapment."

"I'm right with you there, Major," Jim answered. "That's why I said we *could* arrest these five right now. I didn't say we *would*. They're obviously part of a much bigger operation. I'd like to grab every member of the outfit, or at least as many as possible. What I'm proposing is a full-scale investigation, if you approve, Major, and everyone else agrees. It would need to be two pronged. Not only do we need to take down the Black Wolves, I also want to knock out the *La Fronteras*. If we can get some of the *La Muertes* that would be a nice bonus. I want every last one of those sons of bitches behind bars. Bill, that's your territory. Are you with me on this? More importantly, will Major Hardy agree?"

"I am, and I'm positive he would. But will we need to get permission from Austin for an operation this size? Major Trujillo?"

"We would, but I don't see it being a problem. This apparent turf war isn't just endangering the citizens of a small part of Texas. It takes in almost a quarter of the state, perhaps even a little more. An area where law enforcement is stretched so thin there are sections where it's practically non-existent. If either one of these outfits gets a foothold, they'll be able to run their organization with almost complete impunity. We need to stop them before that happens."

"Which what I'm proposing should do is just that, if we execute everything perfectly," Jim said.

"With all due respect, Ranger Blawcyzk, as all of us here know, nothing ever goes perfectly," Quinones pointed out. "Even the best plan has flaws."

"I know, but hopefully we can keep those to a minimum," Jim answered.

"Ranger Blawcyzk, do you have any more specifics for us?" Trujillo asked.

"I do. My intention is to gather enough evidence to raid all three places simultaneously. If we want to put both gangs out of business, we'll have to hit all of them at the same time. If we don't, that will warn off the others. What I'm thinking is I'll handle Presidio and Brewster

Counties. I've got two men, one with the Marfa Police, the other a Brewster County Deputy, in mind to assist. Javier, you'll handle El Paso County. Lieutenant Castellon will be our direct supervisor for the operation. Commander Sampano and Detective Barberry will work closely with you, concentrating on the city itself. Bill, you'll handle things from Del Rio and Val Verde County, along with Lieutenant Montez. Major Trujillo, you, Major Hardy, and Captain Quinones will coordinate the entire operation."

"Ranger, you sound as if you expected us to be here," Quinones said.

"No, I sure didn't. However, I was certainly pleased when I did see y'all. Working together, we can dig up much more information, more quickly, than if this was just a Texas Ranger operation. Major, I apologize. I've overstepped my bounds, just a bit. I'm turning this over to you and the others for discussion. What I just offered is merely a broad outline. There are plenty of details to fill in. Bottom line, I want to round up both the source of the drugs, and the distributors."

"You seem to have forgotten you haven't even seen any proof of drugs yet, Ranger," Trujillo pointed out.

"Not in those suitcases, no," Jim admitted. "But let me remind you the homicide victims' car in Marfa was crammed full of drugs. Ranger Perez has told us the Black Wolves and *La Fronteras* are up to their necks in drug trafficking in these parts, and using new routes to avoid detection. What better way than the train? I'd bet my hat those suitcases you just saw contained drugs and cash. And I'm real fond of my hat. It's certain to be a lot of work, but we're gonna take both those outfits down. So are we a go?"

"Aside from the fact it sounds like *you* were just giving *your superior officer and his equivalents* the orders, I'd say we should discuss the plan further, finalize it, then put it into action," Trujillo said.

"I apologize if I came on a little strong, Major," Jim said.

"I'm not surprised," Trujillo answered. "You always have thrown everything you've got into an assignment, Ranger. Sometimes that tends to get you into trouble, but that's one of the reasons I fought so hard to get you transferred out here. You never give in when you know you're in the right. However, let's hear what the others have to say. Captain Quinones?"

"I believe one law enforcement agency won't be able to handle this situation all by itself, even the Texas Rangers. I feel a joint task force is needed. The DEA is in."

"Understood," Trujillo said. "Commander Sampano?"

"I agree. With all of us working together,

we can put more people into the effort. One advantage that gives us it'll be less likely any of the bad guys will spot one of our undercover officers."

"I trust the rest of you are on board," Trujillo said.

He was answered with a murmur of yesses, including from McCoy.

"I'll give Major Hardy a call as soon as we finish up here, Bill, just to make certain he doesn't have any objections, and see if he might have any suggestions," Trujillo said.

"That'll be fine, Major," McCoy answered.

"Just one thing," Jim said.

"What's that?" Trujillo asked.

"If we have to make certain anyone is 'on board' with this plan, it's AMTRAK."

"Maybe I made a mistake asking to have you transferred to my command after all," Trujillo said, shaking his head. "Let's take a few minutes break, to use the bathrooms and grab some more coffee. Then we can finish formulating our plans."

Three hours later, the final details of the operation were in place. Everyone except Jim, Major Trujillo, and Lieutenant Castellon had left.

"All right, Jim, we don't have to be quite so formal now," Trujillo said. "What's this other case you want to run by us?"

"I'll keep this brief, since I know it's already

been a long day, Major, and I need to get back to Alpine. I've received two credible reports of corruption among government officials in Presidio County, mostly Marfa. I realize regulations preclude me following up on those reports. However, I'm asking permission to handle this myself."

"I see."

"Reliable sources, Jim?" Castellon asked.

"Impeccable. One is the former police chief of Marfa, Georgina Delehanty. The other is a current officer with the department, Nolan Bradford. Bradford is the officer I'm considering asking to help with the drug running problem. Both have also given me more than enough evidence to start an investigation."

"Jim, you do realize what you're asking is highly irregular," Trujillo said. "Even if I agree, I'd have to get the okay from Austin. Then you'd have to get written permission from the Presidio County Attorney to handle the case. You've got to convince me waiving the regulations is feasible, and there has to be a good reason to grant your request. Why in particular do you want to handle this case yourself?"

"There's a few reasons. First, Georgina Delehanty spoke with Leon DaSilva about the alleged corruption quite some time ago. Leon advised her to wait until he retired, and the new Ranger took his place."

"The new Ranger being you."

"That's correct, Major. Me being transferred to Alpine was the worst kept secret in the Rangers, probably the entire Department of Public Safety. I haven't had a chance to ask him yet, since he took his wife on a trip to South Padre Island, but there must be a darn good reason Leon wanted me to handle the investigation. Second, Nolan Bradford came to me with his evidence. I'm not certain he'd be willing to do that with anyone else. Same with Delehanty."

"They could be subpoenaed," Castellon pointed out.

"They could be, Lieutenant, but that makes them hostile witnesses. A smart lawyer could turn that to his client's advantage. And Bradford risked his life coming to me. So did Delehanty, for that matter. Each gave me some pretty damning evidence. I don't want to betray their trust by handing it over to anyone else."

"Anything more?"

"Yes, and this is personal. I'm the brand-new Ranger in town. I can't be accused of favoritism, since I don't know anyone in Presidio County very well yet. I also need to prove that I can't be influenced, scared off, nor bought off by anyone, no matter how much power and influence they may or may not have. Lastly there may be a tie-in between the corruption probe and the gang investigation. That means both may well overlap, or turn into one case. At best, the corrupt politician and court official that are allegedly involved won't realize I'm looking into them. At worst, if any of them do, they'll get scared. And scared people make deals . . . or mistakes."

"Jim, if I can get Austin to agree, and you can get the Presidio County Attorney to go along, you'll have my permission," Trujillo said. "It's against my better judgement, but I'm gonna back you all the way on this."

"*Gracias*, Major. I'm obliged."

"Just don't make me regret my decision."

"I won't, Major. You have my word on that."

"I'll call you as soon as I get an answer from Austin. Don't contact the County Attorney before you hear from me."

"Of course not, Major. I wouldn't even think of it."

"Yeah, right."

This far west in the Central Time Zone in mid-summer, the sun set late. It was still above the western horizon. Jim had just crossed into Presidio County and was about fifty miles from home when he saw a dark gray Nissan Armada SUV bearing New Jersey plates parked on the shoulder of the road.

"What the heck?" he exclaimed, when he saw a family of five, including a toddler being carried by its father, standing in in the field alongside the road. They had evidently left their car, climbed through the barbed wire fence enclosing the field, and were taking pictures of a long-horned cow. The cow's calf was standing at its mother's side. The animal was pawing the dirt and snorting in anger. Jim pulled his Tahoe to a sliding stop and jumped out of the truck.

"Get out of that field, now!" Jim shouted, as he raced toward the family. "Don't run. Back away, slowly and steadily. But move!"

Jim didn't have sufficient time to grab his rifle, so he pulled his Ruger 1911 from its holster as he ran.

Here's hopin' this damn pistol has enough of a punch to stop that cow if she charges. I dang sure hope she doesn't. I'd rather not find out.

His worst fears were realized. Instead of moving, the family stood frozen in place, staring at the angry longhorn. Their making eye contact with the enraged mother cow was infuriating it all the more. Jim dove between two strands of barbed wire, rolled, and came up between the family and the cow. "Now run for it," he ordered. "Don't stop until you're on the other side of the fence. I'll try'n hold her off."

Coming out of their shock, the family broke and ran. Jim put two shots into the dirt in front of the longhorn's lowered muzzle. Pebbles and bits of gravel stung the animal's nose. It shook its head and bellowed. Jim took off his hat and waved it over his head, yelling and screaming at the cow while he ran straight at it. His ploy worked. The cow turned its attention from the family to the Ranger. With a loud bellow, it charged him.

Still whooping and waving his hat, Jim ran for the fence, running parallel to it for a few feet, then jumped through it. As he had hoped, the cow couldn't turn quickly enough to follow him. Had he run straight through the fence, the longhorn would have plowed through the barbed wire like a hot knife through soft butter. Instead, with a final snort, it slid to a stop, then turned to trot back to its calf. Jim breathed a sigh of relief.

Inexplicably, the longhorn, its attention apparently caught by an approaching car, whirled, lowered its head, and crashed through the fence. It slammed into the passenger's side of a bright yellow Volkswagen Beetle, tipping the lightweight vehicle onto its side. The impact had little to no effect on the longhorn. Having vented its anger, the cow shook its head and calmly walked back through the gap in the fence, to its waiting calf. It nuzzled the baby, which promptly started nursing.

Jim ran up to the Beetle. He called to the driver. "Are you hurt?"

"I . . . I don't think so," the young woman behind the wheel answered. "But I'm scared as hell. Get me out of here."

"Cover your eyes." Jim told her. Once she

did, he kicked out the Beetle's windshield.

"Hang on tight while I cut your seatbelt."

Jim took his knife from the sheath on his belt and slashed at the car's seatbelt until it gave way. He carefully pulled the young woman out of her toppled car, made certain she still had feeling in her extremities, and helped her to the side of the road.

"You wait here while I call for help. You need to be checked over for injuries. Will you be all right for a few minutes?"

The woman nodded.

"Thank you."

Jim speed dialed the Presidio County Sheriff's Department Dispatch.

"Presidio County Sheriff's Office Dispatch."

"Dispatch, this is Ranger Blawcyzk. I need a deputy on U.S. 90, about two miles south of the junction with Texas 505. Also need EMS for an auto accident victim. Extent of injuries unknown, but do not appear serious. Hook for one overturned vehicle. Also need owner or foreman of the Rocking Q8 Ranch notified they need to repair their fence at this location. Also will need to examine one of their longhorns for injuries."

"10-4, Ranger. I'll call you right back with ETAs."

"*Bueno*."

Jim walked over to the family, which was now

huddled alongside their SUV. His voice was tight, so as to keep from screaming in anger.

"What in the blue blazes do you think you were doin'? Are y'all plumb *loco*? Walking up to that mama cow was one of the stupidest things I've ever seen."

"We just wanted to get some good pictures of her and her baby," the father answered.

"You nearly got a lot more'n you bargained for," Jim shot back.

"Officer, our children pleaded to see the baby calf," the mother said. "It's so cute. And the mother seemed so friendly. She just kept chewing grass and not showing any sign of being dangerous."

Jim waved at the flipped over Volkswagen.

"She didn't look dangerous, huh? You see that car over there. That could've been you and your entire family. That cow's horns aren't just for show. If I hadn't come along when I did, she'd have put one of those horns right through you. Either that, or trampled you."

"We could have outrun her," the father objected.

"You really think so? Want to go back in there and try it?" Jim challenged.

The man shook his head.

"I guess not."

"What's your names?" Jim asked.

"I'm Barnabus McCutcheon. This is my wife,

Cynthia. We're sorry for causing any problems, Officer."

"Actually, it's Ranger. Texas Ranger James Blawcyzk. I'm not certain an apology will be adequate."

Jim's phone rang.

"Excuse me," he said, then answered it.

"Ranger Blawcyzk."

"Ranger, Presidio County Dispatch. A deputy will be on scene in about ten minutes. EMS is coming from Marfa, their ETA is twenty minutes. Maldonado's Towing has been notified. They advise ETA of approximately forty minutes. Rocking Q8 has someone en route, on horseback."

"Appreciate that, Dispatch."

"10-4, Ranger."

"Are you going to arrest us?" McCutcheon asked, when Jim hung up.

"Me? No. But there's a Presidio County deputy on the way. He may decide charges are warranted. Someone from the ranch that owns the cow and calf will also be here. It's likely they'll want to be reimbursed for the damages to their fence."

"The cow did that, not us," Mrs. McCutcheon protested.

"True, but if you hadn't provoked her, none of this would have happened," Jim answered. "You may also have to notify your insurance company. There's the matter of liability for the wrecked car, and any medical treatment its owner may need."

"You mean we might be responsible for that?" McCutcheon asked.

"It's possible, since your actions led to the accident. Consider yourselves dang lucky the cow doesn't appear to be hurt. If it had been killed, or injured so badly it had to be put down, you'd owe the rancher its value. Probably for the calf, too, since it's too young to survive without its mama."

"You're not going to put my mommy and daddy in jail, are you?" the oldest child, a girl of about nine, asked.

"No honey, that won't happen," Jim assured her. "The most that might will be your folks getting a ticket, just like for speeding. That's all. What's your name?"

"It's Holly. My little brother is Howard. And my little sister is Shawna."

"Well, don't you worry. Everything will be just fine. You wait here with your mom and dad until the deputy arrives. I'm going to stay with the lady from the car until then. All right?"

"Yes, Sir."

"Not sir. Jim. Or Ranger Jim. You stay with your folks. I have to get something from my truck, then stay with the lady until the ambulance arrives."

"I will."

"Thank you. That's a good girl."

Jim retrieved the items he wanted from his Tahoe, then returned to the Volkswagen's driver.

"Are you still feeling okay? No nausea or light-headedness? No sharp pains or shortness of breath?"

"No, just banged up. I'm certain I'll have some nice bruises shortly. I have to say, I never expected this. No one'll believe I was tipped over by a cow. Isn't it supposed to be the other way around? People tip over sleeping cows?"

Jim laughed.

"That's just another urban legend. Even if a person could sneak up on a sleeping cow, which is damn nigh impossible, there's no way it could be tipped over. I didn't get your name, Ma'am."

"It's Stacy. Stacy Lofton."

"I'm Ranger Blawcyzk. Here comes the deputy now."

A Presidio County Deputy's Ford Explorer pulled up. The deputy parked where his vehicle blocked the gap in the fence, then came over to Jim.

"Howdy, Ranger. Deputy Francisco Colon. What have you got here?"

"Jim Blawcyzk. Obliged to you for blocking that hole in the fence. I haven't had the chance. See that family over there? Eastern tourists. The damn fools decided to try'n get up close and personal with a mama cow. You know how well that worked out."

"I have an idea, but maybe you'd better give me the full picture, Ranger."

"Of course. I happened to come along in the nick of time. Spotted those folks in the field, taking pictures, completely oblivious to the signs mama cow was giving 'em she was mad as hell. I managed to get between her and them just in time. I distracted her until they were able to reach safety."

"Seems to me a bit more'n just that happened, Ranger. What about that car layin' on its side in the middle of the road?"

"Yup. Ms. Lofton here had the misfortune to drive past at exactly the wrong moment. The cow had started back to her calf, but it appears Ms. Lofton's car caught its attention. I reckon it was still angry, and decided to take its mad out on somethin'. Unfortunately, that somethin' was Ms. Lofton's car. The cow was fine after the collision, but I can't say the same for the car. That poor Beetle didn't stand a chance."

"I see. You're not injured, Ms. Lofton?" Colon asked.

"Just roughed up a bit."

"The EMTs are on the way from Marfa, just to check her over," Jim explained. "Jesse Maldonado's comin' to retrieve her car, and there's a hand from the Rocking Q8 ridin' over to make certain mama ain't hurt."

"I reckon I'll have a chat with those Eastern

folks first, then. Unless you have any objections, Ranger. And will you be all right until I'm done with them, Ms. Lofton?"

"None at all," Jim answered. "I'll write up my report for you while I'm waitin'."

"And I'll be just fine, Deputy," Lofton added.

Sixty minutes later, Deputy Colon had finished taking statements and concluded his investigation. Bart Quincy, the owner of the Rocking Q8, had come and gone, leaving instructions with the McCutcheons on how to have their insurance company contact him. Luckily, the cow and calf were fine, so the only damages were to the fence. Stacy Lofton had been checked by the Marfa EMTs, who cleaned and treated her only injuries, some minor scrapes. Her Beetle had been uprighted and towed away. It would be up to her insurance carrier to decide whether to simply pay her claim, or subrogate against the McCutcheons' insurer. She would ride with Jesse Maldonado to Alpine, where her boyfriend would meet her, and take her home to Fort Stockton.

Mr. and Mrs. McCutcheon were each issued summonses for trespassing, along with stern warnings about approaching livestock or wildlife. Possible charges of reckless endangerment were held in abeyance.

"You'll receive a notice of court date, with the option to plead guilty and pay the fine by mail," Colon advised them. "Just please, be more careful. The cows you see out here aren't those gentle moo cows you see on dairy farms back East. They've got real nasty tempers."

"So we found out. You can be certain we'll stay well clear of any animals that aren't in a zoo," McCutcheon told him. "Thank you, Deputy."

"Mr. and Mrs. McCutcheon, before you leave, I have something for you," Jim said.

He handed them four tickets, along with a sheet of paper.

"These are passes to the Texas Ranger Hall of Fame and Museum in Waco, with my compliments. I hope you'll swing by on your way back home."

"We certainly will, Ranger. Thank you," McCutcheon said.

"You're welcome. That paper is for the museum staff. When you arrive, give it to one of them. Tell them I've arranged to have your children enrolled as Junior Texas Rangers. I'll call ahead so they'll be expecting you. There'll be a real Texas Ranger like me there, to sign their certificates, give them their badges, and swear them in."

"You didn't have to do that, Ranger," Mrs. McCutcheon said. "Especially since you put your own life in danger to save ours."

"It's my pleasure. All of you will learn quite a bit about the Rangers while you're there. As far as distracting that cow, it was a piece of cake."

"I bet it will be as much fun as Wild West City back home," Howard exclaimed.

"Wild West City?" Jim asked.

"Yes. It's an old-fashioned Western theme park in Stanhope, not far from where we live in New Jersey," McCutcheon explained. "They've recreated an Old West town. They also have rides, animals, and do shootout re-enactments. It's been there since the late 1950s, and is still going strong."

"Well, I can't promise any gunfights at the Ranger Museum, but it's still a great place," Jim said. "*Vaya con Dios*. Have a safe trip home."

"We will. Thank you again. You also, Deputy. And we are truly sorry for the trouble we caused," Mrs. McCutcheon said.

"Ma'am, if your family was the worst trouble I had all day, I'd be mighty grateful," Colon answered. "I'm just glad no one got hurt. Even Ms. Lofton came out of the wreck pretty much unscathed. *Adios*."

Jim and Colon watched while the family got back into their car and drove off.

"Nice meeting you, Ranger, although I wish it had been under better circumstances," Colon said.

"Well, they could've been a lot worse," Jim answered.

"That's right. Where are you headed now?"

"Home. It's been a long day. I had to drive

from Alpine up to El Paso and back. Had a long meeting at Company Headquarters. I'll stop and grab a bite, then turn in. That piece of cake I mentioned sounds mighty good right about now. I haven't eaten since I left El Paso. Been getting by on cashews and Dr Pepper."

"*Amigo*, I've been there and done that, only I prefer pistachios," Colon replied, laughing. "I'll stick with you until we reach Marfa. Then I've got to head for Shafter to finish my patrol."

"That's a mighty lonesome road. Be careful, Deputy."

"Of course. *Hasta que nuestros caminos se vuelvan a cruzar*."

"*Si. Hasta entonces*."

When Jim arrived home, he bade good night to Copper and Sandman, then prepared to take a shower.

"Aw, the heck with another quick shower," he said. "I'm goin' up to the house and takin' a nice, long soak in the Jacuzzi."

He grabbed clean clothes, a towel, washcloth, and bottle of foaming lavender scented bath lotion. He walked over to the house, unlocked it, and headed straight for the master bathroom.

The big house seemed eerily quiet with no one else around, and little furniture. Jim started filling the tub with water as hot as he could stand. He dumped half the bottle of bath lotion into the swirling water. By the time he undressed and stepped into the tub, mounds of bubbles were already high above its rim. Jim sighed as he slid under the water, only his head and shoulders visible.

"I needed this," he murmured. "If Kim were here this would be absolutely perfect. Oh, well, only a few more weeks and the family will be together again."

He sank more deeply into the tub, allowing the jets of bubbles to relax his muscles, and soothe away the cares of the day.

13

It was close to ten o'clock the next morning when Jim walked into the DPS building in Alpine. Miriam Colter, the receptionist, greeted him warmly as she buzzed him in.

"Good morning, Ranger Blawcyzk. You're a mite later than usual. And if you'll pardon my saying so, you look a little angry this mornin'."

"Good mornin', Miriam. I'm not a little angry. I'm a lot angry. Not at you, though. I just got out of the damn DMV office. Almost two hours just to change the address on my driver's license and vehicle registrations."

"I can purely understand that. Dealing with those people is so frustrating. They're enough to try the patience of a saint."

"You've got that right," Jim answered. "Any messages?"

"Just one. Major Trujillo asked that you call him as soon as you arrived."

"That's the one I'm waiting for," Jim answered. "Either my day's about to get a whole lot better, or a whole lot worse."

"It's hard for a day to get worse after it starts out at the DMV," Miriam pointed out.

"True. Let's hope mine doesn't."

Jim went into his office, shut the door, hung up his hat, sat down at his desk, and dialed Company E Headquarters. He was put right through to Major Trujillo.

"Jim, I've been wondering when you'd return my call," Trujillo said. "I thought you'd be in a lot sooner than this."

"I would've been, but I had to go to the damn DMV to change my residence information," Jim said. "Took forever. Those people need some dynamite lit under their butts."

"Should've shown them your badge," Trujillo said, laughing.

"Unethical, but it was a temptation," Jim admitted. "Don't think it would've made any difference. I was on my way in, so I was already in full dress code. My badge was in plain sight."

"Well, at least you weren't tempted to pull your gun."

"I plead the Fifth on that one, Major."

"I think you'd better. Now, to the matter at hand. I had a long conversation with Austin about allowing you to investigate the alleged government corruption in Presidio County."

"And?"

"They agreed you should."

"That's great news. I appreciate you making the case for me. I'm obliged."

"Not quite so fast, Jim. There is one *caveat*."

"As the saying I learned in high school Latin class goes, *Caveat Emptor*. Buyer beware. So Major, what is it?"

"We discussed this at length. You are not to ask the Presidio County Attorney for permission to conduct this investigation."

"Are you or Austin going to handle that?"

"Neither. You were pretty clever, Jim. You didn't say anything when I mentioned seeking his permission. You know damn well he himself might be involved. So this investigation is to be conducted without his knowledge."

"Whoa, Major. And you were concerned about *me* bending the rules? You just twisted 'em into a goldang horseshoe."

"You don't need to remind me about what I already know, Ranger," Trujillo answered. "I shouldn't have to tell you the only regulations we're not observing are internal ones. Since this decision came right from the top, you won't have to worry about your investigation not being legal, or getting yourself in trouble for not informing the Presidio County Attorney. DPS and the Rangers will have your back. If you need warrants I can get those from a state's attorney for you."

"That'll be a change," Jim muttered.

"What did you just say, Ranger?"

"I said I'm out of change," Jim answered. "Need to get a Dr Pepper from the pop machine. Forgot to bring some with me."

"You stickin' to that?"

"Absolutely."

"What can you tell me about the County Attorney? How well do you know him?"

"Raymond Nelson? I've only met him once, when Leon was introducing me to all the county officials. But Officer Bradford tells me he's a straight shooter. Says Nelson's honest as the day is long."

"The days get pretty short come November. Bradford could be wrong. Or covering for Nelson."

"I know, Major, but I doubt it. Bradford came to me on his own volition. Makes it unlikely he's covering for Nelson, or anyone else. And I got a favorable impression of Nelson when I met him."

"And you've got a good instinct for reading people," Trujillo said. "What does Delehanty say about him?"

"I haven't had a chance to ask her yet. We've got to be real careful about communicating. Speaking to her again is on my list of things I've got to get done before I go back to Austin. I'm hoping this afternoon. The movers are scheduled, and I damn sure won't leave Kim alone with that task. I've already blocked off the time, and it's been approved."

"I'm aware of that," Trujillo said. "I'm already planning on having the Rangers from El Paso rotating coverage of your territory. Taking a break isn't a bad idea."

"I'm not certain dealing with moving is a break,

Major," Jim answered. "Plus it'll be a long trip there. Since I've got to drive my personal vehicle back, I'm taking AMTRAK to Austin. They take the long way around. It'll be an overnight trip."

"Maybe the people you suspect of trafficking drugs by train will be on yours."

"If they are, I hope none of them from the bicycle shop recognize me. I doubt they'll remember me from the hotel, but you can never be certain. I don't want to scare them off, not yet."

"Jim, unless there's anything else, I've got a meeting to get to. Keep in touch. I'll advise you of any new developments from our end. By the time you return, every agency on the task force will have their members in place. You be careful."

"Always am, Major."

"That's not what I've been told. Goodbye, Ranger."

"You too, Major."

Jim spent the rest of the day in his office, going through the evidence he'd gotten from Georgina Delehanty. He called her to arrange a meeting, and left a message when he received no answer. About seven o'clock, he decided to pack it in for the night. He stopped for a quick supper at Sazzon Baja Mex, then headed for home.

One thing Jim had learned out here in west

Texas was to leave his two-way radio on at all times. There was nowhere near the traffic and chatter that plagued transmissions back in his old territory. With law enforcement being stretched so thin, and distances so vast, leaving the radio on, in addition to his phone, could mean the difference between life and death.

Jim was almost to the turnoff for his ranch when his radio crackled to life.

"Brewster County Sheriff's Unit 29 to Dispatch."

"Brewster County Dispatch. Go ahead, 29."

"In pursuit of a camo painted Toyota Land Cruiser, eastbound on 67, approximately two miles before the Alpine roadside picnic area. Shots have been fired. Requesting all available units in area to assist."

Jim grabbed his mic.

"Brewster County Dispatch, Unit 29, this is Ranger 810. Westbound on 67, just before intersection for *Tres Alamos* Estates. Will attempt to intercept suspect vehicle."

"10-4, Ranger 810. Brewster 29, do you copy?"

"10-4, Dispatch."

It was only a matter of moments before the pursued vehicle came into sight, with the Brewster County deputy's SUV a short distance behind. Jim turned his Tahoe sideways, blocking the road. He grabbed his Bushmaster, jumped out, and laid his rifle on the Tahoe's hood, using the SUV as a shield. The Land Cruiser kept coming. Jim fired one shot, into the big Toyota's windshield. Its driver swerved off the road, tearing down a section of barbed wire fence. The Brewster County deputy continued after it. Jim got back in his truck and joined the chase. The Land Cruiser continued on, plowing through brush, jouncing across ditches and kicking up gravel. The Brewster County Deputy closed in on the Toyota. When he got within five feet, the Toyota's driver hit the brakes, then spun the wheels. A spray of rocks shattered the deputy's windshield. His SUV spun into a clump of ocotillo.

"Brewster 29, you okay?" Jim called into his mic.

"I am, Ranger. Go get that son of a bitch."

Jim pressed down hard on the Tahoe's accelerator. The big SUV lurched ahead, gaining quickly on the fleeing driver of the Toyota. The suspect swerved, zigzagging in a desperate attempt to shake off the pursuing Ranger.

"You ain't about to lose me that easy," Jim muttered. Not certain how soft the sand on either side of the rutted track was, he was unable to attempt a PIT maneuver, for fear of getting stuck or losing control. Instead, Jim waited until they approached a shallow dry wash. He eased up to the Land Cruiser, then rammed its back bumper. The impact caused the driver to lose control. He spun off the right side of the trail, his vehicle rolling onto its roof. Jim braked his truck to a sliding stop. He grabbed his rifle, jumped out of the Tahoe, and pointed the rifle at the overturned Toyota's driver's door window.

"Show me your hands! Empty! Now!"

There was no response.

"You in the truck. I want to see your hands, now. Lemme see 'em!"

The Brewster County deputy rolled up and stopped. Gene Molson got out, also carrying a rifle.

"You get any response from that bastard, Jim?"

"Not yet. Dunno if he's conscious or not."

"Let me try. Harlan Jefferson, stick your hands out of that window. You've got ten seconds, or I start shooting."

"What're you after this *hombre* for, Gene?"

"Domestic violence case."

"Harlan, you hear me? I've got a Ranger here backin' my play. You ready to die?"

Two hands, one bloodied, appeared from the overturned Land Cruiser.

"No. Don't shoot, Deputy. I'm givin' up."

"You crawl out of there, slow and easy," Molson ordered. "Make even the slightest suspicious wiggle and I'll put a bullet through your useless brain. You're a damned coward, beatin' on a woman who's half your size. Shooting you would rid the world of one more sorry loser."

"I'm done, Deputy. I swear I won't cause you no more trouble."

"I'll not be certain of that until I have you in cuffs, Harlan. You slide on outta there. Stay on your belly once you're out of your vehicle. Soon as you are, put your hands behind your head. Don't move until I get down to you."

"Once you've got him cuffed, I'll call it in, Gene," Jim said. "I'll keep you covered until then."

"I'm obliged. Better call for an ambulance, too."

"Of course. And a hook."

The chase and subsequent wreck had knocked all the fight out of Harlan Jefferson. He gave Molson no resistance when the deputy handcuffed him, pulled him to his feet, and walked him out of the wash.

"EMTs are on the way from Alpine," Jim told him. "Also Maldonado's Towing."

"You gonna let me sit in the back of your vehicle, Deputy?" Jefferson asked. "I'm feelin' mighty poorly."

"And get it all bloody? Not a chance. You'll live to see a judge," Molson answered. "You can sit on the ground right next to it. Rest your back against the wheel if you have to. But first I've got to give you the charges against you, and read you your rights. Harlan Jefferson, you're under arrest for violating a restraining order. Also first degree assault, possibly attempted murder. Also failing to obey a peace officer, and engaging a peace officer in a pursuit. Speeding, reckless driving, and failure to remain in the proper lane. If I could charge you with bein' a damn idiot, I'd add that too."

Molson concluded after reading Jefferson his Miranda rights.

"Now, we just wait for the EMTs," he said. "Did dispatch give you an ETA, Jim?"

"About half an hour. They had to roust out a pair. Seems quite a few weren't available. You probably could have taken your prisoner to the hospital yourself. Might've been faster."

"If he was hurt badly enough, I would have. But he's got just scrapes and bruises. No broken bones that I could find. The EMTs should be able to patch him up right here. Unless they say otherwise, once they're finished, I'll take him straight to the lockup. Jim, while we're waiting, I might as well get your statement."

Jim chuckled.

"What's so funny?"

"Gene, two things. First, for once I won't have to make out a full report. That'll fall on your shoulders, pardner. And you're welcome to it."

"Thanks a damn heap."

"Don't mention it."

"What's the second thing?"

"I won't have to listen to Jake Kearney at DPS

complaining about me scraping up the paint on my truck. He's the DPS head mechanic, and yelled at me every time I chased a bad guy through the *brasada.* I don't know who Company E will tell me to have repair the scratches and straighten out the push bar, but it won't be Jake."

"Good thing he doesn't work out here. In this territory, it's just about impossible to not mess up a paint job," Gene said. "Here's comes the ambulance. That means we shouldn't be here too much longer."

When Jim rolled up to his gate, there was an old, but well maintained, turquoise Studebaker pickup truck pulled to the side of the road. Two people were inside it. Once Jim got out of his truck to unlock the gate, the man in the Studebaker's driver's seat got out and came over to him. He was a Mexican of indeterminate age. If Jim had to guess, he would estimate the man to be in his late fifties to early sixties.

"*Hola, Senor. Indulto. Mi nombre es Miguel Ochoa. ¿Puedo hablar contigo uno momento*?"

"*Si. Habla usted Ingles*?"

"Yes, *Senor.*"

"*Bueno.* My Spanish isn't the best. I'm Jim Blawcyzk. It's lots easier to just call me Jim. What can I do for you?"

"You are the new owner of this ranch, no?"

"My wife and I are, yes. She will be here in a

few days, along with the rest of my family. I have a little boy, and an infant daughter. *Mi madre* will also be living here."

"Ah, you have a family. It is good for a man to have one. Forgive me for being so presumptuous, *Senor* Jim . . ."

"Whoa. Just plain Jim."

"*Si*. Jim. You see, until the last owners passed on, and the family sold the *Tres Alamos*, my wife and I lived here. Her name is Rosita. She is still in our truck. I was a caretaker, handyman, and gardener. Rosita was a housekeeper, and a cook when the family desired. We had a small cottage just beyond the old bunkhouse."

"I remember going through that cottage," Jim said. "It's still in good shape, but does need some updating and TLC."

"TLC, Jim?"

"Tender loving care. Fresh paint, floors resurfaced, things like that. The bathroom and kitchen particularly need attention. The fixtures and appliances have to be replaced. The furniture is also pretty old."

"That is why I am here, Jim. My wife and I would like to make the *Tres Alamos* our home again. We don't ask for much. Just our cottage to live in, and whatever you feel is fair in addition to allowing us to move back, and work here again. This is a beautiful place. It was our home for many years."

"Yes, it is," Jim agreed.

"However, it is much too large for a small family to care for properly. You will need help with repairs and maintaining the grounds. I can clean the stable and corrals, feed and water your animals, whatever they need. If you entertain, Rosita can organize the meals. She is an excellent cook."

"We don't do a lot of entertaining," Jim answered. "My work keeps me pretty busy. My wife also works, but mostly from home."

"I would imagine a Texas Ranger does keep busy," Miguel said. "Another reason you will find it necessary to have additional help. Rosita would also babysit, if you and your wife both need to be away. She loves children, and they love her."

"Miguel, I'm sorry, but you know I have to ask you this next question, especially since I'm in law enforcement. You and your wife are both citizens, or legal residents, of the United States, right?"

"*Si*. Both our families have been in Texas for at least six generations. We were both born and raised in Marfa."

"That's good to hear. Where are you living now?"

"In a small trailer a friend owns, and lets us rent very cheaply. It's in a run-down trailer park at the edge of Valentine."

Miguel shrugged.

"It's not a good place to live, but it's all we can afford."

"I see. Miguel, I'm usually a pretty good judge of character. As far as I'm concerned, you can move back to this ranch whenever you want. I can check references later."

"*Muchas gracias*, *Senor.* I am most grateful. Mary Dobson can vouch for us. Rosita will be so happy. And our little Chico will be able to have more space."

"Chico? Is that your son?"

Miguel shook his head.

"No, *Senor*. We only had one child, who died when still an infant. She is buried in the Holy Angels Cemetery in Alpine. Chico is our little dog."

"Jim, remember? I'm so sorry about your baby."

"She is an angel in Heaven. We will see her again, in *Dios*'s time."

"I'm certain you are right, Miguel. We have two dogs, so we'll need to introduce them to make certain they get along. And don't get your hopes *too* high. My wife makes all the important decisions for our family. I'm not worried she won't welcome you back to the ranch. However, as far as pay, or the amount of your rent, that will be up to Kim."

"What if she asks for more than we can pay?"

"She won't. And if she did, I'd change her mind."

"*Gracias*."

"No problem. When do you think you'll be moving in?"

"Would this weekend be too soon?"

"This weekend would be perfect. I have to go to Austin on Tuesday to help my family with the move. I'll be gone for three or four days. That will give me time to introduce you to my *caballos*. I have two here now, but there will be more coming with my family. Also some barn cats and chickens, and the dogs. With you being here while I'm in Austin, I won't have to ask someone to care for my *caballos* and keep an eye on the place."

"Let me give Rosita the good news. And introduce you to her."

"Of course."

They walked over to the Studebaker. A brown and white Chihuahua who had taken over the driver's seat began barking ferociously at Jim.

"Chico, be quiet!" Miguel ordered. The dog quit barking and wagged its tail.

"Rosita, this is *Senor* Jim Blawcyzk, the *Tres Alamos*'s new owner. *Senor*, may I present my wife, Rosita?"

Rosita was about the same age as her husband. She was pleasantly plump, still attractive, her hair still black as jet. She smiled broadly, revealing dazzling white teeth.

Jim touched two fingers to the brim of his Stetson in greeting.

"I'm pleased to meet you, *Senora* Ochoa. But just call me Jim, *por favor*."

"*Estoy muy contento de conocerlo*, *Senor*."

"Rosita, Jim says we can move back here as soon as we wish. We made arrangements for this weekend," Miguel told her.

"*Senor. Gracias. Muchas*, *muchas gracias*."

Rosita then broke into a torrent of Spanish, speaking so rapidly Jim could only catch some of the words.

"I take it she's happy, Miguel," Jim said.

"*Si*, very happy. We have both missed the ranch so much. We will be good tenants. And we are both very hard workers."

"I'm not worried about that," Jim answered. "By the way, I love your old truck."

"My grandfather bought her, brand new. She was passed down to my father, then to me. She has always been well cared for."

"I can see that. Miguel, Rosita, I don't mean to be rude, but I've still got some work to do, then I want to get some sleep. Would you like to come with me to look over your cottage before you go? Perhaps meet my *caballos*?"

Rosita shook her head.

"No, Jim. We also must be on our way."

Miguel said. "We will see you on Saturday. We don't have much to move, just some personal belongings."

"That'll be fine," Jim answered. "If for some reason I'm not here, I'll leave the gate closed, but unlocked. Same for the cottage. I'll have keys made for you soon as I can."

"That will be fine, Jim. Until Saturday, *adios*."

"*Adios*. That includes you, Chico," Jim said, when the little dog commenced barking again.

The Ochoas waved out the open windows of their truck as they drove off. Jim waved in return. He sighed as he got back into his Tahoe.

"First a horse, and now two people, and their dog," he muttered. "Kim's gonna think I'm picking up every stray in the county. But Miguel and Rosita seem like fine folks. I'm certain all of us will get along just great."

14

Sunday morning Jim had just returned from Mass, when he received a call from Marcus Barberry.

"Good morning, Ranger," the detective said. "Commander Sampano is on the line with me."

"Howdy, Detective. You too, Commander. I thought it was about time I should be hearing from you. What've you got?"

"There's another shipment coming into Alpine on next Tuesday's train."

"Dammit. That's only a couple of days away. I just knew that would happen. I'm taking that same train to Austin. My family's finally moving out here. I've taken the rest of next week off. I reckon I'll have to change my plans."

"Ranger, I said *next* Tuesday, not this coming one," Barberry answered. "That's more like a week and a half from now. Sorry if I wasn't clear."

"No, you were," Jim answered. "I guess I'm still only half-awake. The past several days have really been tough. Besides my usual case load, I'm dealing with this drug gangs' turf war, and another major investigation. Got about three hours sleep last night. Nearly fell asleep during Father Peralta's homily. Anyway, go ahead."

"I'm going to let Commander Sampano speak first, Ranger. Then I'll give you the details on the shipment."

"That's fine. Go ahead, Commander. Speak your piece."

"Ranger, as soon as we've finished this call, I'd like to arrange a conference call with all the involved agencies, including AMTRAK. Have you heard anything from Ranger McCoy?"

"He's putting together some leads. As far as finding Rafael Mendoza, no. He told me his contact said Mendoza had crossed back into Del Rio. But there's no confirmation of that. He could still be in Mexico."

"Let's hope he turns up. Marcus, go ahead."

"Ranger, the delivery will be made by a woman named Jewel Holland. Only her gang name is the *Marquesa de Sade*. She's a female enforcer who's probably more vicious than most male gang members. No one crosses her. If they do, they die. But very slowly. I'll send over her photograph."

"You're positive she's not aware you're a cop?"

"If she was certain, I'd be dead right now. So no. Not yet. But I believe she's getting suspicious. So are some of the others. That's one reason she's making the run, rather than one of the usual couriers. The Black Wolves are nervous about another open run-in with the *Diablos*.

They believe someone from that outfit, or the *La Muertes*, may have infiltrated the gang. Her bringing the drugs to Alpine is a message, not only to the other Black Wolves, but to the Del Rio and *Ciudad Acuna* gangs."

"You think suspicion's fallen on you."

"So it would seem."

"Commander, I don't want to step on anyone's toes, but perhaps it's time to pull Marcus out of the Black Wolves," Jim suggested.

"We've discussed that. I'm all in favor of it. But Marcus disagrees. He made a helluva strong case for leaving him right where he is. I went along with him, for now, since this is such an important operation. But I'm prepared to pull him out at a moment's notice, if it becomes necessary."

"Marcus, you'd better be damn careful," Jim said. "Otherwise, you might end up in a barrel, floating down the Rio Grande."

"I'll do my best. Unless the gang has more on me than it appears, I should be safe for now."

"Will you also have someone on the train?"

"That was the plan we agreed upon, so yes. Franz Hoklztgrein. He's just been promoted from patrol officer to detective, so he's mostly unknown to the street gangs, yet. He also looks about sixteen years old. Which means it's highly unlikely he'll be recognized by Holland."

"Don't let him forget he's just to observe what Holland does, and where she goes, after the exchange is made. I'll follow whoever meets her."

"He's clear on that," Barberry assured Jim.

"Ranger, I've got one thing to say before we start the conference call," Sampano broke in. "If the other Rangers involved, along with DEA, think we should make our move next week, I'm going to recommend it. I'd like to hear your thoughts first."

"I'm reluctant to say we should, at least quite yet," Jim answered. "I'd still like to have more evidence gathered before we move in. The bicycle shop has been under 24/7 observation since we first put the task force together. We've got enough evidence to shut them down right now. However, I'm not certain about Del Rio. What about up your way?"

"We've got sufficient evidence to bring charges," Sampano answered. "Of course, you always want more evidence. But that's not always possible, as you well know."

Jim sighed.

"I know. The bottom line is this. If Detective Barberry has been compromised, or even if the Black Wolves are merely suspicious of him, then we have to move quickly. Without him, the entire operation just might collapse. And I damn sure don't want to wait too long and get you killed, Detective. If you have been compromised, you won't be able to obtain any more information anyway."

"Don't rush things on my account," Barberry said. "I can handle myself. I've been working undercover for a helluva long time now."

"But we all know there's a point when an undercover operative has been too long underground. Their effectiveness is ruined, endangering not only their life, but the lives of others," Jim answered. "You might have reached that point, Detective. Commander, let's put that call together. I'd especially like to hear what DEA's latest information is. We have to be certain we'll get at least some cooperation from the Mexican authorities. Right now, I'm leaning toward agreeing with you, Commander. A week from Tuesday, once the exchange is made, we'll move in on all three gangs. It will be hard work getting everything coordinated in such a short length of time, but it can be done. It just might have to be, if we're to make this operation a success. I'd also rather settle for taking down the Black Wolves and *Diablos*, and let the *Muertes* for another time, if that's what we have to do. Better two out of three than coming up empty-handed, after everyone's hard work. The one thing I for damn certain don't want to happen is losing all three gangs. I'll stay in constant touch while I'm gone. Ranger Perez and Lieutenant Castellon will be covering for me while I'm away, so they'll have no problem acting in my stead until I return. And of course if the situation warrants I can get a DPS chopper, and be back as fast as I can push the pilot to fly."

"Ranger, you do realize we've all been dancing around the possibility that's on each of our minds," Sampano said.

"What's that?"

"That there's a damn traitor in our midst. Someone whom one of the gangs has turned."

"You're right, Commander. It might even be one of us on the phone right now. So let's make that call. Until we do, we're not certain of anything. And some of the others might have valid reasons we should hold off."

"It could take some time to reach everyone. Let's set it for thirteen hundred."

"Thirteen hundred it is."

15

Jim spent the rest of Sunday and all of Monday making phone calls, checking over evidence, and gathering everything together into a comprehensive report, which he would be able to use to obtain search warrants. Although he was exhausted, Monday night was his turn to watch the Big Bend Bicycling Adventures shop. He arrived just before ten, to relieve Nolan Bradford at the observation post Jim had set up in an empty storefront.

"Boy howdy, Jim, am I glad to see you," Bradford exclaimed, when Jim walked in.

"Why? Anythin' interesting happen?" Jim asked.

"Not a damn thing. Took a few pictures of people goin' in and out, but nothin' useful. Most rented bikes. Two bought helmets. That's why I'm glad to see you. I'm dog tired."

"Then go home and get some sleep. I'll take over. See you when I get back from Austin."

"All right, Jim. Have a good night."

"You too, Nolan."

Jim settled in for a long night. He was half-dozing when the sound of an approaching vehicle jerked him back to full wakefulness. The car, a dark burgundy Mercedes sedan, pulled up in front of the bicycle shop. Jim recognized both the car, and the person who emerged from it.

"Harold Boyle. The Marfa City Attorney," he whispered, as he snapped the first of several photos.

Boyle was in the shop for almost forty-five minutes. When he returned to his car, the red-head, Seamus O'Toole, was with him. O'Toole loaded several packages into Boyle's trunk. Once he was finished, O'Toole didn't go back inside. Instead, he locked up the shop, got into the company's Nissan van, and followed Boyle.

"Well, this could turn out to be an interesting night, after all," Jim muttered. He waited until the two vehicles were a good distance ahead, then got back into his Tahoe. Keeping his lights off, he trailed both vehicles until they stopped at an unmarked building, which appeared to be an abandoned warehouse, on Fremont Street, hard by the railroad tracks, between South Sligo and South Hartford. Jim pulled behind a building on Philadelphia Street. He watched and took photos as a number of people from the warehouse helped unload both vehicles. Jim recognized several of the individuals. Once the unloading was complete, both Boyle and O'Toole joined the others and went inside.

Jim waited a few minutes.

I know I'm takin' an awful chance, but I might not get this opportunity again.

He removed his white hat and shiny badge to be less conspicuous. Moving quickly, he walked up to the Mercedes and van.

I'm in luck.

A trace of the packages' contents, a white powder, had spilled onto the pavement. Jim scraped up as much as he could, then placed the substance into a baggie. He took close-ups of both vehicles' license plates, and specks of the same powder on the Mercedes trunk lid. He took samples of that, bagged them, and sealed them.

Time to get outta here, before someone decides to leave and spots me. I've stayed too long as it is.

Jim hurried back to his truck. He waited until he was back on U.S. 90 before he turned his headlights on.

I'll bet my hat I just picked up cocaine, mebbe heroin. The tests will tell me. And if it's either or both, I've just tied "The Club" to the drug traffickers I'm after. And that gives me the probable cause I need to request a search warrant for the premises.

He chuckled softly.

Even better, I can get some sleep tonight.

He whistled *The Cattle Call* as he headed for home. It had been a productive day. And in a few more, he'd no longer be sleeping alone. Kim would once again be at his side.

16

While on his way to the Alpine AMTRAK station, Jim made one last call to Major Trujillo.

"Howdy, Major. Is everyone all set to cover for me? I still have time to not get on that train."

"Jim, will you stop your damn worrying?" Trujillo answered, the aggravation in his voice apparent. "Lieutenant Castellon and Ranger Perez know every piece of information that you know. One of them will be stationed in Alpine until you return. They'll be fine. Hell, they've both been coverin' west Texas a lot longer'n you have. You want me to ship you back to your old company?"

"No sir, Major. Besides, they don't want me back. Although I do miss visiting with folks at the Ranger Museum."

"Then get off your damn phone, get on that damn train, and stop your damn frettin'. That's a damn order. You're to do nothing but relax and take it easy for the next few days. That's also a damn order."

"Can't hardly take it easy with a passel of movers underfoot," Jim answered.

"Then just do your best, Jim. I want you at the top of your game when we spring the traps next week. Finally having your family with you in

Alpine, rather'n back in Austin, will take a big load off your mind."

"You're right on that, Major. I just wish I could've gone to El Paso and caught a plane. But the flight schedules didn't work, plus I still would've had to get back from here to retrieve my vehicle. I still think mebbe you should have had DPS arrange for me to hitch a ride on one of their choppers. That would've given me a couple more days here. I just have an uneasy feelin' about dropping everything into the lieutenant's and Javier's laps."

"Jim . . ."

"All right, Major. I'll do what you say."

"You're certain?"

"It was an order, wasn't it?"

"You don't exactly have a perfect record of obeying orders, Ranger. Need I remind you?"

"This seems like a good time to hang up. Call me if you need me. Wait a second. I've got to turn around."

"What now?"

"I forgot to bring the big net I'll need to catch my train."

"Good*bye, Jim!*"

The Texas Eagle was running about an hour late. Since he was off duty, Jim wandered over to the Century Bar and Grill in the Holland Hotel. He intended to have just a couple of longneck Lone

Stars, but remembered he would be boarding the train too late for dinner in the dining car. He decided to order a chicken fried steak, mashed potatoes, and green beans to go with the beers.

Usually he would ask for a table in the back. This evening, however, he chose a window table, where he could watch the comings and goings of people on the street. He especially wanted to see if anyone who might be gang connected showed up at the station. He'd checked in with Marcus Barberry, who'd reassured him there had been no change in plans. The next drug shipment from El Paso via AMTRAK remained scheduled for Thursday of the following week. Still, gang members, especially those involved in drugs or human trafficking, were clever enough to keep making last minute adjustments to their plans. And if the Black Wolves were indeed suspicious of Barberry, they could very likely be feeding him false information. Jim wanted to be certain there was no exchange of cash and drugs with the Black Wolves' Alpine front members tonight. If there were, he'd have to miss his train.

It turned out Jim needn't have worried. The evening was quiet, highlighted by a spectacular, pastel hued sunset. Stars were pinpricking the indigo night sky when the Texas Eagle pulled into the Alpine station at 21:27, just shy of forty-five minutes late. Jim was the only passenger alighting or departing from the train. With the engineer and conductor trying to make up some of the lost time, the train didn't remain at the station for its full scheduled ten minutes, but rolled out as soon as Jim boarded. He only carried a duffle bag holding his spare clothes and toiletries, so he was soon settled in his roomette cabin. He sent Kim a message letting her know the train was running late, and he'd call in the morning with an updated arrival time. He checked his emails for any messages from Major Trujillo or Lieutenant Castellon. There were none. He started to finish up some reports. Forty-five minutes after departing Alpine, the train made a whistle stop in Sanderson. The next stop after that would be in Del Rio, nearly two and a half hours later. Jim realized he was bone tired, so he summoned the porter. Jim used the bathroom and washed up while the attendant converted the seats into a bunk, and made up the bed. Once the porter was finished, Jim closed and locked his compartment door, then pulled the curtains shut. Space was limited in the cramped cabin, making undressing a bit of a challenge. Jim took off his hat, bandanna, shirt, boots, and socks, but kept his jeans on, then took his Sturm, Ruger 1911 service pistol from his duffle bag. AMTRAK had been advised he was a law officer, and would be carrying his weapon on the train. He placed the gun within easy reach, and stretched out on the mattress, pulling just the sheet over him. He murmured his evening prayers, and settled in for the almost thirteen-hour journey. Lulled by the rocking of the train and the clickety-clack of its wheels on the rails, Jim drifted off into a deep sleep.

A shadowy figure worked his way through the sleeper cars, making certain no one else was about at this time, approximately one thirty in the morning. He stopped when he came to the compartment he wanted, the one where Jim Blawcyzk lay sleeping. He double checked the aisle to be sure no one was in sight, then jimmied open the compartment door. He waited to make certain Jim didn't stir. Once positive the Ranger was still sound asleep, he parted the curtains and slipped inside, sliding the door closed behind him. He removed a hunting knife from inside his shirt.

This was going to be easy. The worn-out Ranger was sleeping on his back, leaving his neck exposed. The killer could slit Jim's throat in one stroke. The move would be brutal. Quick, effective, lethal, and brutal. With his windpipe sliced wide open and blood spurting from his severed jugular, Jim wouldn't be able to cry out as he struggled futilely to pull breath into his lungs while he lay dying. His body probably wouldn't be discovered until later that morning, when the porter stopped by to see what time the now dead man would like breakfast. The killer prepared to strike.

A sudden hard rocking of the train when it hit a rough stretch of track saved Jim's life. The killer was thrown off balance. He gave a yelp of surprise as he threw out his arms to keep from smashing his face into the car's window. The yell awakened Jim. Still groggy, it took him a moment to realize someone was looming over him. In the dim illumination of the night light, he could see the glint of a knife in the person's hand. The killer swept the knife down toward Jim's chest. Jim knocked it aside before it plunged into his lung, the point of the blade leaving a shallow cut just under his left nipple. The knifeman recovered to take another swipe. Jim kneed him, the blow hitting the man hard, whether in the belly or the groin Jim wasn't certain. The man grunted and doubled over. Jim twisted and kicked him. The scream of agony that followed told him his foot had caught the man solidly in his balls. He jackknifed again. Jim kicked him in the face, flattening his nose, crushing his lips, and breaking his jaw. Several broken teeth fell out of his mouth.

Jim's assailant had neglected to lock the door behind him. It slid open when the train started climbing a slight grade. The impact of Jim's last kick threw the man out of his compartment and across the aisle. His head slammed into the window of the opposite cabin, shattering the glass. He slid to the floor. The cabin's two occupants woke up screaming.

Jim grabbed his gun, jumped out of bed, and pointed it at the would-be killer. The man was unconscious, apparently from the impact of hitting the window frame. Blood trickled from the corners of his mouth and a large gash on the back of his head. More flowed in a steady stream from his broken nose. Passengers awakened by the commotion peeked cautiously out of their cabins.

"Texas Ranger!" Jim said. "Signal for the porter. Use the emergency call. We'll need the conductor, too. Now!"

Several of the passengers complied. The porter hurried from his cabin, followed almost immediately by the conductor, who'd been doing paperwork in the adjoining dining car. He called over his radio to order the engineer to stop the train. He looked at Jim, the gun in his hand, the unconscious man slumped to the floor, and the knife he still grasped.

"What's just happened here?" he asked.

"I'm a Texas Ranger. James Blawcyzk."

Jim nodded at the man on the floor.

"This here *hombre* broke into my cabin and tried to kill me. His name's Rafael Mendoza, a suspect in several murders. We get to Del Rio yet?"

"We're about thirty minutes out. Lost more time waiting for a passing freight."

"There cell service along this stretch?"

"No. Not until we're closer to town."

"Is there an AMTRAK police officer in Del Rio?"

"Yeah, but he'll be off duty, sleeping."

"Get this train movin'. Radio ahead. Rouse your officer. Have him call Ranger McCoy, who's stationed in Del Rio, the Del Rio police, and Del Rio EMS. McCoy'll answer, despite the time. Have all of 'em meet this train. Make certain everyone knows they are *not to talk to the media.* The rest of you folks, get back in your rooms. Don't come out until y'all get the say-so. This here train car's now a crime scene. We can't have any possible evidence disturbed. Y'all have to be questioned once we reach town. Conductor, not one person leaves this entire train until me and my fellow Ranger, and your officer, have a chance to question each and every one. *Comprende*?"

"Understood."

"Good."

"What about that man?"

"You have an empty cabin you can put him in? Also, find out if there's a doctor or nurse on this train. I don't know how badly he's hurt. If you can't find one, I'll bandage him up as best I can."

"I can move the passengers out of the busted up

cabin to an empty one, and put him in there. Will that work?"

"It will. That way I can keep watch on him, in case he comes to. Get some protective gloves before we move him. I'll need something to tie him to the bed. Since I was involved in the incident, I can't investigate it. That will be left to your man and Ranger McCoy. You're gonna need a Hazmat crew to clean up the blood, too. Sorry, but it looks like your passengers are gonna be delayed a few hours. Not that it should surprise anybody, if they ride AMTRAK regularly. This car will have to be taken out of service. If the train's full, you'll have to find another one to take its place. I'll also need the seat or cabin assignment Mendoza had. Don't let anyone near them. I don't want any evidence damaged or destroyed."

"What about you, Ranger? Seems like you're hurt?"

"I just need some ointment and a bandage from your first aid kit. I'll be fine. Now, tell the engine crew to get goin', before someone gets curious and wanders back here. The rest of you, do what I said. Get back in your cabins, and lock the doors."

"Sure, Ranger. Folks, you heard what he said."

Once the conductor radioed the all clear, the train resumed its journey. The porter brought Jim the car's first aid kit, as well as nitrile gloves. The passengers from the damaged compartment were moved to an empty one, Mendoza was placed on the bottom bunk, his hands bound with his belt. Jim removed the supplies he needed from the first aid kit, bandaged Mendoza's broken nose and sliced open scalp. He then went back into his own room, leaving the door open so he could watch Mendoza. Not that he expected him to wake up. The man had taken a nasty crack to the back of his head. It would be a miracle if he didn't have a fractured skull, and a severe concussion. He might even have broken vertebrae in his neck.

Jim tended to his chest wound, then redressed. He pinned his badge to his shirt and buckled his gun belt around his waist. He sat on the edge of his bunk. There was just one thought on his mind.

How the hell did Rafael Mendoza know I was on this particular train?

"Ranger, we'll be pulling into the Del Rio station in a few minutes," the conductor advised Jim.

"Good. As soon as we stop, send Ranger McCoy, your officer, and one Del Rio officer to me. The EMTs also. No one is to enter the compartment he used. I've already gone through Mendoza's clothing, so he can be taken straight to the hospital. He's going to have to be guarded continuously until he's well enough to be transported to prison."

"What about the passengers?"

“No one gets off this train until they’re questioned. It shouldn’t take all that long. I’m certain few, if any, actually saw Mendoza.”

“None of my people did, except for the attendant in his car. He went into his cabin and stayed there, as far as anyone knows. He didn’t have supper in the dining car.”

“They’ll have to provide statements.”

“I understand that. Look, I have to get back to my post. I’ll make certain your instructions are carried out. Mendoza’s cabin has already been sealed off.”

“I’m obliged. See you at the station.”

When the train stopped, the only door which opened was the one at the front of Jim’s car. From his window, he could see a number of police officers on the platform, but no civilians. Not even any television or newspaper reporters. Apparently, Bill McCoy had issued orders for people waiting for the Texas Eagle to be kept inside the station’s waiting room. The conductor stepped from the train, spotted McCoy, and indicated the Ranger should come with him. McCoy, an AMTRAK Railroad Police Detective, and two EMTs followed the conductor to Jim’s car. McCoy ordered the others to wait outside until he had the chance to speak with Jim, alone.

“Jim,” Bill McCoy said, as they shook hands.

"I sure didn't expect to meet you like this. What the hell happened?"

"Well, I found Rafael Mendoza. Or I reckon I should say he found me. He's right in there."

Jim nodded at the compartment where he'd had Mendoza placed.

"Mendoza? Damn," McCoy said. "Is the bastard dead?"

"No, but not for lack of me tryin'," Jim answered. "The son of a bitch tried his damnedest to kill me."

"He followed you onto the train?"

"*Quien sabe*? He didn't get on in Alpine, and the only other stop between there and here is Sanderson. Since the train doesn't stop between El Paso and Alpine, he must've boarded there. He'd be taking an awful chance, goin' into Black Wolves territory, but that has to be what he did."

"So someone tipped him off."

"Either that, or he's been followin' me for a spell, but I doubt that. I can usually spot a tail. And you told me he dropped out of sight once he crossed from Mexico back into Texas. Listen, let's get the EMTs in here and send Mendoza on his way to the hospital. I took the liberty of going through his pockets, so he could be removed as soon as the train arrived. Got his stuff in a bag for you."

"All right. You mind if the railroad detective joins us?"

"Not one bit. I'd sure like to know if anyone from the railroad is involved with one of the gangs. If anyone can find out, it'll be an AMTRAK officer."

"Okay."

McCoy summoned the EMTs and AMTRAK detective into the car, along with one of the Del Rio police officers.

"Your transport is right in here," he said to the EMTs. "He's lost quite a bit of blood. Been unconscious for, about how long, Jim?"

"About forty minutes, more or less, I'd say," Jim answered.

"He needs to be taken to the nearest hospital. Officer Dugan," McCoy continued to the Del Rio policeman, "he's a known gang member, and a suspect in several murders. He's to be kept under guard twenty-four hours a day, until he's well enough to be transferred to a prison medical facility. Name's Rafael Mendoza. I'll get the rest of his info to your department later."

"Right, Ranger."

The EMTs went to work. McCoy waited to introduce Jim to the AMTRAK detective until after they, and the policeman, had taken Mendoza off the train and put him in an ambulance.

"Now we can talk," McCoy said. "Jim, this is Chelsea Greene. She's AMTRAK's senior detective for this region. Chelsea, Ranger Jim Blawcyzk."

"I'm pleased to meet you, Ranger."

Greene was Black, in her mid-thirties, of average height and weight. Her brown hair was cropped short under her uniform cap.

"Same here, Detective. Listen, I'm certain you're aware, if Bill hasn't already told you, I can't take part in the investigation of an attack on myself. I'll give a sworn statement, of course. However, off the record, someone must have put Mendoza onto my trail. Bill, have you . . . ?"

"Yes, I've provided Chelsea with the necessary information on the gang issue we're working on. We've worked together on several cases. You can trust her as much as you trust me."

"Hmm. I'd better think about that," Jim said.

"Don't mind him, Chelsea," McCoy said. "Jim's sense of humor is, well, unique."

"It's been called far worse than that, Bill. Seriously, Detective, I have no idea how Mendoza learned I'd be traveling on this train. I would hope there's no one from the railroad involved with him."

"But if there is, you want me to find that person. Which I will," Greene finished for him.

"I'd be obliged. Bill, the next step is up to you."

"Let me take your statement, Jim, before we start processing evidence," McCoy answered. "That way you can get some rest. You look like you need it. You also should have let the EMTs check you over. There's blood on your shirt, and it's not a splatter pattern, as it would be if it came from Mendoza."

"It's just a little cut. I've already patched it up. Some blood must have seeped through the bandage, but it's stopped. Mendoza tried to slash my throat. When I knocked his hand aside, the tip of his knife caught my chest. I didn't have a shirt on at the time. It's nothing to worry about. The knife's with the other stuff I got from him."

"Uh-huh." McCoy looked doubtful. "Well, let me take your statement. Then we can go from there. The conductor's already giving Chelsea a hard time about delaying the train. I don't want to hold it up any longer than necessary."

"Hey, delays are SOP for AMTRAK," Jim said. "No offense meant, Detective."

"None taken, Ranger. Everyone's aware of our late train problems. You won't mind if I also have a few questions for you?"

"Not at all," Jim answered.

"Then, Bill, let's get started," Greene said.

The Texas Eagle pulled out of Del Rio just before six a.m., nearly five hours late. Jim waited until seven to call his wife.

"Hello, Kim."

"Jim! Where are you? Are you getting close to Austin?"

"I'm afraid not, honey. The train lost more time overnight. There was a slight problem that held us up in Del Rio. It should reach Austin around two-thirty. I'm sorry, but there's not a thing I can do. I'm as frustrated as you must be."

"If you hadn't insisted on keeping your old truck, you wouldn't have had to take the train back home to get your good one. You could have just driven yourself. Now I'll have to pick you up right in the middle of the packers being here. They're due any time after eight."

"I know. Mebbe I should have junked the old pickup. But I just couldn't give up that truck. Not yet. And she'll make a good ranch truck. How's Ma and the kids doing?"

"Don't try and wiggle out of this, Jim. They're fine."

"I'm not. And just think. A few more days and we'll all be together again. On our own ranch, with room to spread out. No more traffic, no more polluted air and dirty water. Moving's hard, but it'll be worth it in the long run. You haven't changed your mind, have you?"

"No, of course not. It's just with so much going on, and you not here."

"I'll make it up to you, I promise. Why don't you send Ma to pick me up?"

"She's just as busy as I am. I'm counting on her to keep Josh from underfoot."

"I'll tell you what. Don't worry about picking me up. I'll order an Uber. Will that make things easier for you?"

"You wouldn't mind?"

"Not at all. Besides, the way this trip has gone, there might be more delays before we reach Austin."

"It would make things a lot easier."

"Then that's what I'll do."

"Josh is still sleeping. So's Katerina. Your mother's at her place, so I can't put any of them on the phone."

"That's all right. I'll see them soon as I get home. I'll call you when I get to Austin. Love you."

"I love you too, although why, I'll never know. Tell the Uber driver to step on it."

"I will. If I knew how to run a train, I'd commandeer this one. Bye, honey."

"Bye, cowboy."

17

When Jim arrived home, no one was in sight. Even the dogs weren't around. There were two box trucks from Berger, the local Allied Van Lines agent, at the house. One was a smaller sized packing van, the other a larger moving van.

Might as well see how things are comin' along.

Jim went inside to find several packers wrapping and boxing up items in the living room. A good number of boxes were already stacked, waiting to be moved.

"Howdy," Jim said. "Can any of you tell me where my wife's at?"

A woman looked up from the vase she was wrapping. She nodded toward the back of the house.

"She's in the kitchen. Least she was, last I knew."

"Appreciate it," Jim answered. He headed for the kitchen. Kim was indeed there, gathering items for Friday's trip to Alpine.

"Jim, there you are. Where in the world have you been?"

Jim kissed her.

"I'm sorry, Kim. The darn train took forever. I told you there was an issue outside Del Rio. I'll explain that to you later."

Kim didn't fail to notice the dried blood on Jim's shirt.

"What happened to you? No. Don't tell me. Let me guess. Whatever that incident was, you were somehow involved. I saw a brief story on the news, about a wanted man being captured on a train, but they didn't give many details."

"Yes."

One of the packers came into the kitchen.

"Mrs. Blawcyzk, we're going to start working in your boy's bedroom now. Have you gotten everything you need from it?"

"Let me make certain. Jim. You can explain later. As long as you're all right."

"I am. How can I help?"

"Josh is at your mother's. So are the dogs. If you could take them off her hands, that would be a great help."

"I can do that. Mebbe I'll take Josh to the Dairy Queen, then come back and we'll go for a swim."

"That's a wonderful idea."

"How many people are here from the movers? I'll bring back Blizzards for everyone. You and Ma too, of course. And Katerina."

"Katerina?" Kim echoed.

"Well, just a small cup of vanilla for her," Jim said. "Don't worry. I'm only joshing you. Katerina can't have ice cream for another couple of weeks."

"Jim . . ."

One of the packers broke in.

"There are six of us here all told, Mister Blawcyzk. I'm Maria Hernandez, the packing crew chief. There's four of us, and also two movers who have gotten started emptying out your mother's place. You needn't bring us anything."

"I needn't, but I will," Jim answered. "And I'm Jim."

"Then I say *gracias* in advance."

"Kim, is there anything else you need before I leave?"

"No. Just come home in one piece. That will be a change. We'll talk tonight, once everyone's left and the kids are sleeping."

Jim winced.

"Ouch. And *touche.*"

"Jim, I've got to go with Maria. Things are a bit hectic."

"So I see," Jim answered. He kissed Kim again.

"I love you, honey."

"Tell me that after we're settled in our new place," Kim answered.

Thursday, the movers emptied out the Blawcyzks' old house. They would deliver the furniture on Saturday. Jim and his family spent the night at their neighbors' house. The Howfields had leased Jim's family's place for guest houses.

Friday morning, Jim and his mother made a final visit to the family cemetery, at the back of their property. After that, Jim hitched his antique 1989 Texas Ranger Chevy station wagon to the back of his pickup. He then hitched the four-horse trailer to Kim's Suburban, and hefted all the horses' gear into the tack compartment, while Kim and his mother loaded the luggage into their cars. He then slid the chicken coop into the bed of his Silverado, making certain the doors were secured so none of the hens could escape, and be turned into chicken cacciatore when they landed in the road, to be run over by an eighteen-wheeler. Lastly, he put the three barn cats, Hilda, Matilda, and Gilda, into carriers. They would go with his mother to Alpine. Josh and Katerina would ride with Kim. The dogs, Frostie and Fritz, would travel with Jim.

"Unless there's anything else, I'm ready to load up the horses so we can be on our way," he said, once the coop was lashed in place. "Quiet, girls," he soothed the nervously clucking hens. "You'll be fine."

"We're ready," Kim said.

"All right."

Jim led Slacker, Freedom, Peach, and Halle into their trailer. Once the horses were loaded, he put the cats in the back of his mother's Equinox. He opened the back door of his pickup to let Frostie and Fritz jump in. Josh and Katerina were belted into the cars seats behind their mother.

"Kim, you're taking the lead," he said. "Ma,

you stay behind her. I'll follow you both. There's no hurry, so whenever you feel the need to stop, just let me know."

"Betty, mark this date down. You'll never hear Jim say that again. 'There's no hurry.' "

"That's for certain," Betty answered, laughing. "Let's hit the road."

The drive from San Leanna to Alpine would normally take about six and a half hours. With their young children requiring rest stops, and their animals needing to be checked and watered, it took the Blawcyzk family just under eight hours to complete the trip. When they pulled into their yard, the first thing they noticed was a large sign reading *BIENVENIDO FAMILIA* hanging over the front door.

"Jim, what's that all about?" Kim asked, as they got out of their vehicles. Frostie and Fritz hopped out of Jim's pickup. They both put their noses to the ground, sniffing the unfamiliar scents.

"I have no idea," Jim answered. "I didn't hang that sign."

Miguel and Rosita Ochoa came outside.

"*Senor* Jim and *Senora* Blawcyzk. Welcome home!"

"What the . . . ?" Kim exclaimed.

"That's one of the surprises I told you about. Kim, Ma, meet Miguel Ochoa and his wife, Rosita. They used to work at the *Tres Alamos*.

Lived right here on the ranch. Miguel asked if they could have their old home again, along with helping care for the place. I said yes, with your approval, of course. Miguel, Rosita, *amigos mio*, this is *mi esposa*, Kimberly Tavares Blawcyzk, *y mi madre*, Elizabeth. Our *nino y nina*, Josh and Katerina, are in Kim's car. *Uno momento* while I take them out."

"We are so happy to finally meet the rest of your family, Jim," Miguel said. "*Senoras*, Rosita and I have prepared a small welcoming *fiesta* for you. It is in the back yard. I hope we haven't been too forward."

"Not at all. And call me Kim, *por favor*."

"And I'm Betty."

"Your *nino y nina* are so precious," Rosita exclaimed.

"*Gracias*," Kim answered.

"Come, let's eat," Miguel said. "We can make conversation as we do."

"An excellent idea. I'm starved," Jim said. "Just let me get the cats out of my mother's car. And open the horse trailer doors. We'll put them in their stalls as soon as I get something to drink."

"Jim, from the little I know of you, you are always starved," Rosita said.

"She knows you already," Betty said.

After Jim took the cats, leaving them in their carriers on the shaded front veranda, everyone headed for the back yard. The Ochoas had laid out a spread of Mexican food, platters piled high.

"This is far too much!" Kim exclaimed. "But it all smells and looks *muy deliciosa.*"

"You must sample everything," Rosita insisted.

"Don't worry about that," Jim answered.

"*Cerveza* or pop, Jim?" Miguel asked.

"*Cerveza.*"

Miguel opened a cooler and removed two bottles of *Dos Equis*. He handed one to Jim.

"*Gracias*, Miguel."

Copper had heard Jim's voice, and caught his scent. He began whinnying. Sandman joined in.

"Jim, there seems to be an extra horse in the pasture," Kim said.

"Really?"

"Don't play innocent. The buckskin who keeps calling even more loudly than Copper."

"Oh, you mean Sandman. He kind of adopted me. I'll tell you the whole story after we get the rest of the horses in their stalls, fed and watered. It won't take all that long. Then we can resume the *fiesta*."

"Can I help you with that, Jim?" Miguel asked.

"No, but I do have a chore you can handle," Jim answered. "The keys are in my truck. If you would take the chicken coop to where we agreed it should go, and get it in place, that would be really helpful. Give the hens some water and feed. Once the animals are settled, then we can celebrate."

"Where are the barn cats going, Jim?" Betty asked.

"In the last stall on the left. They'll stay in there a few days, until they realize this is their new home."

"I can take the *gatos* there," Rosita said.

"No, you stay here with Kim and the children," Betty said. "I'll take care of the cats."

"*Si, Senora.*"

"Betty."

"Of course. Betty."

Jim and Kim were finally alone, getting ready for bed.

"Are you happy?" Jim asked.

"Very. But very tired," Kim answered.

"Well, it's been a hectic few days," Jim answered. "What with the long drive, movers delivering everything yesterday, getting the house at least partially set up. I think everyone's tired. Even Josh. And I have to get back to work in the morning."

"Thank goodness we have Miguel and Rosita to help us," Kim said. "They're real gems. And the food they had for us! If that was a small spread, I'd hate to see a large one."

"I'm glad you like them. I took a chance you'd want them to stay on."

"Well, they certainly didn't ask for much. I had to insist they accept what I offered."

"I'm sorry about springing all this on you, especially about the *hombre* who tried to ambush me on the train."

"Jim, much as I hate to admit it, I've kind of gotten used to things like that. Yes, they still frighten me, but I can't live my entire life in fear. I knew what I was getting into, marrying a Ranger."

"I love you, Kim."

Jim kissed her on the cheek.

"Not so fast, cowboy. There is one thing."

"There is? What?"

"That horse, Sandman. Does he ever shut up?"

"Very seldom. He *is* a talker."

"No kidding. Almost as much a one as you."

"Possibly. But right now I have an idea that won't require any words, at all."

"And just what might that be?"

"It's time to try out that big tub. We both could use a nice, hot soak. Plus there's a full moon, shining through the skylight."

"Are you certain a soak is all you want?"

"We'll see," Jim answered.

A mischievous grin spread across his face.

"Then lead the way, cowboy."

18

Jim had just hung up with Lieutenant Castellon when his phone rang.

"Texas Rangers Alpine. Ranger Blawcyzk."

"Ranger, this is George Delehanty."

"George! I was worried about you. Thought perhaps you'd left town. Or worse."

"No, I'm fine. Just keepin' a low profile. But I have heard some rumors around town."

"Such as?"

"Word is some of the people behind 'The Club' are getting nervous. They've caught wind of something. The next city council meeting, the chief's gonna ask for Nolan Bradford to be fired. Of course, the council will vote to let Bradford go. The chief has something on just about every one of 'em. Your making Bradford look like a fool over the ticket he gave you is the excuse they needed."

"We can't let that happen. I can't say more than that. When's the meeting?"

"Friday night. Seven o'clock."

"That gives me time. Thanks for giving me the heads up, George."

"No problem. Nolan's a decent guy. I'd hate to see anything happen to him. And I wouldn't be surprised if firing him is just the first part of their plan."

"You mean they intend to kill him?"

"I mean he knows too much for his own good."

"Nothing will happen to him. I promise you that. Lemme get to work on this. And you be careful. You're a brave woman, Georgina. Braver than most men. But I'd bet my hat these *hombres* also have a target on your back. Let me know if you hear anything else."

"Will do."

After Delehanty hung up, Jim dialed Nolan Bradford's personal number.

"C'mon, Nolan, pick up the damn phone," Jim urged, when it rang several times. "I don't want to leave a message."

Bradford answered just before his phone went to voice mail.

"Howdy, Jim. What's up?"

"I just got a call, Nolan. You heard anything about the chief wanting to fire you?"

"Only this morning. He intends to bring it up before the city council this Friday. But I'll have thirty days to contest the move."

"I'm not worried about thirty days. As long as we make it to Thursday. I'm told some of the people we're after are suspicious that you're gonna turn on 'em. And that getting fired might be the least of your worries."

"That makes sense. Chief Asher's been unhappy about me workin' with you. Of course, he thinks I'm just helping stake out the bike shop. I think he and his pals are worried we might be doin' a little more diggin' than that. They'd be right, of course, at least you are, based on the evidence me'n Georgina gave you. Mebbe you should pull me off the task force."

"It'd be the smart thing to do, all right," Jim agreed. "But it's too late. Takin' you off now would look mighty funny. At least we've suspended our surveillance of the shop for now. You just go right about your normal routine, best you can. But watch yourself."

"Part of the job. Talk to you later, Jim."

"Later."

Jim leaned back in his chair and sighed. He got up and poured himself another cup of coffee.

"I reckon I've got to let Major Trujillo know we have a problem. We'll have to decide how to handle it. One thing's for certain. We're too close to putting a stop to the drug trafficking and killings that have been plaguin' this territory. We can't let anything happen to ruin our operation now."

19

Thursday night was the most nerve-wracking of any Jim had spent in his law enforcement career, except for the day of his father's death. Everyone was in place at Alpine, Del Rio, *Ciudad Acuna*, and El Paso. AMTRAK's Detective Greene, along with Andrew Moyers, a member of the State Highway Patrol's Drug Interdiction Task Force, were riding the Texas Eagle, along with Ranger Javier Perez. Jim's assembled members of the Alpine/Marfa segment of the task force were ready. Nolan Bradford, Marfa Police Chief Barry Asher, and Presidio County Sheriff Jacob Marlin, along with several of his deputies, were waiting to move in at the bicycle shop, once the couriers arrived with the drugs. Jim and Perez would follow the couriers from the train station. Greene and Moyers would take whoever brought the drugs from El Paso into custody. Lieutenant Castellon, Commander Sampano, and DEA's Captain Quinones had their El Paso team assembled and ready to move. So did Texas Ranger Lieutenant Gabriel Montez and Bill McCoy down in Del Rio. The *Ciudad Acuna* police were prepared on their side of the border. If all went according to plan, a major drug ring would be broken up this night, and a large dent put in the criminal activities of three border gangs.

However, as Jim well knew, the unexpected always happened with an operation this large. The biggest question was if there'd been a member of the task force who'd turned informer for the gangs. That was an especial concern with the Mexican authorities. The drug cartels south of the Rio often had more power than the police. Also, exactly what did the Marfa police chief have on Nolan Bradford? With an operation of this magnitude, there was no way to leave the local law out of the mix. Major Trujillo had agreed with Jim they needed to keep Bradford as part of the team. And Asher had to take part in the raid.

Then there was the biggest question mark of all. What time would the Texas Eagle actually arrive in Alpine? Between having to deal with poorly maintained rails, and waiting for slower freight trains to clear the main line, AMTRAK, often through circumstances beyond its control, quite often ran late. Sometimes very late.

Jim was parked at the Alpine railroad station, in his faded old Silverado. No one would ever suspect that beat-up pickup was a police vehicle. He had a portable Brewster County Sheriff's Department two-way radio with him, along with his phone. The radio was set to both the Brewster and Presidio County Sheriff's Department bands.

The truck's air conditioning had long since died. Even with both side windows, and the rear sliding window, open, there wasn't a breeze stirring. Jim was sweating profusely under the bulletproof vest he wore over his shirt. His clothes were drenched with perspiration. He took the bandanna from around his neck to wipe his brow, then checked his watch. It was a little past seven thirty. He couldn't notify the other teams to move in until he was certain the drugs were on their way from the station to the bike shop, and the couriers from El Paso in custody. He had to fight the temptation to call Perez or Greene. He started a bit when his phone dinged. It was a text message from Greene.

Train running about twenty minutes late. Will message again when we reach Marfa.

Jim breathed a sigh of relief. He messaged the other teams with an updated ETA.

Just before eight o'clock, the bicycle company's van pulled into the railroad station's parking lot. Not having to worry about watching the actual delivery and exchange take place, Jim was also in the lot, at the far end. It was doubtful he'd be recognized, but he wasn't taking any chances. He slid down in his seat, and pulled his hat low over his eyes. To anyone passing by, he would appear to be just another rancher or cowhand, sleeping in his truck, probably waiting for someone arriving on the train.

It seemed an eternity until Greene messaged Jim that the Texas Eagle was rolling through Marfa. It seemed even longer until he heard the train's whistle as it approached the Alpine station. Greene messaged him everyone was in position.

"Time to roll," Jim muttered. He watched Raymundo Carillo get out of the red van and walk into the station.

"Now I know who's gonna meet the person from El Paso," Jim said. "Just a few more minutes."

The train pulled to a stop. Jim kept close watch on the station's doors. In about five minutes, Carillo reappeared. He carried two large suitcases. Jim waited for Carillo to get in his truck and drive away. As soon as it pulled out, Javier Perez came from the station. Like Jim, he was dressed in a range hand's clothes. He carried a battered duffle bag, and a soft-sided rifle case.

Jim sat up.

"Howdy, Javier," he said, when his fellow Ranger got to the truck. "Slide on in. We don't want to lose our *amigo*. Not that I'm worried about it. I know where he's headed."

"Howdy yourself, Jim."

Javier tossed his duffle and rifle onto the Silverado's bench seat, then slid in alongside them.

"Damn, Jim. You told me to look for an old pickup, but I didn't expect a total wreck. You mean to tell me this truck's gonna make it all the way to Marfa?"

"She's never let me down yet," Jim answered. He turned the key and the truck's engine fired to life. The clutch screamed for mercy as Jim pushed it in, and the transmission sounded like a coffee grinder on steroids when he put the truck into first gear.

"This junk ain't even gonna make it outta the parking lot," Perez said.

"She'll make it all the way to El Paso if I ask her to," Jim retorted. "Was Holland picked up?"

"I can't say for certain. But Moyers won't let her get away. Neither will Greene, from what I've seen of her. One of 'em'll message me once they have her in custody."

"*Bueno.* Do me a favor. Message the other teams and let them know it's time to move in. I can't text and drive. That's against the law, you know."

"Yeah, right. As if either one of us cares," Perez shot back. Nonetheless, he started sending messages, while Jim hit the speed dial on his phone.

"Sheriff Marlin. What've you got, Ranger?"

"Our pigeon is on his way to the home roost. It's Carillo. I'm gonna stay about a quarter mile behind him. Don't want to take a chance on spookin' that *hombre.* Don't forget, you don't move in until I arrive on scene."

"Correct. Has Moore been picked up?"

"It wasn't Moore. Still waiting to hear if the woman was."

"A woman?"

"Yup. One you don't want to tangle with, from what I've been told. See you in a bit."

"Damn straight you don't want to mess with that Holland woman," Javier said, when Jim hung up. "She's a real mean lookin' mother. Wouldn't surprise me if she carries more handcuffs than we do. Also whips and riding crops. She had a leather collar around her neck which was heavier, and with more studs, than you'd see on a pit bull."

"We might need some extra cuffs before this night is through," Jim said, laughing.

"Hold on," Javier said. "Just got a message."

"What's it say?"

"Gimme a minute. It's from Moyers. They've got Holland and two others in custody. Taking them to the Brewster County lockup for processing."

"Three down, and who knows how many more to go. Our boy's movin' right along. We'll reach Marfa in just a few minutes. You might want to slip into your vest."

"Good idea."

• • •

Jim drove past the bicycle shop, went around the block, and turned off his lights. He put the Chevy in neutral, shut it off, and let it coast to a stop. He and Javier had a clear view of the shop's rear doors.

"Wait until they start unloadin' the van," he told Marlin, over the phone. "I'll give the word."

"You ready, pardner?" he asked Javier.

"Locked and loaded."

"Then it's time. They've started unloading. Sheriff, move in. Now!"

Jim started his pickup, turned on the lights, and sent it screaming into the bike shop's lot. At the same time, several Presidio County Sheriff's units, and Marfa's two patrol cars, roared out from their hiding place behind the Dairy Queen.

Jim skidded to a stop right behind the suspects' van, while the local and county officers surrounded the building. Rifles in hand, he and Javier jumped out of Jim's pickup.

"Texas Rangers! On the ground, now! Do it!"

"You're surrounded," Javier added. "Don't try anythin' stupid."

Caught in the glare of Jim's high beams, the four suspects stood frozen like deer in the headlights. By now, Sheriff Marlin, three of his deputies, and both Marfa officers were out of their vehicles.

"I said down, or we start shootin'," Jim ordered.

“Don’t, don’t shoot,” Seamus O’Toole pleaded. He flopped to his belly on the hard packed dirt lot. His partners followed suit.

“Hands behind your heads,” Jim ordered. The prisoners complied.

“Javier, you and the sheriff go ahead and cuff this bunch, while I read ’em the charges, and their rights.”

“With pleasure.”

Jim slapped several papers onto the back bumper of the suspects’ van.

“Those are duly authorized search and seizure warrants, allowing us to search and seize these premises, this van, and their contents. There are also arrest warrants for each of you. Seamus O’Toole, Raymundo Carillo. Juanita Ortiz, and Julie Ann Huntress. You are all under arrest. The charges are possession of drugs with intent to sell, illegal transportation of drugs with intent to sell, including across an international border, sale and distribution of illegal drugs, and racketeering. More charges may follow. You have the right to remain silent . . .”

Once Jim finished reading the prisoners their rights, they were placed into two deputy’s vehicles, to be transported to the Presidio County Jail.

“Let’s tear this place apart,” Jim said. “Not literally, but y’all know what I mean. Chief, I’ll want you with us inside. Sheriff, you and two of your deputies. The others, stay out here and keep everyone away."

The search proved fruitful. In addition to the drugs Carillo had picked up, there was a large quantity stored in a back room of the bicycle shop. A substantial amount of cash was found in an unlocked safe.

"Rather careless of them, wouldn't you say, Javier?"

"Jim, that's a helluva lot of *dinero.* I'd say more like damn foolish."

"Can't argue with you. Do you mind finishin' up here? It's high time I got the second part of this *fandango* goin'."

"Not one bit. Things are pretty much under control. I know what's left to be done."

"*Bueno.* I'll meet you back at the county courthouse."

"See you there."

Jim went outside. He signaled to Nolan Bradford and two of the sheriff's deputies.

"I've got to make a couple of phone calls. Soon as those're done, I need you three to come with me. We've got another stop to make. I've already cleared this with the sheriff and police chief. Officer Bradford, you know where we're headed. You and one deputy'll come in from South Hartford. Me'n the other'll come in from South Sligo. Soon as we get there, I'll bust down the front door. You do the same with the back. The deputies'll follow us in."

"You mind if I take Deputy Torres?"

"Not at all."

"I guess that means I'm goin' with you, Ranger. Deputy Samuel Forester."

"Jim Blawcyzk. Glad to meet you. Same situation as here. We go in fast and hard."

"All right."

First, Jim called Lieutenant Castellon in El Paso.

"Lieutenant, it's Jim Blawcyzk. How did things go?"

"A little better than we dared hope. The gang put up a fight, of course. Three of 'em are dead, several more shot. Don't know their conditions. We did have two personnel injured. One of the DEA agents was shot in the chest, but she'll be okay. Just got a bad bruise from the slug striking her bulletproof vest. Marcus Barberry's in worse shape. One of the Black Wolves recognized him and shot him in the back of the neck. Dunno if Barberry's gonna be paralyzed or not, that's if he lives. But the son of a bitch who shot him won't be doin' any more shooting, except in Hell. How about at your location?"

"Not a shot fired. Moyers and Greene took the courier from the train into custody, and the others gave up without a fight. I'm gonna call Lieutenant Montez, to see what the situation is in Del Rio, then move to the next part of this operation. Keep me posted."

"Will do."

Jim next called Del Rio.

"Lieutenant Montez. Jim, I've been expecting your call. What's the status?"

"We mopped up here with no real problems whatsoever. I just spoke with Lieutenant Castellon. The Black Wolves wouldn't give up without a fight. Three of them were killed, a number shot. Two of our people were wounded. Marcus Barberry from the El Paso Police, and a DEA agent. The agent's wound isn't serious, but Barberry's might leave him paralyzed, if he pulls through. How about at your end?"

"We weren't quite so lucky. Two Del Rio officers were killed. We also lost three Val Verde County deputies. Bunch of others shot up. But the gang got it worse. There's at last ten of the bastards who got themselves blasted straight to Hell."

"I'm sorry, Lieutenant."

"It's been rough. But it was even worse on the Mexican side. Six *Ciudad Acuna* police officers and two *Federales* killed. A dozen or so *Mano de la Muertes* bit the dust. Plenty more shot up bad. However, there is some real good news. The Mexican authorities caught the leader of the *Gatos del Diablo* cartel, and his chief lieutenant, at the *La Muertes* headquarters. The damn sons of bitches are both on their way to the morgue. What's left of them. Despite our losses, the raid was a success. The *La Muertes* have been pretty much dismantled, and the *Gatos* will start a power struggle over who'll take over the outfit, so that'll keep 'em busy. Maybe even lead to the cartel falling apart. Not that another won't take its place."

"Good versus evil. The eternal struggle," Jim said. "Keep me updated. I'm headed to the second part of the operation here in Marfa. Also, call Major Trujillo. I know he's waiting to hear from one of us."

"I will. And you be careful."

It was only a few blocks from the bicycle shop to "The Club." As expected, the door was locked when the lawmen arrived. Jim spotted Harold Boyle's Mercedes in the lot.

"That'll save me one stop, anyway. Here goes."

He smashed his pickup through the building's wooden double doors, and came out of the truck with his Remington shotgun in hand.

"Texas Rangers! Nobody move. This place is officially shut down."

"Don't anybody think of sneakin' out the back way, neither," Bradford added. The front end of his Explorer was halfway into the building. He stood in front of it, also holding a riot gun.

"What's the meaning of this?" Boyle shouted. "Who authorized this, this travesty?"

Jim couldn't help himself. He grinned.

"State's attorney. I've got a search and seizure warrant, allowing me to search this place, and seize any unlawful gambling equipment, drugs, and liquor. We have solid evidence of after hours serving of alcoholic beverages, illicit drug use, prostitution, and possibly other illegal activities. I've got a warrant for your arrest, Mister Boyle. I have one for you also, Mayor. Your police chief is being taken into custody as we speak. In addition to the charges based on your activities here, you two are also being charged with falsifying official records, fraud, embezzlement, and I've also got warrants for several others, as well as sufficient John Doe and Jane Doe warrants. Some of the rest of you folks may be released tonight, on your own recognizance. Some may not face any charges. The others will have to make bail. Now pay attention. I'm about to read y'all your rights."

"But, I'm merely an entertainer," one woman, blonde and tall, dressed in a form fitting, low cut, ankle length gold lame and sequined gown, wearing stiletto platform sandals, protested. "I was only hired for tonight."

"What's your name, Ma'am?"

"It's Peachy. Peachy Keene. But that's not my real name. It's Gerard Custer."

"Drag queen?"

"How could you tell, Ranger?"

Jim had to laugh.

"It wasn't easy. You play the part well. If your story checks out, you'll be on your way in a few hours, at most. I'm sorry to inconvenience you."

"*Danke schoen.* It's no inconvenience at all," Keene purred. "I just *adore* men in uniform."

"Rangers don't wear uniforms. And I'm sure not dressed for duty as I normally am."

"No, but those three men with you do. Quite well, I might add."

Keene smiled at the other three officers, then blew each a kiss.

"*Enchante.* It's a pleasure to meet y'all."

After the suspects from "The Club" were taken to jail, Jim and the two deputies spread out through Marfa, serving more arrest warrants. Judge Cummings protested loudly when Jim took her into custody.

"This is just a vendetta on your part, Ranger. You're getting even because of the traffic ticket you were issued. Need I remind you I dismissed the case? I also reprimanded both the officer and prosecutor."

"Not hardly. This is strictly about preying on innocent people visiting Marfa, so certain individuals could take kickbacks and funds from false traffic summonses. You'll have your day in court. Only on the other side of the bench."

By the time all the arrestees were processed, it was nearly four in the morning. Jim went straight to his ranch. Finishing up with the prisoners from the train could wait until later. Right now, he badly needed sleep. When Jim got home, he didn't want to disturb his family, so he went to his barn apartment and stumbled into bed. His phone rang just as he collapsed onto his mattress.

"Ranger Blawcyzk."

"Ranger, this is Detective Greene. Please forgive me for calling so late. It's the first chance I had."

"I just got home, so I was still awake."

"Yes, it's been a long night for all of us. I just wanted to let you know about the person who told Rafael Mendoza which train you'd be on. It was our station agent in Alpine, Cletus McGraw. He was in the pay of the Black Wolves, to look the other way when they delivered drugs. Since he saw all the passenger manifests, he knew which train you'd be on, and even your car and room number. Now he's behind bars. So are Holland and another gang member who accompanied her, Pozenda Simmons."

"Glad to hear it," Jim said.

"I'm glad you were able to let AMTRAK take part. I'm most appreciative."

"That means the hell with the other stuff. Tell your deputy I'm on my way. Where should I meet him?"

"At the east entrance to the park. Even though the murders took place in my county, they were much closer to Brewster County. So my deputy went there. I've already notified Sheriff Zuniga, just to maintain protocol. You know where that is?"

"Yup. Sure do."

"Good. My deputy says you'll need a horse. That park's real isolated, and the terrain in many places can't even be handled by an ATV. He'll have one ready for you."

"I'll bring mine. I've got to pick up some supplies, too. Tell your deputy I'll see him in about two hours. Also, I'm gonna call Ranger Perez. He stayed in Marfa overnight. I'll have him cover for me in court today. Can you go with him? Looks like our job ain't quite finished."

"Yes, and it seems as if," Marlin said. "Good luck, Jim."

"I may need it."

Jim hurriedly changed into fresh clothes, jeans, a long-sleeved denim shirt, with a teal silk wild rag tied around his neck, not bothering to shower or shave. He slipped into a brown roughout leather vest, and pinned his badge to that. He got spare underwear and socks, went into the barn and stuffed them into his saddlebags. The horses whinnied at him, and stamped their feet.

"It's not feedin' time yet," Jim scolded. "Except for you, Copper. You're gonna be eatin' breakfast on the road."

He went outside, hitched up his horse trailer, and backed it nearer the barn.

"Here comes the worst part. Tellin' Kim."

He went inside the house. Kim was just waking up.

"Jim. Good morning. I'd hoped you'd sleep in. I heard you come home this morning."

He kissed her before answering.

"I'd planned to, but I've got another murder to investigate. This one's way down in Big Bend Ranch State Park. I've gotta run. Don't know how long I'll be gone, but I'd count on a few days."

"But you've been going practically non-stop for days."

"I know. However, this murder has four victims. And it may be tied into the case I've been working on. So I don't have a choice. I'd hoped that was over yesterday, but it doesn't look that way."

He kissed her again.

"Love you. Gotta run."

"You be careful. And call me."

"I'll do my best. I'm probably gonna be in the back country, where there's no cell service, so don't worry if you don't hear from me for a few days. But I'll call when I reach Terlingua."

He grabbed a case of Dr Peppers from the refrigerator, along with two cans of cashews from a cabinet. None of the Alpine stores would open for at least another half hour. With no stores, except a small country store that kept irregular hours, between Alpine and Terlingua, in fact the entire length of Texas 118 being virtually unpopulated, those nuts and pops would have to be his breakfast, until he could purchase supplies in Terlingua or Lajitas. Once he stopped to fill his gas tank, he'd drive straight through.

Jim hurriedly put his horse's gear and feed in the trailer, along with four covered five-gallon buckets of water. He hung a full hay bag for Copper, then loaded the paint. He gave him a carrot.

"Sorry, but you'll have to wait until we reach the park before you can have your grain. You've got enough hay to munch on until then."

He patted Copper's nose, closed the escape door, and fired up the Tahoe. He turned on its strobe lights, but left off the siren.

Wonder what the devil I'm gonna find, he thought, as he pulled out of his driveway.

Texas 118 was always deserted. A person could drive forty miles or more without encountering another vehicle. It had long, flat stretches with no curves. For most of the way, Jim kept the Tahoe at ninety miles per hour, slowing only for the occasional curve or rare side road. He reached the east entrance to the park an hour and fifteen minutes after leaving home. The only vehicles in the lot were the gate attendant's, a Presidio County Sheriff's Deputy Ram pickup, and a Texas State Parks Police Silverado. Both men got out of their cars when they saw Jim approaching.

"Howdy, Ranger. You made good time. I'm Deputy Harley Silver."

"My handle's Hiram Mattson," the park policeman said.

"Jim Blawcyzk. We can talk soon as I feed and water my horse. He hasn't had his breakfast yet."

Jim opened the tack compartment. He removed one of the buckets of water, and allowed Copper a short drink, then hung a bucket of grain for him.

"Okay, what have we got?"

"Four victims. They were riding along westbound on 170. Their bodies were found at the old abandoned Contrabando movie set. They hadn't been there for long."

"Who found them?"

"A park ranger. She called it in. There's another park police officer with her."

"Let's go take a look."

Jim followed the two men a little more than six miles into the park. They stopped at the old Contrabando movie set, which was alongside the Rio Grande.

Mattson introduced Jim to the two persons waiting there.

"Ranger, this is Felicia Guerrero, who found the bodies. Frank Lofton, another park police officer. Frank, Felicia, Ranger Jim Blawcyzk."

"Howdy. Tell me what you found while I have a look at the bodies."

"They're in the picnic shelter," Guerrero said. "I knew they were dead, so I called the park police. The tire tracks indicated they came in from the east. They ended at the shelter."

"This was no random robbery," Lofton said. "It was a premeditated, cold-blooded slaughter."

They'd reached the shelter. Four bodies, two male and two female, were sprawled underneath it. Blood pooled around the bodies, covered much of the shelter's floor, and was splattered on the surrounding rocks, soil, and plants. Hundreds of flies buzzed about, feeding on the still damp blood. Shell casings were scattered on the ground.

"You're right, Officer Lofton. This was no crime of opportunity. Notice anything strange about the bodies?"

"You mean other than the fact they were all shot in the head? No."

"There's no backpacks. If these people were on a bike trip through the park, they should've been wearing backpacks. Also, the fact they were all shot in the head tells me they knew their killer or killers. They didn't expect to be executed. There's also too much blood from just the head wounds. Let me take a look around."

Jim walked around the shelter.

"Footprints, coming from and then down to the river. Let's see what we find there. Lofton, come with me."

They followed the tracks down to the riverbank. Jim took photos as they went.

"Two sets of tracks coming up from the river, four going down, then two more coming back. All made by men wearing boots," Jim said. "That means they don't belong to the bicyclists. They all wore sneakers."

When they reached the Rio Grande, Jim pointed to a large, disturbed area in the sand. Still damp blood stained some of the ground a rust color. Four shell casings glittered in the sunlight.

"Two bodies. Must've been shoved into the water. Call it in, and have an eye kept downstream. I'd bet my hat we're lookin' at a drug deal gone bad. Let me take some samples and pick up those casings, then we'll get back to the bodies."

It only took a few minutes for Jim to take the photos and gather the samples he needed.

"Find anything?" Silver asked.

"Plenty. Appears as if these people were here to pick up drugs. Two men came out of the river, which means they crossed over from Mexico.

They were killed, and the bodies shoved into the Rio, the evidence indicates. I'd say things went like this. The drugs and cash were exchanged, then the shooters waited until the mules started back to Mexico. They killed the bicyclists, then caught up with the mules and shot them, dumping them in the river. The big question is where did they come from, and how did they leave? There's no fresh tire prints, except from our vehicles. I'll take a fast look at the bodies, then try'n figure that out."

Jim hunkered beside the nearest corpse, a male who was lying face down. He took photos, then rolled the man over. Several stab wounds punctured his chest and abdomen.

"Now we know where all the blood came from. Whoever did the killing wasn't satisfied just to shoot their victims. They wanted to leave a clear message."

Jim took photos of the other bodies, and made some notes. They were all dress in Spandex bicycling suits. None had any identification. He then took photos of the bicycles.

"These bikes were from the Big Bend Bicycling Adventures Company. That confirms what the sheriff told me. I've got a hunch."

He took out his pocket knife, and sliced open one of the bicycles' seats. A white powder spilled out. Jim touched his finger to the powder, put it to his lips, and tasted it.

"Heroin. Looks like our killers made a mistake. They took the backpacks, which I'm certain contained drugs, but didn't check the bikes. Dollars to doughnuts the tires are also filled with heroin. Let's find out."

He sliced open the same bike's front tire. Again, a thin stream of white powder spilled out.

"Looks like you were right, Ranger," Guerrero said.

"Yep. I've got another hunch. Be right back."

He headed across the road. Behind a screen of scrub brush, he found an area of dirt, packed down by horses' hooves. Vegetation had been nibbled on by the animals. There was also a pile of horse droppings. Jim picked up one of the balls of manure, and crumbled it between his fingers. The tracks of two horses led into and out of Contrabando Canyon. He hurried back to the picnic shelter.

"You find something, Ranger?" Silver asked.

"I sure did. The killers came in on horseback. They left a clear trail goin' into Contrabando Canyon. I'm not surprised. That canyon's been used by smugglers since before the days of the Texas Republic. That's how it got its name. I'm goin' after them."

"By yourself?"

"They've got about a four hour head start. I don't have time to wait for anyone else. Deputy Silver, since there's no phone service out here,

I need you to notify Company E and have them send another Ranger down here. Let them know what I'm doin'. Also tell them I've collected some evidence, which I'll get to them as soon as possible."

"You want us to gather any evidence while we wait?" Lofton asked.

"Yes, as long as you're careful. Don't touch the bodies. Leave that for the Ranger. But taking pictures of the scene, marking where the shell casings landed, taking soil and blood samples, all that's fine. I've got to get moving. Every minute I stand here is another minute the killers are gainin' on me."

Jim got Copper out of his trailer. He tacked up the gelding, filled his saddlebags with supplies, including extra ammunition, and tied his bedroll to the saddle.

"Tell Company E Headquarters I'll be in touch soon as I can," he said, as he swung into the saddle. "*Adios*."

He never realized he'd forgotten to call Kim and let her know he had reached Terlingua.

21

"We've got to move fast, but not push too hard, if we're gonna catch up with those *hombres*, Copper. We'll keep a steady pace. Unless they've stopped for some reason, and I don't know why they would, we won't catch up to 'em today anyway. So far, it appears they're sticking to Contrabando Canyon. We'll have to see which way they head when they reach the top."

Copper shook his head and snorted. Jim leaned forward and patted the big gelding's neck.

"Don't worry. I hung a sack of grain from the saddle horn. You won't have to settle for mesquite pods and dried-out grass tonight."

Where the soil was sandy, it was easy to follow the hoof prints of the killers' horses. In addition, until they reached the head of the canyon, beetling cliffs and loose talus slopes made it impossible to turn off the trail.

"I reckon these *hombres* are gonna head north, stickin' to the trail for a spell, then cut back east. Unless I miss my guess, they're from the *La Fronteras* gang. They probably have a truck and horse trailer hidden somewhere along 118. There's plenty of places to stash a rig along there. Even if someone did spot it, they'd just figure it belonged to horseback riders or hunters."

The terrain got more rugged as Jim continued on. The tracks were more difficult to follow. Jim was able to keep on the killers' tails by finding a broken twig, a length of horsehair, or the scratch of an iron horseshoe on rock. Even a misplaced pebble hinted at the direction his quarry was taking. He would stop every so often to examine a pile of horse droppings, crumbling them between his fingers to check the moisture content. He and his horse were alongside Fresno Creek, in one of the few places its bed contained water, not just damp soil or quicksand.

"Seems like we've gained an hour and a half or so on 'em," he said to Copper. "But why the devil are they still headed north? It looks like they're following the creek. I figured for certain they'd have cut east by now. We'll rest here a spell. You can get a drink, and graze a little while I do some thinkin'."

Jim got out of the saddle. He allowed Copper to drink his fill, then stretched out on his belly to quench his own thirst. He dunked his face into the cooling water, then sat in the shade of a struggling cottonwood.

"Let me go over this situation," he said aloud. "It's plain the four murdered folks didn't realize the bike shop had been raided. It's also one hundred percent certain they were part of, or workin' for, the Black Wolves. So the most logical conclusion is they were killed by either the *La Fronteras* or *La Muertes*. But how would those outfits know about the shipment? And why are the killers still headed north? And why didn't the dead cyclists put up any kind of a fight? The logical thing for the bushwhackers to do would've been goin' right back into Mexico, or toward Del Rio. Only thing that makes sense is they're gonna deliver the drugs to the customer. And that means one thing. There has to be a traitor in the Black Wolves, as Barberry suspected. Someone on the inside who has the information on when and where shipments are being made, and can turn that over to the other gangs. That's the only thing that adds up. Might could be just about any member of the gang. It does have to be somebody close enough to the head honcho, Rolando DeJesus. Marcus Barberry? Wouldn't be the first time a good cop has gone bad. But he doesn't seem the type. Besides, we caught the gang flat-footed. If Barberry was workin' for them, he'd have warned them of the raid. Well, when I catch up with these two sons of bitches, I'll find out."

He got up and stretched.

"Sorry, Copper, back to work."

Copper nuzzled his vest pocket.

"Of course I've got your treat."

Jim pulled out a honey oatmeal granola bar, unwrapped it, and gave it to his horse. Copper happily crunched down on the treat. Jim mounted his paint, and turned his nose northward once again.

The brutal Texas sun beat down on both man and horse. It forced Jim to slow the pace. As the afternoon wore on, heat radiating from the rocks only added to their misery. The blazing heat had dried out any horse droppings, to the point Jim could no longer tell whether he was gaining on the killers or not. Afternoon dragged into the evening, the sun seeming to fight every effort to go below the horizon. Jim stopped when they reached a small *cienga*, where water seeped out from the base of a mesa. It formed a shallow pool in a depression in the rocks, the overflow sinking into the sand and evaporating.

"Time to call it a day, pard," Jim said to Copper, as he pulled the saddle and blanket off his horse. He replaced Copper's bridle and reins with a halter and lead rope. He poured a quarter of the contents of the grain sack on the ground. Copper ate while Jim rubbed him down, removing dried sweat and dirt from the overo paint's sorrel and white hide.

In the clear desert air, even the flame on a matchstick could be seen from miles away. Jim didn't dare chance a fire. His supper was jerky and biscuits, washed down with water from his canteen. He'd refill the vessel before leaving in the morning.

After supper, Jim rolled out his blankets. He pulled off his boots, then lay on his back. Big Bend Ranch was also an International Dark Sky Park. The innumerable stars seemed close enough to touch. When the Milky Way rose, it flooded the night with a soft, eerie light. Jim drifted off to sleep while gazing at the incredible celestial display.

Jim was in the saddle as soon as it was light enough to trail. Tracking someone through the wilderness was both a science and an art, along with plenty of instinct. It was a forgotten skill by most modern law officers, including the Texas Rangers. However, the knowledge passed down by six generations of Jim's forebears made him an expert at reading sign. A few times he lost his quarry's tracks, but cast back and forth until he found them again. The killers had left any known, maintained trails. They were now headed slightly west of due north.

"We're gainin' on them, Copper. Just wish I could figure out where the hell they're goin'. Guess we'll find out. They seem to be movin' slower. If they're carryin' four backpacks full of heroin, the extra weight will tire their horses out, especially in this damn heat. They'd have been smart to bring a pack horse."

The tracks continued in the same direction, working their way around the base of an ancient volcano's eroded cone. The land was rugged, the almost invisible path working its way between rocky escarpments, ridges, and scattered boulders. The hoof prints Jim was following turned gradually more toward the northeast.

"Wherever those *hombres* are headed, they're sure takin' a roundabout route," Jim muttered. "Seems as if they're gonna circle all the way around this old volcano. Must want to make certain they don't come across anyone. I sure hope they don't. They wouldn't have any compunction about killin' anybody they met. They're not about to leave any witnesses."

The tracks continued northeastward, occasionally jogging more north or east to go around a sharp ridge. Copper was weary, but kept on moving under Jim's urging. Jim stopped, poured half the contents of his canteen into his Stetson, and let Copper drink. He then took two swallows for himself.

"The airport!" he exclaimed. "That's gotta be it, Copper. They're meetin' the buyer at the park airport. Lemme think. Goin' all the way around like this, that's still about a two days' ride, unless they kill their horses by pushin' 'em too hard. We've got them now. There's not a horse in Texas that can match you over rough ground and long distances."

Jim climbed back into his saddle. Knowing

it was useless, he still turned on his phone. No service. He was on his own.

Jim kept riding steadily for the rest of the afternoon. He was north of the volcano's cone now. The tracks he was following had turned due west. Now it was evening, the setting sun casting long shadows.

Jim was approaching a gap between the main caldera and a smaller cinder cone. He saw the flash of a rifle. Copper's head exploded in a spray of blood. Jim felt an agonizing pain in his belly. He kicked his feet out of the stirrups as his horse began to crumple. The echo of the first rifle shot hadn't faded away when the hidden gunman fired again. A hot poker seemed to slam into Jim's groin. He slumped over his falling horse, lying atop the downed gelding.

Both man and mount lay motionless as *Muerte.*

22

Jim came to when he landed on the ground with a thump. It was now full dark. Copper was standing over him, snuffling his face and nickering. Blood stained the horse's bald face.

Dazed, it took Jim a moment to react.

"Copper! You're alive, boy! I reckoned we were both goners. Lemme get my bearings and I'll see how bad you're hurt."

Jim waited a few moments to catch his breath. When he stood up, pain shot through his belly and groin. He had to lean against his horse for support until the pain subsided somewhat.

"Okay, pal, let's have a look at your head."

There was a deep groove along the top of Copper's head. A large tuft of his mane was missing. Half an inch lower and the bullet would have lodged in his brain.

"Your skull must be as thick as mine, horse," Jim said, with a grim chuckle. "The bullet bounced right off your head. Then it ricocheted into my gut. I guess you saved my life. If the slug hadn't hit you first, it would've torn a hole clean through me. Let me get some salve on that, to keep the flies off."

He dug in his saddlebags, and removed a bottle of Wonder Dust and a tube of antiseptic ointment.

"This might hurt a little."

He poured the Wonder Dust powder into the wound to staunch any further bleeding, then coated it thickly with the ointment.

"That takes care of you. You'll be fine. Now to take stock of my own injuries."

Jim replaced the equine medications, then removed his medical kit from the saddlebags. Blood soaked the crotch and most of the right leg of his jeans, as well as the left side of his shirt. He sat down on a low rock ledge.

"Those sons of bitches just might've killed me," he said. "I've got two bullets in me, and I'm liable to bleed out. Possibly pass out again, and die from dehydration. Well, I'm not about to feed the buzzards and coyotes without a fight. Lemme see what I can do."

Jim removed his vest and shirt first. The bullet which had taken him in the belly was still lodged in his stomach. Blood continued to ooze from the wound.

"I can't do anything about this one except pack it, dress it, and tie it off."

Jim took a bottle of Betadine, tube of triple antibiotic ointment, and thick piece of gauze from the medical kit. He poured the Betadine directly into the bullet hole, gritting his teeth against the pain. He coated the gauze with the ointment, and stuffed it into the wound. He taped the gauze pad in place, then tore a strip of cloth from the bottom of his shirt. He tied that around his middle.

"That should hold until I can reach help. Now to see how bad the other one is."

Jim removed his gun belt, unbuckled his belt, and lowered his jeans and briefs. The second bullet had buried itself high in his right leg, just missing his right testicle. It had come so close the slug had burned hair off his scrotum, and left an angry red burn mark.

"Dammit! That bullet's gotta come out," Jim exclaimed. "And that's as close to bein' gelded as I ever want to come. This should be fun."

Jim had removed bullets from wounded men before, even once from his own chest. But never in an area so sensitive. This would be a delicate operation. One slip, and his knife could slice open his femoral artery. In that case, he would bleed to death within minutes.

"Well, there's nothing to do but get at it."

Jim took out his Bowie knife. He had to tape his genitals to his left leg to keep them out of the way. He doused the blade with Betadine, then poured more into the wound. This time he couldn't hold back the scream when the burning liquid hit.

"Sooner I get this over with the better," he muttered, through clenched teeth. He slid the knife blade into the hole in his leg, probing until it hit the bullet. He eased the blade alongside the slug as a guide. Using a pair of forceps, he removed the chunk of lead, and set it aside. He pulled his knife from the wound.

"I've gotta stitch that up. No doubt about it."

Jim removed a heavy needle and surgical thread from the kit. He dipped them in the Betadine, then sutured the wound. He finished by coating a gauze pad with antibiotic ointment, taping it over the wound, then ripping off a shirt sleeve to tie it in place.

"Now comes the worst part."

Jim ripped the tape off his genitals, in one quick motion. The pain was almost unbearable. He fell to his back, gasping for air.

Copper gave out what Jim swore was a horse laugh.

"You think it's funny, horse? Or are you just gettin' even over you losin' your nuts? Well, I've got news for you, pal. I've still got mine," Jim scolded. He sat up. He got his jeans back on, then his vest. There was no use bothering with the ruined shirt, except as evidence, so he stuffed it into his saddlebags.

"Copper, we're gonna keep after those *hombres*. The bullets they put in me just might kill me. But if I'm gonna die, I'm taking those men with me. They'll have stopped for the night. They figure I'm dead. The last thing they'd expect is for me to ride all night to catch up with 'em. You up for a chase?"

Copper whinnied, and tossed his head.

"Then let's go."

Jim struggled, but managed to pull himself onto Copper's back. He yodeled like Wiley Gustafson when he hit the saddle.

"We're both hurtin', so we'll keep to a walk most of the way, Copper. We'll still be movin', while our friends won't, at least not until daylight. This is one meeting I'm really lookin' forward to."

23

"Copper, looks like those hombres are gonna make the airport ahead of us after all, damn it," Jim said.

It was about eight in the morning. Clearly, the men Jim was pursuing had gotten an earlier start then he'd hoped. The only chance he'd have of capturing them now would be if he caught up to them before the plane arrived. Or if they weren't in fact going to the airport.

"I dunno if I'm gonna make it either, pal," Jim continued. "I'm still leaking blood. I'm not certain how much longer I can stay in the saddle. But I'm not quittin' until I catch up to those *hombres*, or I'm dead. The airport's only about a mile off now. Give me a bit more, if you've got it in you."

He dug his heels into the big paint's ribs, urging the weary animal into a slow gallop. Ten minutes later, the airport came into view.

"There they are, Copper!" Jim yelled. Two men were waiting alongside the runway, their horses picketed. They were waiting for a plane which had just landed to turn, and taxi up to them. Jim forced Copper into a dead run. He wasn't worrying about the men hearing his approach over the sound of the red and white Cessna's engine. He pulled his horse up a hundred feet from the pair, yanked his LaRue .308 Bushmaster "Ranger Rifle" from its saddle scabbard, and threw it to his shoulder.

"Texas Ranger! Don't move. You're under arrest!"

One of the men turned to face Jim. He held an AR-15. Jim shot him through the chest. The second man hesitated for a moment, then turned and started to run.

"You want to die like a coward, then?"

Jim took aim, fired, and shot the man in the back. He ran for several more steps, stumbled and fell.

The pilot of the single engine Cessna saw the men go down. He pulled back the throttle of the plane, hoping to fly off and escape. Jim emptied the chamber of his rifle, riddling the plane's fuselage, disabling the engine and puncturing the fuel tank. The Cessna crashed off the runway and burst into flames.

Jim rode up to the men he'd shot dead, and dismounted. One was a Mexican whom he didn't recognize. He rolled the second man, the one he'd gunned down in the back, who was lying face down, over. He sucked in a deep breath when he saw the man's face.

"Thomas Moore. The 'White Shark.' That explains all the knife wounds in the bodies at Contrabando. It also explains why the cyclists didn't realize they were bein' ambushed. So you were the turncoat. I can't say I'm feelin' guilty about back-shootin' you. I should, but I don't. Not one damn bit."

He glanced at the burning plane. Anyone still inside was beyond help.

"Copper, let's see if I can raise the Sauceda Ranger Station."

He took out his cell phone. It showed half a bar.

"Well, half a bar is better than none, horse."

Jim dialed the station. A park ranger picked up, then the signal faded away.

"They couldn't hear me, Copper. Looks like we'll be here awhile. Not to worry. Someone'll see the smoke from the fire and come up to investigate. Meantime, all we can do is wait."

Copper nickered, went to his knees, and lay on his side.

"Take a nap? That's not a bad idea," Jim said. "Reckon I'll join you. Mind if I use you for a pillow?"

Loss of blood, and pain from his wounds, finally overcame Jim. He twisted and fell, his head and shoulders resting on his horse's neck.

24

Jim awakened to see the vague faces of two people leaning over him.

"Ranger, you're awake," one of the faces said. "We thought we were going to lose you."

The voice sounded as if it were in an echo chamber, or at the bottom of a deep well.

"There's a Medevac chopper on the way. It will be transporting you to the Alpine hospital."

"Hold on just a doggone minute," Jim said. "Where's my horse?"

"He's with one of the other park rangers."

"How's he doin'?"

"He seems to be just fine. You need to worry about yourself more than your horse."

"Uh-uh. He got shot. He needs to see a vet. I'm not goin' anywhere until I know Copper's on his way to an equine hospital."

"That's not possible."

"I mean it. Until one of you assures me a vet's been called, and Copper's on his way, I'm not goin' anywhere."

"Once you're sedated you won't be able to fight the EMTs."

"No, but I can put up one helluva battle until they manage to stick that needle in my arm."

"Not in your condition!"

"You want to bet your hat?"

"Hold on, Ranger," the other face said. "I'm calling Alpine Veterinary right now."

Jim could hear the second voice talking into its phone. After a few minutes, he heard it get ready to end the call.

"Uh-huh. Uh-huh. Thank you, Doctor. Hold on a minute. Perhaps you should speak to the horse's owner. Let me see."

"Just hand me that phone," Jim said.

"This is Doctor Clark. Are you the Ranger who owns the horse I was just called about?"

"Sure am, Doc. Jim Blawcyzk. Are you going to take care of him for me?"

"Just as fast as someone can get him here."

"*Muchas gracias*, Doc. I'm obliged. He just saved my life. Dunno how soon I'll be able to pick him up, or pay your bill."

"I understand. Don't worry about anything. Your four-footed partner will get the best of care. Just get better yourself."

"I'm feelin' better already, just knowin' Copper's in good hands."

"That's fine. Goodbye."

"Bye, Doc."

Jim felt himself slipping back into unconsciousness as he handed the phone back to its owner. Later, he had a vague feeling of floating through air.

Guess I'm dyin' after all. Sure hope I'm takin' the elevator up, not down.

25

When Jim first regained consciousness, he was in a hospital room. He could hear the beeping of machines monitoring his vital signs. IV tubes ran in and out of his body. He was also hooked up to a catheter. When he shifted just a bit, one of the machines' alarms went off. A nurse hurried into the room.

"Ranger Blawcyzk. You're awake."

"Seem to be," Jim said. "How soon until I'm outta here?"

"I'm afraid that will be a while longer," the nurse said. "Let me get the doctor."

Jim glanced at the chart on the wall.

"Nurse Sullivan?"

"Erin."

"Erin, could you call my family? I'd sure like to see them."

"Of course. Your wife just left a short time ago. I'm certain she'll be so happy to see you're awake."

"I sure hope so," Jim said, under his breath, once the nurse left to get the doctor. "She's probably none too happy with me."

A physician walked into the room. He was in his early fifties, with graying hair and sharp blue eyes.

"Ranger Blawcyzk, hello. I'm Doctor Julius Patch. I performed your surgery. I must say, for all you've been through, you're doing very well indeed."

"Howdy, Doc. Doctor Patch? Like in you patched me up?"

"Perhaps you're not doing as well as I thought, Ranger. I did quite a bit more than just patch you up. Do you realize how much blood you'd lost?"

"Well, Doc, lots of people have told me I'm a quart low. Also that my elevator doesn't go all the way to the top, I'm not the brightest bulb in the box, not the sharpest tool in the shed . . ."

"Enough. I get the idea. You nearly killed yourself going after those men. Why didn't you turn around and go for help as soon as you were shot?"

"Couldn't do it, Doc. Not in my code. If I hadn't gone after those *hombres*, they would have gotten clean away. Probably be in Central America by now."

"It still wasn't a good idea. I had to do quite a bit of reconstructive surgery inside your abdomen. Also, the bullet which hit your leg came very close to the femoral artery. You really should have been taken to a larger hospital in El Paso, but your condition wasn't stable enough. You would never have survived the trip. The EMTs tell me you must have removed the bullet and sutured the wound yourself. Is that true? If so, you did a good job, especially under what must have been excruciating circumstances."

"Yes. Did the best I could with the belly wound, too. It was either that or bleed out. Besides, that bullet in my leg came too dang close to where a man never wants to get shot."

"Yet you still continued your pursuit. Amazing."

"I can be stubborn sometimes. Doc, has anyone from the Rangers been by?"

"More than I can count. Also from other law enforcement agencies. I'm supposed to call your commanding officer as soon as I feel it's safe for you to speak with him. If you agree, I don't believe tomorrow will be too soon."

"Today would be better."

"Let's settle for tomorrow. I have another patient to check on. I'll come by a little later, just to see how you're doing."

"I'm ready to go home, Doc. Unlike you, I don't have any patience."

"Right."

Twenty minutes later, Jim's wife Kim, his mother Betty, and son Josh came into the room.

"Daddy!"

Before he could be stopped, Josh jumped on Jim's bed. He hugged his father tightly.

"Josh! Remember you have to be careful with Daddy," Kim chided. "He's hurt."

"That hug was the best medicine I could have, next to one of your kisses," Jim said.

"Was that a hint, Ranger?"

"I dang sure hope you got it."

Kim crossed the room and kissed her husband. Betty also gave him a kiss.

"Jim, I don't know whether I'm happy to see you, or whether I'd rather shoot you," Kim said.

"You're too late. The shooting part's already been taken care of."

"Jim, why?"

"Because I'm a Ranger, that's why. Maybe a bit old school, but it's what I am."

"I know. And I can't help loving you for it."

"Jim, you are so much like your father was. He drove me crazy, and so do you," Betty said.

"I'm sorry, Ma."

"Don't be."

"Kim, how's the baby?"

"She's just fine. Rosita is watching her. And yes, before you ask, Copper is doing well too. He's home."

"Thanks, honey."

"Jim, your doctor said we can only stay a few minutes. I have two things to say before we leave."

"What are they?"

"First, you didn't call when you reached Terlingua, like you promised."

"I didn't?"

"No, you didn't. I spent all the while you were missing not knowing what had happened to you. Then I had to worry you'd survive the operations."

"I must've just plain forgot. I'm sorry. What's the other thing?"

"I know the reason you got yourself shot."

"You do?"

"Of course I do. You'll do anything to get out of helping me rearrange furniture, put up paintings, and hang drapes. But getting shot? Really? That's going just a bit too far, Mister."

"You mean everything's in place?"

"Thanks to Miguel and Rosita, yes."

Nurse Sullivan poked her head in the door.

"I'm sorry, but Doctor Patch says your visiting time is over, Ranger."

"Already?"

"Yes."

"Jim, we'll be back tomorrow," Kim said. "I know it will be hard for you, but obey your doctor's orders. You'll mend more quickly if you do."

"You just want me home to shift the sofa and chairs around."

"Well, now that you mention it . . ."

Kim leaned over and kissed him.

"I'll be waiting for you, cowboy."

26

"Ranger Blawcyzk, Major Trujillo, Lieutenant Castellon, and Ranger Perez are here. Shall I send them in?"

"Of course, Erin."

Jim let out a nervous sigh. Now was the moment of reckoning.

"Jim. How long do you keep intending to stay in that bed?" Major Trujillo boomed, when he walked into the room.

"If it was up to me, I'd be out of it already," Jim answered. "Howdy, Major. Same to you, Lieutenant. And especially you, Javier. I'm sorry for stickin' you with all the paperwork."

"If I had a choice between paperwork or takin' a couple of bullets, I'd take the bullets like you did," Perez answered. "How you feeling, Jim?"

"Like a man who took a bullet in the belly, and came too damn close to not bein' able to play tennis," Jim answered.

"Huh?"

"Javier, Jim means you need balls to play tennis. And he nearly lost his," Castellon explained, chuckling. "Now give us a serious answer, Jim. *Por favor.*"

"Not bad, all things considered. I'm just goin' stir crazy in here. And what happened with the gangs, and the Marfa cases? No one'll tell me a thing."

"Except for the people we lost, the operation was a success," Trujillo answered. "We just might've put the Black Wolves and *Diablos de la Fronteras* out of business for good. And the *Mano de la Muertes* took a big hit. Of course, there are always others waiting to take their places."

"Sadly, you're right, Major. How's Marcus Barberry?"

"He's in rehab, expected to make a full recovery."

"That's good news."

"As far as Marfa goes, Jim, every one of the people who were arrested is trippin' all over each other, tryin' to blame someone else. They're all singing like canaries. You really made your mark in west Texas already, Jim. One helluva mark. I'll leave copies of the reports here for you to peruse at your leisure. Of course, you'll have to file some too. But that can wait."

"Of course."

"So tell us what happened at the park," Castellon said.

"I'll do my best. I'll start after I got to the scene. You already know it was another gang robbery of drug mules. The bikes they were ridin' told me they were workin' for the Black Wolves. I found hoof prints, heading deeper into the park.

Two horses, meant two men. I knew if I didn't go after those *hombres* right then they'd disappear into the tall and uncut. So I took their trail. At first, I had no idea why they were headed north, then west. Then it hit me. One of them had to be a Black Wolf who'd gone over to the other side. As I kept trailin' 'em, I realized they had to be heading for the park airport. But they caught me in an ambush. Shot poor Copper in the head. That bullet ricocheted off his skull and into my belly. As he was fallin', I took another bullet. When I came to, it was dark. I was mad enough I decided I was goin' to find those men, or die tryin'. Patched myself up as best I could, then took their trail again. I caught up to them at the airport, just as they were getting ready to hand over the drugs. They wouldn't surrender. One tried to take a shot at me. Dunno his name. But I nailed him first. The other one tried to turn and run. I plugged him, too. That was Thomas Moore, aka 'The Shark.' He got the name because he liked to cut people up. He did exactly that at Contrabando Canyon. He was the turncoat."

"What about the plane?" Trujillo asked.

"The pilot tried to take back off. He would have flown right into me if he could've. So I shot his plane up. Didn't have a choice."

"Then?"

"I checked Moore and the other *hombre.* They were both dead. I couldn't do a thing about anyone in the plane. It was already engulfed in flames. Next thing I sorta remember is seeing some folks lookin' down at me. Then I woke up here. That's the *Reader's Digest* version."

"Well, Ranger, I have to say, you've certainly got *grandes cojones*," Trujillo said.

"If that second bullet had hit me just a bit to the left, I wouldn't have any *cojones* at all," Jim answered, eliciting laughs from the group.

"Jim, I'm certain you realize, once you're strong enough, there will be a lot more before the investigation is closed," Trujillo said. "The man with Moore was Floyd Dummer. He was a member of *La Frontera.* There was only one man in the plane. His name was Dwayne Hoffman. His daddy's one of the biggest oilmen in Tulsa. He's gonna try'n make waves."

"He can make as many as he wants, Major. I don't get seasick."

"One last question, then we'll leave you to rest. It appears Moore was shot in the back."

"He was, Major. I plugged him in the back, and I'd do it again if I had to. He had to be the ambusher who almost succeeded in killin' me. I was in no shape to chase him into the *malpais.* If I hadn't gotten him, I'm positive he would have turned and gotten me. Then he and that oilman's kid would have gotten clean away. Moore was involved in the killing of four people at Contrabando Canyon, and who knows how many others. I wasn't about to let him get loose to kill more."

"I see."

Trujillo stroked his chin. There was silence in the room for several minutes, before he spoke again.

"So Moore was facing you, getting ready to pull his trigger. Instead, just as you fired, he turned to run. You aimed at his chest, but when he turned, your bullet struck him in the back. Does that about sum up what happened?"

Jim looked from Trujillo, to Castellon, to Perez. All three men nodded.

"Yeah, Major. I reckon that's exactly how it happened."

"Good. Jim, I knew I made a wise decision, asking you to transfer out here. It seems I was right. You were made to enforce the law in west Texas. The Rangers need you out here. Get out of that bed as quick as you can."

"Is that an order, Major?"

"It certainly is."

"Two weeks, tops," Jim said. "I'm chompin' at the bit."

"We talked to your wife earlier," Castellon said. "Seems she mentioned something about you coming home to help finish the decorating. And also about rearranging your office. And looking at paint color swatches and flooring samples for the caretaker's cottage."

“Major, suddenly I’m not feelin’ so good,” Jim said.

“Better you than me,” Trujillo answered. “Ride easy, Ranger.”

About the Author

While a native New Englander, James J. Griffin has been a student of the Texas Rangers from a young age. He is considered an amateur historian of the organization. His extensive collection of Texas Ranger artifacts is now in the permanent collections of the Texas Ranger Hall of Fame and Museum in Waco.

Jim is a lifelong horseman. Horses always play a major role in his stories. He travels out West frequently, both on vacation and to do research for his books. He has visited most of the famous Old West towns. His travels have taken him to all fifty states, and several Canadian provinces.

Jim makes his home in Keene, New Hampshire.

Learn more about Jim, and his extensive catalogue of traditional Western novels, contemporary Texas Ranger Mystery novels, Young Adult Western novels, and children's picture and chapter Westerns at his website, www.jamesjgriffin.net

Center Point Large Print
600 Brooks Road / PO Box 1
Thorndike, ME 04986-0001 USA

(207) 568-3717

US & Canada:
1 800 929-9108
www.centerpointlargeprint.com